LADY LIGHTFINGERS

Janet Woods

Severn House Large Print
London & New York

This first large print edition published 2013
in Great Britain and the USA by
SEVERN HOUSE PUBLISHERS LTD of
19 Cedar Road, Sutton, Surrey, England, SM2 5DA.
First world regular print edition published 2011 by
Severn House Publishers Ltd., London and New York.

British Library Cataloguing in Publication Data

Woods, Janet, 1939- author.
  Lady Lightfingers. -- Large print edition.
  1. Poor women--England--London--History--19th century--
  Fiction. 2. Theft--Fiction. 3. Aunts--England--Dorset--
  Fiction. 4. London (England)--Social conditions--19th
  century--Fiction. 5. Love stories. 6. Large type books.
  I. Title
  823.9'2-dc23

  ISBN-13: 9780727896599

Severn House Publishers support the Forest Stewardship Council™
[FSC™], the leading international forest certification organisation. All
our titles that are printed on FSC certified paper carry the FSC logo.

Printed and bound in Great Britain by
T J International, Padstow, Cornwall.

One

London, 1850
There were about two hundred rats trapped in the enclosure. Not that they'd be missed by the thousands still running loose in the city, Celia Laws thought.

Outside the enclosure several men and a few light-skirts chatted. Not all were slum dwellers; some were toffs, and many were businessmen with side whiskers, cutaway coats, high hats and fancy waistcoats – and in pursuit of certain types of amusement. They had braying laughs, fat wallets and high cravats.

There were women too, dressed in silk, fringes, fancy bows and lace. Hats ranging from demure bonnets to outrageous creations adorned their heads as they sought adventure and amusement amongst the lowest of the low.

Money changed hands as bets were laid.

The terriers were brought in, blindfolded, but yapping with tension as they smelled the rats. The rags were removed from their eyes and the dogs' yaps became squeals of bloodlust as they were thrown into the enclosure, where they set to work snapping the necks of their prey.

The rats' squeaks rose to a high-pitched crescendo as the creatures sensed the fear of the

5

others. They scrambled and piled one on top of the other for safety until a booted foot scattered them into the middle of the ring. Blood ran. Some of the crowd began to shout and yell, counting in unison the number of corpses being tossed aside. Some vomited, adding to the already decomposing street detritus.

Celia felt slightly sick, not at the demise of the rats because there were too many in London to count, and death came swiftly to them, but at the concentration of enjoyment painted on the faces of the watchers. But she was not here to watch rats being slaughtered, she was here to earn a living, she reminded herself.

She made her move. Dressed in her ragged grey cloak, a garment that made her indistin-guishable from all the other beggars, her face smeared with dirt so she couldn't be easily recognized by those who might take coin for reporting her to the authorities, Celia sidled swiftly round the outside of the circle, her fingers dipping lightly into pockets, extracting a watch from a waistcoat, a coin or two from an inside pocket, the metal cold and satiny against her fingertips. A loose ring was slipped from a finger and a purse containing several coins exchanged for a few pebbles wrapped in paper.

There was a young man leaning against the wall watching the proceedings with an amused smile on his face. He seemed to feel her gaze on him, for his eyes, as dark and shining as liquor-ice, met hers. He smiled, sort of lopsided and bemused, then winked. Celia didn't stop to admire him because his coat was hanging open and she was hungry, and what might be inside it held more appeal. She closed in on him.

'Hello, my pretty,' he said.

She pretended to trip on a cobble and he automatically reached out to steady her. As smooth as if it were sliding on butter she sent her hand journeying amongst the silk layers of his waistcoat. For a moment his heart beat a lively dance against her palm, then she dipped her fingers inside his pocket and brought out something metal, tucking it into her sleeve.

Awareness came into his eyes, and she realized he wasn't as drunk as he seemed.

Celia didn't linger. Slipping the spoils into the canvas pocket secured inside her skirt at the waist, she walked rapidly away through a rubbish and dung-filled passage to a court similar to the one she'd come from. She began to twist and turn through the maze of passages until she was half a mile from the entertainment she'd just witnessed.

She stopped by a shop to gaze around her and get her bearings, her eyes alert as she scrutinized the crowd. A lad came to look in the shop window. He wore a red kerchief around his neck and his glance was on her reflection.

She'd seen him at the rat pit. He'd marked her and considered her to be easy prey, she thought. She could see the outline of the ned under his jacket, a bag filled with sand. Stuffed in his belt he would use it to stun his victims before he stole from them. There was also a knife in a sheath strapped to his wrist. This lad meant business.

Her blood ran cold. He was dangerous, for he

wouldn't hesitate to use his weapon on his unsuspecting victim, especially one who was too weak to fight back. She wasn't going to allow him to help himself to the pickings she'd worked for. But though she couldn't fight him she could outwit him.

Beyond him was the gentleman with the handsome eyes. He lifted his arm when he saw her, and she hunched her shoulders to disguise the small jutting breasts that had grown shortly after her fifteenth birthday. She hated men staring at them.

Better to be safe than sorry. Celia picked up speed, threading in and out of the people, scattering wandering chickens. Pigs and dogs snapped at her heels and a couple of curses followed after her ... a sound that continued behind her as the lad speeded up. Mingling with a cluster of people, she ducked down a flight of steps. Pausing for just a moment, she turned her cape inside out to reveal the dull green-checked lining.

She didn't have long to wait. A few seconds later her pursuer ran past, his shabby boots a soft clatter on the spread of dung coating the cobbles. Pulling the hood up over her hair she headed back up and retraced her steps, walking like an old woman and not looking at the gentleman, who didn't give her a second glance as they passed each other.

She took a look behind her. Of the lad or the gentleman there was no sign now. She picked up speed, heading towards home; though she felt uneasy, as if she were still being observed. Celia was soon tucked out of sight in the basement hovel she shared with her mother and sister.

Their home was one miserable cellar, which was damp with mould in the winter. The ceiling pressed down on them, so her mother had to bow her head if she stood. At the moment, Alice Laws was stitching the seam on a pair of trousers she was making, a garment that would earn her eight pence. If she was diligent and trade was good, the occupation of trouser hand would earn Alice three shillings a week. But she had to buy her own thread and needles, so the pittance didn't go far enough.

Her mother didn't talk about it, but Celia knew she earned money in other ways as well, but she never brought men home. Here, her mother had her own sleeping arrangement, a mattress spread on the table.

At the back of the cellar a small and grimy barred window allowed a grey smear of daylight to penetrate. Barely three feet away they had stretched a ragged sheet across on a length of string. Behind that sheet, Celia slept with her sister Lottie. It provided an illusion of privacy.

'You can't trust men, Celia,' Alice Laws had told her. 'It was your father who brought about my downfall.'

Her mother didn't often bring up her past. She spoke, and sometimes acted, as if she hadn't been brought up to such a life as the one she now led. And indeed, she hadn't been. She'd been the eldest of three daughters, and had taught in the church school for two mornings a week.

Celia had listened with interest when her

9

mother said of the man who'd fathered her: 'Jackaby Laws was his name, and I still use it because, as far as I know, I'm still legally married to him, and I have the papers to prove it. He was a charming rogue. It was my father, Richard Price, who brought Jackaby home to dinner.'

Celia loved it when Alice Laws spoke of her past life, which was very different from the one they led now, but something Celia aspired to.

'Jackaby was a theatre impresario looking for investors. We married and came to London, staying in a fancy hotel while he did business. The show didn't eventuate. A month later Jackaby left for America to seek his fortune. He took my money with him, but left me you to remember him by, and a note to say I was to go home to my father, and he'd join me when he'd made his fortune.'

Celia stored each crumb of information in her memory. 'What did you do then?'

'I stole out of the hotel at midnight and made my way back home. My father was a broken man when I told him. He'd invested heavily, you see, and although he didn't tell anyone lest he look like a fool, it got out because Jackaby had persuaded father's friends to invest too.

'When Jackaby didn't return for me, my father was convinced that his good name was ruined. And indeed, the family was no longer welcome at the local social gatherings. He needed someone to blame, and although he didn't turn me from his door, he sent me to be a companion to his cousin in Scotland.'

A stern-faced old man with a funny voice

10

snatched at Celia's memory.

'That's where you were born. We lived there for five years, with father supporting us, until his cousin died. I'd hardly got back home when my father followed her into the grave. My stepmother accused me of bringing about his death, and used it as an excuse to turn us out of the house.'

'What about your half-sisters ... my aunts?'

'Harriet and Jane?' Her mother had given a slight shrug. 'They were young, and in no position to argue against her authority. Though Harriet pleaded with her mother to allow us to stay, she wouldn't hear of it. I haven't seen any of them since the week following my father's funeral. What my father had left went to his wife. I was given the coach fare to London and twenty pounds, and advised not to go back to Hanbury Cross again.'

'That's not fair,' she said hotly. 'It wasn't your fault that Jackaby Laws turned out to be a liar and a trickster. You were as much a victim as they were. One day I'm going to hunt the man down and do the same to him. I'll trick him out of everything he's got, and see if he likes it. And I'm going to find those sisters of yours too, and give them a piece of my mind.'

'Don't be so passionate, Celia. Jackaby was a bad money manager, that's all. As for my sisters ... let sleeping dogs lie. It wasn't their fault. They were young and they didn't have much say in the matter. It's not worth getting angry over after all this time. Just know that your life can be different if you work at it. There's a world outside

London where it's clean and green and the air is sweet. Now, fetch your slate and the dictionary and get on with your lesson. As soon as you've copied down every word in it, learned to spell them, and can understand the meaning of them, I'm going to buy you a book.'

'A proper book with a story in it?' Celia said eagerly.

'*Robinson Crusoe*. It's an adventure story about a man who's marooned on a desert island.'

'What's a desert island?'

'It's a small piece of land surrounded by sea, usually unpopulated. The air is fresh there and the palm trees provide shade when it's hot. There, you can walk for a whole day without meeting anyone else and not be frightened by anything, except for a snake perhaps, or a coconut falling from a palm tree on to your head.'

'Is that like the countryside you grew up in?'

A smile inched along Alice's lips when she saw how absorbed by the thought of it her daughter was. 'Dorset doesn't have any palm trees with coconuts as I recall. Compared to London, it's like the Garden of Eden, though. You'll be able to read about such places if you work at it.'

Over time Celia copied all the words in the dictionary, and in doing so learned to read and write ... but it had taken a long time. By that time, she realized that any money they earned was needed to feed and shelter them, and *Robinson Crusoe* would have to wait. Celia could read well when she came across any printed material, and she could write with a neat hand, make up her own stories and poems, and do her numbers.

* * *

Alice Laws bit through the cotton thread and glanced at Celia now, managing a weary smile. 'I'm glad you're home,' she said. 'You're breathing fast. Have you been hurrying?'

'I was marked, and had to shake someone off.' She looked around for her sister. 'Where's Lottie?'

'Asleep. She had to go without breakfast, so she's been fractious. How did you get on?'

Celia avoided her mother's eyes as she emptied her pocket on to the bed.

Alice raked a finger through it. 'You've been on the dip again. I told you to beg for money.'

'There are too many beggars out there already. I'm fifteen, and getting too big to beg. The toffs like the younger children. I should take Lottie with me. With her curls and sweet smile she'd do well. All I get now is lewd suggestions.'

'I want you and Lottie to grow up decent, so don't you listen to them. You don't want to end up like me?'

Celia didn't, but if there was a way out of life in the London slums, where everyone seemed to prey on everyone else, she had yet to discover the secret. 'I'll be careful. Just take a look at that watch. It's real gold,' she said proudly, and examined the house key hanging from the chain.

She'd taken it from a well-fed-looking gentleman who she'd seen in the district many times before. He'd been totally distracted by the entertainment, tearing his eyes away only to write notes and make sketches in a notebook. She'd seen him coming out of the print shop on several occasions before. Celia was curious about what he put in his notebook, and why he was doing it, and was surprised that his watch hadn't been lifted before.

'How do you expect me to sell that without arousing suspicion? It's got a name etched on it. Thomas Hambert. Besides, I didn't bring you up to be a thief. Dipping becomes a habit.'

'I'll give the watch back to him, and tell him to keep a better eye on it next time.' She didn't tell her mother about the card case she'd taken from the young toff. He'd been too quick to alert himself to what was going on, and might come looking for her.

'That man will have you arrested.'

'Don't worry, I was just teasing. If I can take it from his pocket I can just as easily put it back in again. Or I can follow him home and hand it to a servant. I'll tell him that I found it. He might offer me a reward.' She giggled at the thought. 'It's just a game, Ma.'

Celia drew her mother's attention away from the watch as she handed over a fat coin purse. 'Here's some money for you.'

Her mother's eyes widened. 'How did you get this?'

'It was my lucky day. I was reciting poetry and a drunken man gave it to me. "Keep it," says he when I went to hand it back. "I won't need it where I'm going." Where's that, sir? I asked him, all polite and ladylike. "To hell, my little beauty ... hell is where I'm going," says he. "You can join me if that's your fancy."'

Her mother managed a small smile as she cut

through Celia's embellishment of the situation. Celia had been prone to melodrama when they'd travelled the country fairs for a short time with the Wentworth Players. Her daughter had enjoyed watching the actors and had been influenced by their play-acting. Sometimes she'd been given children's roles to play. Alice herself had been employed playing small roles, and making and repairing costumes, but Mrs Wentworth had accused her husband of flirting with Alice, and had dismissed her.

'How did you really get this money?' Alice insisted.

Celia modified her earlier lie. 'It dropped from someone's pocket when he gave me thruppence, and I put my foot on it. He was as drunk as a lord and said I could have it for my trouble. It was a good poem, worth every penny, and one that took me a whole week to learn – the one Lord Byron wrote about walking in beauty. The toff said it reminded him of his true love, who he was parted from, and so did I. Then he tried to kiss me.'

'You didn't fall for that man-talk, did you?' her mother said, her anxiety all too apparent. 'You're old enough to know about men and their ways, and don't need to gain experience the hard way, like I did. Get the ring on your finger first, and make sure he's an honest man. Women are easily duped.'

Celia did know about men. In this part of London you learned quickly if you wanted to survive – and she did intend to do that. She knew what her mother had to do on occasion to keep food on the table, and how much she hated it. Celia was learning other skills of survival, but they didn't include accommodating the appetites of men.

She snorted. 'Do donkeys fly? There were others waiting to relieve him of the purse if I hadn't planted my foot on it. That's why I was marked myself, I reckon.'

Celia grinned. Her explanation had been accepted. She must have inherited her father's skill where lying was concerned. Or perhaps her mother chose to believe her because they were in need.

Her smile faded as a second thought intruded. Watch out, Jackaby Laws, I'm only fifteen at the moment but I'll soon be grown-up. If I ever run into you I'll find some way to relieve you of the money you took from my mother and grand-father. When I do, my mother will be able to hold her head up again and so will her children.

Lottie called out and her mother sighed. 'Look after her, Celia. I'll go out and buy some milk and bread, and some pies and fruit. We'll eat like princesses tonight.'

'I'll go if you like.'

'Not if you're marked. He'll be hanging around where he last saw you, waiting for you to emerge.'

'You can't miss him; he's wearing a red ker-chief, and there's a ned in his belt. I haven't seen him round here before, and I spotted him easily. What about the watch? Shall I try and sell it?'

'You must find some way of giving it back to the gentleman, but don't get caught, Celia. I couldn't bear it if you were put in prison or transported to the other side of the world and I never saw you again. And get rid of that ring at the same time. It's too noticeable.'

It was a pretty trinket with a green stone in the middle, surrounded by small, creamy pearls. It fitted her middle finger perfectly.

Lottie came in and climbed on to her lap, her eyes widening when the watch began to chime. Celia held it to Lottie's ear. She was three years old, and she had light-blue eyes and soft, brown, curly hair, the same as Alice, so she looked as though she belonged to them. Celia had darker eyes. Cornflower blue.

Celia could remember cornflowers in the fields when they'd toured with the Wentworth Players. She resembled her father, her mother had told her. His eyes had been the same colour, as was his hair – dark brown, almost black. Not that Celia had ever met him. He didn't even know of her existence – not yet! But one day she'd find him, even if it took the rest of her life.

As for Lottie's parentage, it was a mystery. Her mother had found her as a newborn baby, abandoned amongst the rubbish on the riverbank. She'd been left for the tide to carry away, something that was a common practice. She'd probably been born there and left where she was dropped.

At first, Alice had intended to ignore the child, but her thin little cry as the cold and dirty water began to lick at her naked body had touched her, and Celia had begged her mother to save the baby's life. They'd called her Charlotte, quickly shortened to Lottie, and thus Celia had gained a sister.

They'd lived in a real house then, the room and board paid for by her mother's efforts at housekeeping. Another child in his home, especially one that cried at night, was too much for the owner to bear, and he'd sent them packing.

They'd gone downhill. Nobody would employ her mother and she sent Celia begging. But Celia couldn't earn enough to keep them all.

They'd been lucky and had found the cellar that they'd called home for the past three years. But it was a struggle to pay the rent and buy food. Now, when it seemed that they couldn't go any lower, her mother seemed resigned to her lot in life.

Life wasn't fair sometimes, Celia thought, kissing her sister's soft curls. But she had no intention of trying to earn an honest living by sewing seams in trousers or being a housemaid and a dollymop on the side.

Celia learned things easily, and she didn't intend to stay. When she was old enough she would leave this place. Using her wits, lying, stealing, dramatics, begging – or even marriage to a rich man – she'd be the very best at what she did, and she'd look after her family while she was doing it.

Her gaze went to the watch. She was tempted to keep it, but just as she thought she might, Lottie's exploring fingers found a hidden catch and the back sprang open. Celia laughed when Lottie's eyes rounded with surprise and she clapped her hands. Revealed was a small sketch of a child's face surrounded by a wreath. RIP

Celia Jane Hambert it said on the back, and there was an address.

For reasons unknown, tears sprang to Celia's eyes.

The man had lost a child he loved and he carried a memorial of her around with him. Odd that they bore the same name. Celia didn't believe in signs ... until now. It was as if the ghost of the girl was whispering to her, asking to be taken back to the father who loved her. She must take the timepiece back; if she didn't something bad would happen to her.

Her fingers touched against the dangling door key. She had the address and she had a way in. There was bound to be cash at the house and she could leave the watch and help herself to the reward at the same time. All she had to do was watch and wait, and seize her chance.

Two

It didn't take Celia long to discover where Thomas Hambert lived. It was apparent that he was a pleasant gentleman, tipping his hat when the need arose to people he passed, especially the ladies. He had an air of absent-mindedness about him that was endearing. Celia followed him around and learned his habits, which proved to be just as much fun as the thrill of dipping her fingers into pockets undetected. He seemed unaware of her presence.

It never ceased to amaze her how careless people were with their purses. Just that morning she'd taken one from a woman's basket, handing it back to her, lighter by several coins.

'Excuse me, ma'am, but you dropped this,' she said, handing it over with as much humbleness as she could muster.

The woman's male companion fished a penny from his pocket and dropped it in her hand. 'Here, girl.'

The purse was placed back in its basket, while the man automatically patted his inside pocket to make sure his paper money was secure, revealing exactly where it was kept. Celia could almost guarantee that by the time they reached the end of the lane, both purse and pocket would be emptied. She was tempted to do it herself, except she'd spotted Thomas Hambert standing outside a bookshop.

She sidled up beside him and looked in the window. When she was sure he wasn't looking she slanted a glance at his notebook. He was making a sketch of the alley with quick, sure pencil marks.

She lowered her gaze when he gave her a quick glance and her eyes fell on a book in the window. 'Robinson Crusoe,' she whispered, her eyes shining as she wondered if she should duck through the door and grab up a copy. But there was a barrier made of wire across the back of the display.

'I beg your pardon, young lady. Did you say something?'

'*Robinson Crusoe*.' She pointed to the book. 'See, it's there. Four shillings and nine pence. Who would have thought words would cost so much?'

'It's good value, because when you've learned them the words are yours to keep and do what you like with. People who arrange words into stories earn money from them. Also, the publisher who makes the book earns money, and so does the shopkeeper who sells the book.'

'So if I wrote a book and it sold for four shillings, I would only earn about...' She stopped to count it on her fingers... 'One shilling and four pence. That's very little for all that work.'

'If it was accepted by a proper publisher and displayed in a bookseller's window, I'd expect more than one person to buy it.'

'Ten perhaps?'

'Easily ... more ... one hundred copies perhaps.'

Her eyes widened. 'That many; would you buy a copy?'

He smiled at her. 'If it was well written, most certainly I would. Such enterprise would need rewarding.'

'Then I'll write a book, and it will be a good one. I'll write down my life story.'

'An autobiography?'

'Yes, an autobiography.'

He gave her a faint, and rather superior smile. 'You're rather young to have accumulated enough adventures with which to write an autobiography. Do you know what it is?'

She shrugged as she threw at him, 'Of course.

21

My mother made me read all the words in the dictionary. I learned their meaning and how to spell them. She promised to buy me *Robinson Crusoe* when I'd learned them all. I thought she'd forgotten, because she didn't keep her promise; but it must have been because she couldn't afford it. She used to be a teacher before she met my pa, you know. He turned out to be a trickster of ill repute. She's frightened that I'll take after him.'

His smile was one of amused indulgence. 'And will you?'

She laughed at his question and shrugged. If only he knew!

'You've evaded my question, and now you tell me you can read all the words in the dictionary?'

'No, I didn't evade it, and yes, I do know what an autobiography is. It's an account of someone's life as written by the subject herself ... or himself, whichever the case may be.'

'My goodness, you've been educated in letters with a vengeance. Like a little parrot you repeat back the words you've been fed.'

Her hands went to her hips. 'There's no need to mock me.'

'Indeed, I'm not mocking you. I'm lost in admiration that one so young could display such a retentive mind. The dictionary, no less?'

There were little red dents at each side of his nose where his spectacles pinched. 'It's the only book we have at home.'

'Samuel Johnson's edition one would hope. Your mother has indeed been industrious on your behalf. Tell me, what are you going to do with all those words now you have them at your disposal?'

'I'm going to write an autobiography.'

'Ah yes, my dear,' and his pencil flew over the page. 'I believe we've already established that. Because it's fact, you must be careful what you put in it, since it could land you in trouble, especially if you'd done something wrong, or blackened somebody else's name.'

'Like stealing, you mean?'

He nodded. 'I'm not suggesting that you would have, of course. You look like an honest and open person to me.'

Guilt prodded at her conscience. 'Perhaps I'll write about the people who live in the district. I can make up poetry and stories about them instead. All I will need is a book like the one you use. Then if I sell it I can keep all the money and will write another one.'

Finished with his task he snapped his notebook shut and pulled a fresh notebook from a satchel he carried. 'Are you sure you can write? If you can I'll give you this to start off with.'

'Test me. Ask me a word ... any word,' she said, unaware that her eyes were as fierce as a bird of prey on the prize.

'Frequently,' he came back with.

'Something that happens often.' She spelled it for him.

'Can you spell the word *enough*?'

She did.

'Through...?'

She gave him a bit of a smile. 'Easy. I can also spell *though*, *tough* ... *thought* and *cough*.' Her fingers closed around the offered notebook and she prayed it wouldn't be withdrawn. 'Thank you, Mr Hambert. My first book of fictional stories and poetry will be for you at the cost of four shillings.'

The smile he gave was loaded with amusement. 'But I paid for the notebook in the first place.'

'But you didn't pay for the future content. You may deduct the cost when the time comes.'

'I'm impressed by your business acumen, young lady. In fact, I'm impressed by you altogether.' He raised a peppery eyebrow and gazed at her through eyes so astute that they seemed to skewer her to the spot. 'Don't forget to keep a copy of your work, and state that it's yours on the title page.' He chuckled. 'I might steal it and pretend it's mine, otherwise.'

The watch in her pocket began to chime. Damn! She'd forgotten about the timepiece she'd lifted from him the last time they'd met. She'd meant to slip it back into his pocket.

Her heart began to thump erratically as he gave her a puzzled look. His fingers automatically slid into his waistcoat and felt about, then he patted his jacket pockets and mumbled, 'I thought I'd lost it. It must have slipped into the lining somewhere.'

'I won't forget to keep a copy; thank you so much,' she said with enough faked graciousness to disguise her mounting panic. While he was distracted Celia edged away to merge with the jostling crowds. She had no choice, because once he realized she had stolen his watch he'd have her arrested and charged with stealing it. She liked Thomas Hambert and had enjoyed their interesting conversation.

But she hoped to talk to him again. First, she'd make sure he got his watch back. After that she wouldn't steal anything but money, until she made her fortune writing enough fictional stories to amaze and delight people. She might even write a play for Mr Wentworth. She had lots of stories inside her head, mostly about the people who lived in the slums. Once she was rich she'd stop stealing altogether, she promised herself.

Thomas Hambert lived in Bedford Square. The three-storey house at the corner of the row was made of dark brick and six oblong windows supported curved recesses. Two attic windows peered from the roof. The double doors were set to one side with a decorative portico, and there was a bridge of steps over the basement area. Over the past week Celia had observed several entrances to the square, through Bayley, Caroline and Charlotte Streets, should she need to make a quick escape.

Her gentleman had one housekeeper, a skinny streak of a woman who looked as though a puff of wind would carry her off. She came in daily and left about four o'clock, just as winter began to cape them in the gruel of twilight. Thomas Hambert usually arrived home about an hour later, after eating a pie and having a pint of ale in a public house.

Celia chose a day when the fog closed in early, muffling the street sound. She knocked first, in case the woman hadn't left. She had. The key fitted in the lock and turned smoothly, giving a well-oiled clunk. She found herself standing in a hallway with a flight of steps to her left.

She had never entered a stranger's house without permission before. It felt strange as though something hovered, watching her every move and breathing tension into her ear. She wondered if it were her own conscience. The house smelled of beeswax mixed with stale tobacco smoke, but it wasn't unpleasant. It was a warm house, not at all like her cold cellar, which lacked a good fire to toast them. The faint smell of stew made her stomach rattle.

A creak came from upstairs and she held her breath, expelling it when a plump tabby cat came racing down to weave around her ankles. When she tickled its chin its purring rattle ceased. It stalked off towards the back of the house, tail up, stopping only to offer her a disapproving look over its shoulder before it disappeared through an open door, as if to say it'd thought she was someone else and the friendly gesture it'd initially offered her was a mistake.

Somewhere, a clock gave a quiet tick, reminding her of why she was here. The empty spaces of the house pressed against her ears as she opened the door to the nearest room.

Where should she leave the watch? When Thomas Hambert found it she wanted him to think it had been there all the time. She found herself in a comfortable drawing room with blue, winged chairs and a chaise longue. The room had a chill to it, as though the fire wasn't often lit. Over the fireplace there was a picture of a woman, unsmiling and stern. Her brown eyes seemed to follow Celia around the room.

'It's all right, missus, I won't steal anything, I promise,' she whispered.

The next room made her gasp. Here, the fire was ready to light in the grate. Here, were two leather chairs either side of the mantelpiece, an occasional table and a sideboard with a decanter of brandy and glasses on a silver tray. Here, there was a whole wall of books, brown, green and red with gold lettering, and of all different sizes. Envy grew in her. He had books – so many that if she took one he wouldn't even miss it.

On the small, highly polished table there was a statue of a bronze goddess with a bow and arrow in one hand, while the other rested on the head of a dog pressed against her leg. She hung the watch around the woman's neck. Thomas Hambert was bound to see it sooner or later, since the chime would alert him.

Her hand slid along the books, and she smiled when she saw a copy of *Robinson Crusoe* by Daniel Defoe. She pulled it out, opened it and read aloud, *'I was born in the year 1632, in the city of York, of a good family...'*

Her mother had been born of a good family too. Celia was about to curl up in the chair and read more when she heard the key slide into the lock at the front door. Startled, she threw the book on to the chair, hurried out of the room and bounded up the stairs.

She should have realized that the fog would have driven Mr Hambert home early. She watched from the landing as he took off his greatcoat and made a fuss of the cat, which had come running to greet him.

'What have you been up to today, Frederick? Not annoying Mrs Packer, I hope.'

Frederick gave a bit of a trill.

'Ah, you need some milk, do you? Then we'd better go down to the kitchen,' he said. The cat meowed in agreement, as though the pair of them were having a proper conversation. Celia smiled as they headed away out of sight, Mr Hambert chatting to the cat and the cat looking up at him and talking back. She was lucky that cats didn't really speak, else Frederick might be telling him there was a stranger lurking in the house.

Seizing her chance, she ran lightly down the stairs to the front door. She fumbled with the catch. Footsteps came from the back of the house and she just managed to open it and slip through the crack in time. Pulling the door behind her with some force she leaped on to the pavement and began to run.

Just as she turned the corner she collided with a man coming from the opposite direction. He was almost into middle age, but not quite, for the light-brown hair that winged from under his hat contained no grey. Still, he was handsome. He grabbed her arm, steadying her. Grey eyes stared into hers. 'What the devil are you in such a rush about? You nearly bowled me over. What are you doing here in Bedford Square, anyway ... begging?'

She nodded. It was easier to let him draw his

own conclusion, and she used her usual excuse. 'My mother is sick, sir, and she needs some medicine.'

'Then she must have it.' To her surprise he put his hand in his pocket and brought out a shilling, handing it to her.

It might be worth going door-to-door with a sorry tale in this area, she mused. She could take Lottie with her. A young child in hand always softened the women. Although she was taken aback, she didn't forget her manners. 'Thank you, sir, that's generous of you. I'm sorry I bumped into you. I must get mama's medicine and find my way home before the fog gets any thicker.'

'Off you go then, girl.'

'You still have my arm,' she pointed out.

'So I have.'

She was gone in the instant when he released her, springing away from him in case Thomas Hambert took it into his head to come out of his house to raise the alarm. The man looked fit, and he would easily catch her before she was swallowed by fog.

It didn't take long to get home despite the drifting fog, though she lost her bearings on a couple of occasions.

Her mother was sewing to the light of a solitary candle. 'Where have you been for all this time, Celia? I've been worried sick about you.'

'I took the watch back.'

'What did the owner say? Did he give you a reward?'

Celia remembered the shilling the young man

had given her and handed it to her mother. 'His housekeeper gave me a shilling.'

'Well, I hope the constables don't come knocking at the door looking for you.'

'Don't worry, Ma. The woman didn't ask where I lived and I didn't tell her.'

'You should inform the police,' James Kent said to his uncle.

'For what reason? Nothing is missing.'

'How did they get in? You said all the windows and doors were shut when you got home. Either they picked the lock, or they had a key.'

Thomas gave his nephew a sheepish grin. 'I've just remembered that there was a spare key on my watch chain, in case I forgot to take my usual door key.'

'Then you must have the locks changed tomorrow.'

'I'm sure I heard the watch chime amongst my clothing a few days ago, but when I looked I couldn't find it. I thought that it might have got caught in the lining of my coat. Let me have a good look through the house again tomorrow.'

'But you said you caught a glimpse of someone closing the door behind them.'

Thomas shrugged. 'I could have been mistaken. I was home early and perhaps it was Mrs Packer I saw, or I might have left the door open when I came in and it simply banged shut. Then again, it might have been a swirl of fog ... or ... or a *ghost*.'

James laughed. 'Now there's a comforting thought.'

'I wouldn't mind too much if it were my wife or daughter.'

'No ... I don't suppose you would.' James patted his uncle gently on the shoulder. 'That was a long time ago. You should have married again. You should sell this house and your half of the printing business and move back to the country to be near my mother. You could then enjoy the fresh country air in your old age. You know she'd enjoy having you to fuss over.'

'My dear James, I don't want to be fussed over, even by my sister. Also, you haven't lived long enough to advise me on what I should, or should not, be doing. As for marriage, may I remind you that it's eluded you so far ... or you have eluded it.'

James laughed. 'My apology, Uncle. At the age of thirty-three I should know better than imagine I've gained any wisdom from living.'

'Apology accepted. And please don't pat me as though I'm the family dog, something I find intensely irritating. Besides, you're forgetting I have my book to write.'

'You could write just as easily in Dorset; you must have finished researching it by now.'

Thomas grinned. 'Not at all; London changes all the time. Besides, I have a rival. I've recently run into someone who intends to do exactly the same thing. The odds of running into someone in London with exactly the same idea for a book as I have, must be almost nil. The girl looks to be all of fifteen years old, and she has learned to spell and write, and she understands the meaning of every word in the dictionary, or so she told

31

me.'

'Really? How interesting. It must be the daughter of a friend of yours, no doubt. Will you make her your protégée?'

'But no, James, she is not someone I know. The child is a beggar I befriended.'

'Ah...' James said, and he began to laugh. 'That's typical of you. And you wonder where your watch has gone. This girl of yours ... Is she about this high?' He placed his flattened hand at the height of his armpit. 'And does she wear a ragged grey cape, and have striking blue eyes?'

'It sounds as though you've met her.'

'Just as I turned the corner she came from the opposite direction as if her feet were on fire. Is it possible that you saw your beggar girl leaving your house? She may have robbed you of the watch earlier, using the key to let herself in with. It's possible she intended to rob the house as well.'

'But nothing is missing as far as I can see.'

'Perhaps because you came home earlier than usual and disturbed her.'

They were standing in the hall. Into the sudden, reflective silence, the sound of chiming suddenly intruded. Thomas gave a broad and satisfied smile. 'There, you see, James, my boy, she didn't take my watch. It's simply that I mislaid it. How odd. It's two minutes ahead of the clock, when it usually keeps good time.'

The sound was coming from the library, where he spent most of his time. The fifth chime died away just as they entered. It was James who found the watch dangling from the statuette of

32

Diana, the huntress. He handed it to his uncle then set a match to the kindling. As he straightened up he saw the book on the chair and picked it up. 'Robinson Crusoe ... I thought you'd read this.'

'I have. Mrs Packer must have taken the book out and forgotten to put it back.' Thomas slid the book back into its slot. 'I expect she found my watch somewhere and put it where I could find it, too.'

Thomas didn't really believe his own explanation. It was too much of a coincidence that the girl had mentioned Robinson Crusoe. But he didn't want to blame the girl. She was a treasure of a child, like a flower growing in the wilderness, delicate but tough enough to survive. Her mind was fresh and fertile, and open to teaching because she was eager to learn. It was such a shame to allow it to go to waste.

It had struck him also that somebody must have kept his watch wound up. As for the glimpse of someone leaving ... well, it could have been the beggar girl. But had she, distracted by the book, come to return the watch, or had she simply forgotten to take it with her when she fled? He remembered too, that the last time they'd met she'd called him by his name. Where would she have learned of it, except from the inscription on the watch?

He picked his notebook up and opened it, gently turning over the pages. He stopped and gazed at a drawing. There she was, her sweet little face wistful, her cupped hand outstretched and her eyes full of dreams.

'Look, here she is,' he said and James came to look over his shoulder.

'She recited a Shakespeare sonnet to the crowd that day. Her voice was clear and rang out with great feeling, but her actions were too dramatic for my taste. She collected very little in the way of money for her efforts. On the whole, the crowds were intent on a more colourful and exciting entertainment.'

'That's the girl who bumped into me in the street. She managed to get a shilling out of me with some tale of woe about a sick mother. As soon as she got the coin she went running off as though the devil himself was after her.'

'Perhaps her mother *is* sick. A girl like that can't enjoy having to live a life of poverty and be obliged to beg. You know what the next step will be for her.'

James shrugged. 'I suppose you're going to make it your mission in life to save her. You should have taken up missionary work. Be careful, Uncle Thomas, she's probably as cunning as a river rat.'

'So would you be if you'd had to fend for yourself from an early age. That's enough now, James. I'm not the old fool you tend to think I am, and I still enjoy a challenge.'

James grinned widely at him. 'I think nothing of the sort. I think you are the most compassionate man I know.'

'Only within reason, my boy. Tell me, what would you make of a thief who steals goods then returns them to her victim?'

James considered it for a moment, his eyes

reflective. Wide blue eyes with dark lashes came into his mind. She'd been a pretty little thing despite the dirt on her face and the rags she wore. 'I'd think that the girl saw the memorial to your daughter in the back of your watch, and her conscience was rattled.'

'Which indicates that she isn't dishonest by nature, and has been brought up to be honest. And yes, I do believe she has a good mind, and because her needs in that area are not really satisfied she employs and enjoys using trickery. She put the watch where she did to trick me into thinking it's where I left it, and it had been there all the time. What she forgot was, if it had been left there for all that time, the spring would have wound down and it would have stopped. She had kept it wound up while she had it, you see.'

'What if she'd left it there by mistake?'

'She would have snatched it up as soon as the key went in the latch. She could also have taken several things on the way out. The silver snuff-box, spoons, ornaments and coins. All this in-dicates to me is that she thieves or begs only to survive.'

'You have an odd sense of what's honest and what's not, Uncle.'

'Perhaps I'll be able to prove it to you before you return to take up that legal partnership in Dorset. I'm going to find out more about this girl. She interests me.'

James sighed.

Three

Thomas didn't see his light-fingered friend for two weeks.

He thought she might be avoiding him, which as far as Thomas was concerned was a sure sign of her guilt in the matter of her uninvited intrusion into his house. Nevertheless, her lesson had been driven home and he no longer wore such a valuable timepiece when going about his day, but a rather ordinary metal watch that didn't keep perfect time like his other one.

In his satchel he carried a gift, with which to entice her.

He was observing a sideshow of tumblers when he saw her again. It was a cold, still day. The sky was high, a sweep of thin cloud brushed across it by a wind that hadn't yet found its way down to ground level. Dark hair tumbled down her back. Her eyes were wide, her expression absorbed. She had a wall at her back and her occasional glances kept her aware of what was going on around her.

She must have sensed his interest for she gazed more carefully at the crowd. Her glance wandered past him and then came back. She didn't avoid his eyes, but cocked her head to one side and offered him a faint, but altogether mischievous smile.

He beckoned.

She shook her head and pointed to a notice on the side of a cart before pointing to herself. *Prize of five shillings for the best amateur acts, voted on by audience acclaim. Thruppence to register your act. Spectator entry fee, sixpence.*

Thomas paid his sixpence and joined the rest of the people crushed shoulder-to-shoulder into a small tent. The smell of humanity was ripe, but after a while Thomas got used to it. At thruppence for registration and sixpence each from the audience, this little travelling entertainment venture could prove to be quite lucrative. And it all packed away into a gypsy caravan pulled by a sturdy carthorse.

A stout lady singer faced the audience first, and was pelted with cabbage stumps. Number two on the bill was a man with one leg who played a tune on a wheezing hurdy-gurdy while his dog danced on its hind legs. Another man whistled a tune, one that was drowned out by a chorus of louder whistles and boos. A soldier marched up and down, clicked his heels, saluted the audience and cried out, 'God save the Queen.'

'Save her from what?' someone shouted. 'Piss orf, will yer! Go and march upp'n down outside the palace with the 'orses.'

Behind the tent the carthorse whinnied loudly, as if it were laughing.

It was then the girl's turn.

'For our final act, Miss Celia Jane Laws will recite a poem of her own composition called, Only a Poor London Girl.' He helped her up on a box for all to see.

Celia Jane! The name gave Thomas quite a shock, and a painful feeling of grief for his deceased daughter attacked him. He suffered a moment of resentment that this beggar shared his dead daughter's name. No wonder the girl's conscience had pricked her. Celia Laws had discarded her cape, but her blue dress was just as patched and ragged, the hem stained with mud.

There was dignity in the way she stood still, her head bowed until the audience became quiet. From behind the curtain came a few plaintive notes played on a violin. Only when it stopped did she lift her head to look up at the expectant crowd. Her face was tragic, her eyes filled with tears.

'What am I? Only a poor London girl brought down by poverty, begging for a penny piece, trying to stay honest in the company of many a thief.'

Thomas winced, but the audience didn't seem to notice anything amiss with the rhyme. She fell to her knees, put her hands together in prayer and gazed up to heaven.

'Lord, help my mama to recover from her malady. Save her from the appetites of men and the sweet, long sleep of the dreadful opium den.'

Startled, Thomas' eyes flew open and he whispered, 'Good grief!'

Somebody from the back yelled, 'Where does your ma live, sweetheart?'

She stood and glared at the speaker, then picked up a cabbage stump and hurled it at him. Everyone clapped and laughed until she assumed a dramatic stance once more, her hands against her chest. Thomas wanted to laugh then. He was certainly getting his sixpence worth.

'I'm just a poor girl on the dusty streets. I'm waiting for papa to return from war and to gather us in his arms when he marches through the door.'

Several women in the crowd had begun to sob.

'I'm just a beggar girl filled with London pride, doing my best to stay alive in the cruel, cold city. I'm as gentle as a dove, so on poor me, please take pity.' She finished with a limp hand against her forehead, and a loud sigh, then came the *coup de grâce*. *'Alas ... poor me!'*

There was a moment of silence before somebody at the back gave a piercing whistle. Somebody else shouted 'Bravo!' as though it was a signal.

With tears streaming down her face Celia bowed to tumultuous applause. 'Thank you, my dear friends; I'm humbled.'

Thomas very much doubted it and he had to stifle the urge to roar with laughter.

'Judging by the applause there's no need to count votes. I hereby declare Miss Celia Jane Laws the winner,' the tumbler said. 'Come and get your prize money, girl.'

Celia curtseyed and smiled tragically through her tears before walking regally off the makeshift stage. She disappeared behind a curtain.

Thomas pushed through the tide of the departing crowd and joined her. He was in time to see the tumbler handing her two shillings.

'I thought the prize was five shillings; don't let

the man cheat you,' Thomas said.

Her glance slid to his, eyes still wet but drying rapidly. She shrugged as she pocketed the money. 'You don't have to be clever to work it out, professor,' and she indicated the tumbler. 'This is my friend Benito. Benito, this is Professor Hambert, the man I told you about.'

Benito smiled at him and extended a hand. 'I'm pleased to meet you, professor. I'll be over at St Paul's tomorrow if you want to earn a little extra, Celia. Same time. You always go down a treat with the audience.'

'I'll be there, Benito. How's your wife. Has the baby been born yet?'

He beamed a smile. 'Just a couple of days ago, so Marie isn't up to getting back to work yet so she's staying with her parents till I get back. We have a son ... His name is Gulio and he can already juggle.'

She laughed. 'Give him a kiss from me, then.'

Thomas raised an eyebrow after they left. 'Professor?'

'Well, you are, aren't you? You've got lots of books.' She slid him a sideways glance. 'Are you very angry with me?'

Thomas should be, but he wasn't. In fact, he rather admired her enterprise.

'I'm sorry. I'd intended to put the watch back in your pocket that day when we talked. Then it chimed and I didn't want you to think I'd stolen it.'

'But you *had* stolen it.'

'I didn't intend to keep it, so it was only borrowed ... but if I hadn't taken it, somebody else would have. I only did it for fun, you know. You're careless with your belongings. It was silly to leave your house key on the chain, and your address inside. You could have been murdered in your bed.'

'Yes ... It was rather silly of me. I certainly won't do it again.' She'd turned the tables on him and made him feel as though he was in the wrong. 'Why did you give the watch back?'

'My mother told me to. She doesn't like me being dishonest.' Her eyes narrowed slightly. 'I notice you aren't wearing it today.'

Thomas smiled and patted his pocket. Then he patted it again. His smile fled, to be replaced by a frown. 'I don't believe it.'

Pulling his watch out of her sleeve she dangled it in front of him, laughing. 'Are you looking for this? You should secure the watch chain and sew a button on your watch pocket, one slightly bigger than the buttonhole, so it's hard to unfasten.'

'When did you do it?' he said, taking the watch from her.

'I lifted it when you shook hands with Benito.'

He sighed. 'I really don't think I can trust you now.'

'I was showing off. I don't usually steal from my friends. Did you like my poem, professor?'

His inclination at the thought of it was to laugh, but she wasn't quite a woman yet. She was still a child – if a rather precocious one – and he didn't want to hurt her feelings too badly. 'I thought it was rather ... well ... florid, I suppose.'

Her eyes sharpened. 'I haven't come across that word before. Is that good or bad?'

41

'It means it's overwritten. That's not good.'

A tiny exasperated sound left her mouth. 'Now who's being florid? If it's not good then it must be bad ... how bad is it?'

He gave her what she didn't really need to hear. 'It was terrible.'

Now he'd offered her the bald truth, he wished he hadn't. She looked crushed by the observation. But then she rallied and spoke in defence of her composition. 'The audience liked it, and you must remember it wasn't written with a learned gentleman like yourself in mind.'

'Oh, I'm not saying that the poem didn't have its good points. It did. The rhythm of it was ... *unusual*, but it worked as you recited the piece, which you put across well. Most of your audience could connect with the emotional content because poverty is something they all know about. You also know how to work a crowd.'

She nodded. 'Before my sister arrived, my mother and I toured with a theatre company. After that she became a housekeeper. I was only young then, but I learned a lot. So what was so terrible about the poem?'

Now she'd put him on the spot again, not with any thought of embarrassing him, but because she seemed to have a genuine need to know. 'The second verse was rather vulgar for a girl of your age, I thought,' he ventured. 'What do you know of men's appetites and opium dens?'

'I've been to Limehouse, haven't I? Besides, that poem earned me two shillings today. And it will earn me two shillings tomorrow and another two the day after, and for the rest of the week.

That's ten shillings, which is better than one shilling and four pence from a publisher or a shilling for...' She bit her tongue, mumbling red-faced, 'Well, you know ... at least ... that's what I'm told it costs.'

Hiding his shock, Thomas stopped to buy them a bowl of pea and ham soup and a thick chunk of bread to soak it up with. He carried his own mug and spoon with him, but Celia drank hers from the wooden bowl. When it was empty her tongue came out and lashed around the bowl as far down as she could stretch it, licking up the residue. She fished out the leftover shreds of ham with her fingertip. She sighed and smiled at the stall-holder when she handed the bowl back. 'That was good.'

Thomas wondered how many people had drunk from the bowl, and shuddered.

When they resumed walking, she said, 'I'm sorry I entered your house without your permission. I liked your cat.'

'Frederick is a good companion.'

'Do you understand him when he talks back to you?'

'In a way. Humans and animals communicate in the only method they can. Usually Frederick's demands are small. He's hungry, or he wants to go out into the garden, or to sit on my lap and have a fuss made of him. Sometimes he just wants to be amused and sometimes he's a dreadful show-off and keeps me amused.'

A smile touched her mouth.

He remembered the gift he'd bought her. Taking it out of his satchel he held it out to her.

'Here, this is for you.'

She undid the knot in the string holding the brown paper in place and gazed unsmilingly down at the book, then at him. *'Robinson Crusoe*? This is the one from the shop window. Why are you giving me this?'

'Because it's a book you wanted to read.'

'And what do you want in return?' She then moved on to display that she did have some knowledge of men's appetites, pushing the book back at him. 'The same as all men, I suppose. Well, I'm not about to sell myself for anything, and especially a book. I could easily ... *get* one if I wanted one. Worse, somebody might think I stole this one from you, and you might say it's true, unless I do your bidding.'

Thomas laughed at her indignation. 'My dear child, you have too vivid an imagination for your own good. This is a gift, pure and simple, and with no strings attached.'

She dangled the string. 'Then what do you call this?'

He sighed. 'I'm talking figuratively ... that is a length of string, literally.'

She examined it more closely before giving him a pitying look. 'It looks like ordinary string to me.'

He stifled his chuckle. Now was not the time to explain. He led her to the stall of a letter writer, an ageing Jewish gentleman. He placed a coin on his desk. 'I would like to hire a pen and ink, if I may, and perhaps you would witness me giving this young woman this book, so she cannot be accused of stealing it.'

'The young lady may come to me for witness if needed,' the scribe said with a smile.

Thomas wrote on the flyleaf, *A gift for my dear friend, Celia Jane Laws. May her dreams come to fruition in the fullness of time. With sincere best wishes, Thomas Hambert.*

Handing the book back to her, he said, 'There, nobody can accuse you of stealing it now.'

She ran a finger gently over the lettering and a grin flirted about her mouth as she hugged it against her chest. 'It's the best gift I've ever had. I'll give you my first book free of charge in return ... that's if you still want it ... you didn't like the poem.'

'That doesn't mean I'll dislike everything else you write. I was too forthright, and I'm sorry if I upset you.'

'You didn't. I know it wasn't good, but sometimes the words rhyme and the meaning of the words don't.'

He offered her a little encouragement. 'Actually, the more I think of the poem the more I like it. It worked very well at a performance level, you know.'

'Perhaps I should just stick to stories. They're easier to write.'

'Have you started on the stories?'

She nodded. 'It took me nearly two weeks to finish a story, and write the poem for Benito's show. Then I had to make a copy like you said. I liked writing the story best.'

So, Celia had been bitten by the writing bug. It was a pity her education hadn't continued, but what did he know about her circumstances? She was better educated than most people around here, in the basics at least. She obviously took every opportunity to earn enough money to exist on. 'Do you have a title for your book?'

'Famous Fictional Tales from the London Slums.'

'An excellent title.'

Her smile was like the sun coming out. 'It took me a long time to think of one. My mother helped me. She thought I should leave the first word off, though. She said it was showing off.'

'It is in a way, but such initiatives must be taken if one's work is to be noticed. If people think the stories are already famous they'll buy them. I would rather like to meet your mother. Why don't you bring her to my house to tea one day?'

'Which day?' she said eagerly before her face fell. 'Her visiting dress is beyond repair so she might be too ashamed.'

'It's not her dress that will be doing the visiting, and I promise not to notice the patches. Bring her tomorrow if you can spare the time. Two p.m.?'

'My sister will have to come too. Lottie is only three, and too young to be left behind by herself.'

'Of course she is. I'm sure I can cater for Lottie.'

'Why do you want to meet my mother?'

'Because if we are to be friends she should be made aware of that friendship, and approve of it.'

Her look assessed him and she gave a wry smile. 'You can come and meet her now if you

46

have the time; then you can decide if you want to remain friends. Our *home* is just round the corner.'

He glanced at his watch and nodded. 'Yes, I do have time.'

It took them three minutes to get there. They went down a few stairs and she banged on a door and called out, 'It's me, Ma. I have a visitor. May we come in?'

There was a muffled reply.

Celia turned to him. 'The ceiling is low so watch your head.'

Through a door of rotting wood and over a solid stone step designed to keep rain from trickling in, Thomas found himself in a damp cellar with a flagged floor. There was a small grate with a stewpot hanging from a hook.

'Mr Hambert. This is my mother, Mrs Alice Laws.'

The woman stood, automatically bowing her head from the danger of the low ceiling. She had a pale, pinched face, in which gaunt traces of a former beauty could be found. 'How do you do, Mr Hambert.' She crossed to where Celia stood. 'You're not in any trouble are you, Celia?'

'No. Mr Hambert thought he should meet you so you'd know he was respectable.' Her hand went to her pocket and she handed over the two shillings she'd earned to her mother. 'I earned this reciting a poem.'

'Good, that means we have enough to pay the rent with this week.'

Thomas was getting a crick in his neck so he went down on his haunches and spoke to the small child who was gazing at him. 'Hullo, my dear. What's your name?'

The infant gave a soft giggle.

Mrs Laws smiled. 'Her name is Charlotte, but we call her Lottie. Would you take a seat, Mr Hambert? You will be much more comfortable.'

Thomas was horrified by the accommodation, but he realized it was as clean and tidy as one could make such a place. The tiny fireplace gave out very little heat, and in places mould slimed the walls where dampness had risen from the ground and was progressing upwards. Such cellars were not designed to accommodate anything but wine and rats, and it had a peculiar odour. His nose wrinkled. It was not one he wanted to identify.

He took a seat at the rickety table and found his notebook. 'Would you mind if I sketched the interior of your home? It's for a paper I'm writing about social conditions of our time.'

Mrs Laws gave her permission and took the child up on her lap. Celia bent to stir the stew.

He chatted to Alice Laws while he worked, introducing topics she might be familiar with. She was intelligent, but ill at ease, appearing embarrassed by the squalor she was forced to endure.

Footsteps pattered overhead and dust drifted down.

Bit by bit he dug her story from her. A hasty marriage followed by desertion. She was middle-class and down on her luck, a country girl taken advantage of, but doing her best to survive. She had a persistent cough too, which boded ill for her future. Thomas wondered if she'd seen a doctor about it.

'I'm so pleased that Celia was able to return the watch she found, Mr Hambert. Thank your housekeeper for giving her a reward. I understand that you were absent at the time she went to your house to return it, so where did you make the acquaintance of my daughter?'

He shifted his glance to Celia, who had the grace to look ashamed as he was forced to find the wit to lie. 'I sought her out. Celia was pointed out to me on the street and I introduced myself.'

'Mr Hambert has bought me a copy of *Robinson Crusoe*.' She handed it to her mother. 'See, he has written a message inside.'

She read the inscription and looked him straight in the eye. 'That's kind of you, sir. How odd that you picked the very same book that Celia has always coveted.'

This woman was no fool, but she had a disillusioned air about her. She was nicely spoken and everything Celia had said she was. As far as he could tell the slums had not sucked either her or her children completely into its social maw yet.

'I would offer you tea, but we have none.'

'I'm not thirsty, Mrs Laws. I'm here because the information Celia gave me about you piqued my interest. I wanted to reassure you that your daughter will not be in any danger in my company.'

The woman gave her daughter a searching look. 'Celia has a vivid imagination and she is prone to exaggeration.'

'I've noticed.'

'What do you want with her?'

Thomas didn't really know. It was unlike him to become involved in the life of those he observed. 'I might be able to help you to better yourself.'

She shrugged. 'I would prefer my independence than be under an obligation to any man.'

'I want nothing from you. Let us be frank with one another. It seems to me that you and your children have nowhere to go but down. Celia is on the brink of womanhood. She's got a good brain on her and already has quite a bag of tricks at her disposal; most of them dishonest, for even begging is illegal. She's also an accomplished liar.'

Celia gasped.

'I can only guess at how you are able to support your children, Mrs Laws, but if Celia is any indication they haven't got much of a future. I'm not without influence. Perhaps if I were to inform the parish of your circumstances—'

'They would give me a place in a workhouse and deprive me of my children. They would then be worse off because they'd be hired out to anyone who would offer for them, and would be at the mercy of people who didn't care what happened to them. Have you seen the children starving, or frozen to death on the streets? I don't want that to happen to my children.'

'And if anything happens to you?'

She avoided his eyes. 'Celia is better educated than most, and she's old enough and sensible enough to care for Lottie.'

'So are you, my dear, but you can't earn enough to afford decent lodging.'

Celia put an arm around her mother and gazed fiercely at him. 'Was it your intention to insult us when you came here?'

'Hush, Celia. Mr Hambert has never been in the position we're in, while I have the advantage of being familiar with his. He's attempting to educate himself under the guise of educating us ... is that not so, Mr Hambert?'

Thomas squirmed at the resounding put-down. That's exactly what he'd done. How could he have been so patronizing? 'You're right, Mrs Laws. I'm not usually so crass, and I hope you will forgive me, and come and have tea with me tomorrow. As Celia so rightly reminded me, that's why I came here ... to meet you, and invite you.'

Would misplaced pride make her refuse the offer of a free meal, though?

The woman gazed down at her dress and sighed, but said nothing of her poverty. 'Afternoon tea ... it's been a long time ... yes, I think I'd enjoy that.'

'I'll get along home, then.' Flustered, he stood up too quickly and banged his head on the roof.

Celia smothered a laugh.

When Thomas told James of the invitation his nephew flopped into a chair, looking clearly astounded. 'You've invited a family of thieves to tea? Good Lord, Uncle ... whatever next? The people in the square won't appreciate your home becoming a meeting place for such people.'

51

Thomas ignored the suggestion. Bedford Square was mostly inhabited by artisans, writers and scholarly people like himself. Some took in lodgers to help pay the rent. 'You'll like Celia when you meet her. Her mother is unusual in that she was a teacher in a church school before she fell on hard times.'

'A likely story.'

'James, you're being much too cynical. Please reserve your judgement until after you've met them.'

His eyes lit up with amusement. 'You mean that you expect me to attend your tea party in an effort to further my social interaction?'

'Damn it, James, yes, I most certainly do,' Thomas growled. 'You must be obliged to mix with all classes of people in your legal profession, so I'm sure you'll carry it off admirably. In fact, I'd be interested in what you make of them. If nothing else it might encourage you to appreciate your own circumstances and opportunities a little better. Besides ... I thought the family might be a suitable study for the paper I must present to the Anglican Philanthropic Society I belong to.'

'Ah ... so that's it. Perhaps I'll be able to keep an eye on the teaspoons for you if I join you then. Have you told Mrs Packer that you're expecting beggars as guests tomorrow?'

'I've told her I'm expecting guests for tea, and to light a fire in the drawing room. That's all she needs to know. I've asked her to buy some muffins from the vendor in the morning, and she has promised to bake a madeira cake.'

James' laughter rang out. 'It'll be worth coming to your tea party just to see her face when she sets eyes on them.'

Four

The walk to Bedford Square tired Alice Laws more than she cared to admit. Celia strode on ahead, her sister carried warmly under her cape. Lottie rode astride Celia's hip, small and thin.

'Celia, wait.' She stopped to catch her breath and was overtaken by an irrepressible urge to cough. Her handkerchief displayed tiny flecks of red afterwards. Alice knew what that usually signified, though she'd avoided thinking about it so far. She'd just turned thirty-eight, yet she felt like an old woman. It occurred to her now that she must make arrangements for the welfare of her children. She had no doubt that Celia would manage without her, but it was *how* her daughter would manage that worried her.

An offer had been made recently that her daughter didn't know about. Celia possessed a certain quality that had attracted the notice of a gentleman. Innocence! Through a broker he'd offered a great deal of money for the girl, trying to tempt Alice to hand her over.

Alice had turned the offer down, but she suspected that she was simply postponing the inevitable. It wouldn't take much to snatch Celia from the street. Children of all ages disappeared every day, some turning up on the Thames river mud a few days later, their bodies broken.

Alice always worried when Celia went out, just going about her business and looking for work to help them provide for their daily needs. Her daughter was lovely and drew the eye.

Concern in her eyes, Celia came back to where she stood. 'Are you all right, Ma?'

Alice nodded, her breath a harsh rasp. She felt the cold, deep down inside her bones. 'Yes, my love. I just need to catch my breath. It's years since I walked this far, and you're hard to keep up with.'

'I should have walked slower. It's not much further, just around the corner.'

When Alice's breathing quieted Celia took hold of her hand and placed it on her shoulder. 'Lean on me.'

'Celia,' Alice said urgently. 'If anything happens to me I want you to take Lottie and go and ask my sisters for help. Beg if you have to. I don't want you and Lottie to be forced on to the streets.'

'I know better than that.'

'You might not be given a choice, so be vigilant. A gentleman noticed you and his agent approached me. I don't want you to live that sort of life.'

Celia looked shocked for a moment, then placed a kiss on her mother's cheek. 'Neither do I, Ma, so don't worry so much. I'll be careful.'

'I don't know why I agreed to have tea with your friend. You can't trust any man and we

54

could be walking into the lion's den.'

'Oh, Ma, you can't blame all men for what happened in your past. Think about it. We'll get something nice to eat, and the bread and broth we were going to eat today will then last us until tomorrow.'

'There's that.' There was also the thought that she wouldn't have to find some man to give her the price of a meal for her favours. Celia didn't mention it, but Alice knew that her eldest daughter was well aware of the way of things. She was sure that's why Celia had taken up dipping ... to earn more money for them all. Alice was ashamed of herself and hated what she was forced to do to survive. She definitely didn't want her daughter to sell herself. It was demeaning.

'Cheer up, Ma. You haven't had a cup of tea to drink for months, and now you'll get more than one,' Celia teased.

'That will be wonderful. I'm really looking forward to it. Perhaps there will be muffins and cake, and little sandwiches.'

Celia grinned. 'And four-and-twenty blackbirds baked in a pie, perhaps.'

Alice laughed and placed a hand on her daughter's shoulder. They moved forward at a slower pace and turned the corner into Bedford Square. Celia knocked at a door with ornate glass panels.

A thin streak of a woman opened it and gazed down her nose at them. She was wearing a silver-framed lorgnette on a cord around her neck. 'Yes?'

'We're here to see Professor Hambert.'

'For what reason, may I ask?'

Thomas Hambert called out, 'Are those my guests, Mrs Packer? Let them in.'

'I don't think so, sir. They look more like beggars to me.'

The blood rose to Alice's face and she bit back a retort. She couldn't blame the woman for thinking that, though, and began to wish they hadn't come.

Her daughter called out, 'It's me, Mr Hambert ... Celia Laws, with my mother and sister.'

He bustled forward, a smile on his face. 'Celia my dear ... and Mrs Laws. How lovely to see you again. Don't stand out there in the cold.' He drew them inside. 'Hello, Lottie dear, what a dear, sweet child you are. Shut the door if you please, Mrs Packer, you're allowing the cold in. May I relieve you of your capes, ladies?'

The door closed with a thud to signify the housekeeper's displeasure, and, as she went stomping off towards the back of the house, Mr Hambert called out to her retreating back, 'Serve tea in fifteen minutes please, Mrs Packer. And use the best china for our guests. The child will have milk.'

'Can I be of help, Mrs Packer?' Celia offered.

The woman turned and gave her that tight-lipped look of hers. 'I can manage.'

A word of thanks wouldn't have gone amiss, Alice thought. Brought up in a house with servants, she was now being scorned by one. It would have been a different attitude if she'd turned up in a satin gown.

When Mr Hambert chucked Lottie under the

chin she put her hands up to her eyes and peered through her fingers at him. She giggled when he said, 'Boo!'

There was a faint smell of lavender in the room and a fire burned brightly. A woman gazed down at them from a frame. The late Mrs Hambert, Alice supposed. She looked rather serious, but there was a soft curve to her mouth and the beginnings of a twinkle in her eyes, as though her expression disguised a nature that was both frivolous and mischievous.

A man rose to his feet. He had a natural, easy smile and eyes that displayed an intelligence that had not yet been satisfied.

'This is my nephew, James Kent. He has cut his teeth at the Old Bailey, and is shortly to join a legal practice in the country, where he will eventually take up the post of magistrate. He's a clever young man who should go far.'

'Now, now, Uncle, your pride is showing.'

James kissed Alice's hand. It had been a long time since that had happened and memories surfaced of evenings spent in the drawing room with her family and their friends. How easily those particular worms had turned when she'd needed them.

'Mrs Laws; how nice to meet you. You look cold ... come, take my seat by the fire.' When she did he placed a cushion at her back and turned to Celia. 'Miss Laws, we meet again. How are you?'

Celia busied herself with Lottie. 'I'm well, Mr Kent.'

'Good. My uncle tells me you've taken up

acting. You must recite your poem for us.'

Celia turned a rosy shade of pink. 'I don't think so, Mr Kent. I'm not a real poet and your uncle thinks my poem to be ... *florid,* so I won't bore him with it again.'

'I wouldn't have thought that a young woman who performs in public would be shy of performing in the drawing room. What say you, Uncle?'

The man was subjecting Celia to some light teasing.

Mr Hambert beamed a smile at everyone. 'There's a big difference in acting a part, and in being connected to a poem for the love of it. One is performed with the head, the second with the heart.'

Spontaneously Celia said, 'Oh, I know exactly what you mean.'

'Do you, my dear?'

'Some poems hide inside you, and little snatches of it visit from time to time. Sometimes the scenes created by the words are so beautiful they make me sad.' She looked from one to the other and shrugged. 'I imagine that sounds silly.'

Alice rescued her daughter. 'Not at all, that's exactly how it is. Now, you might prefer to recite another poet's work, Celia. Keats perhaps.'

Mr Hambert smiled at her. 'Ah yes, John Keats. It's a long time since I've heard his work recited. Do you know *The Human Seasons*, Celia? It starts with: *Four seasons fill the measure of the year.'*

'Not very well.' Shyly, Celia picked up on it. *'There are four seasons in the mind of man: He* has his lusty spring, when fancy clear, takes in all beauty with an easy span.'

When she hesitated Thomas prompted, 'He has his summer...'

They picked through the poem together, and Alice received a nervous glance from Celia when it came to her turn again. '...on mists of idleness – to let fair things pass by unheeded as a threshold brook.' Celia spread her hands. 'It's been a long time and I forget the rest.'

James smiled at her. 'He has his winter too of pale misfeature...'

'Or else he would forgo his mortal nature?' Celia finished.

'A wonderful joint effort.' Thomas said with a smile.

'Why is the poem called The Human Seasons when it refers to men all the time? Women are human, too.'

James laughed. 'Answer that one, Uncle?'

'I'm afraid I can't. Perhaps because the poet was a man, and perhaps because women are the beauty he perceives in his lustful spring and the honeyed cud of his summer.'

James gently coughed and Thomas looked a bit flustered.

'Perhaps my daughter is too young to be expected to understand such poems yet,' Alice told him.

'Of course she is, but she recited the lines she remembered quite beautifully, I thought.'

When Celia beamed with pride and said, 'It's easier to perform to a bigger audience of strangers than to a small group,' they exchanged smiles.

'That's because it's more intimate with friends present.' Thomas asked, 'How are you getting on with *Robinson Crusoe*, Celia?'

'I haven't had time to read any of it yet. I've been writing my stories ... five in all, and I'm just about to finish the sixth. And I've been ... working.'

'Doing what?' James asked her innocently.

Celia saw no reason not to say out loud what they all knew. 'Begging, amongst other things.'

'Really ... what are the other things?'

Into the sudden silence the door opened and Mrs Packer came in with a tray of tea things. She placed it on the sideboard out of Lottie's reach, then left, coming back again with a tiered cake stand holding delicious-looking sandwiches, steaming muffins soaked with melted butter, and slices of cakes. She didn't look at anyone, but followed her nose back out of the room.

'Oh dear, I seem to have upset my house-keeper.' Thomas turned, his eyes laced with amusement. 'Perhaps you wouldn't mind pouring the tea for us, Mrs Laws.'

Alice barely heard him. Her gaze was on Celia, who was looking at James with a frown on her face.

He merely smiled at her. 'What other occupation did you say?'

Celia gave her a quick glance of reassurance and quietly informed him, 'I didn't say, but I act in plays.'

His smile teased her. 'Ah, you're an actress.

Are you famous?'

'I used to perform for the Wentworth Players.'

'I imagine you did perform, though I can't say I've ever heard of the theatre company.'

'I don't suppose they've heard of you, either. Are you going to prod at me all day, Mr Kent?'

He gave a bit of an abashed chuckle. 'I'd heard you had various talents. Being rude seems to be one of them.'

Calmly Celia informed him, 'It's you who is being rude. You are being inquisitive, and I was merely reacting to it.'

When James said, 'I must humbly beg your pardon, Miss Laws,' Celia's face flamed and she looked vexed.

'Enough James,' Thomas said mildly and turned to Celia. 'I do wish you'd brought your stories for me to read. Perhaps you'd drop them off sometime so I can offer my advice in editing them.'

'Perhaps I will, after I've got them exactly as I want them.'

'Which defeats the whole object of editing,' James said with a faint smile.

Colour rose high in Celia's face as she realized her mistake and she took him back to their spat, obviously unwilling to abandon it. 'I suppose it must do. What had you heard about my *various* talents, Mr Kent?'

'Oh, nothing that should alarm you.'

When Celia's eyes narrowed Alice thought it was time to intervene. Patience wasn't one of her daughter's virtues. 'Celia ... see to your sister if you would. Take her on your lap and give her

61

some cake to eat. Make sure she doesn't drop crumbs.' Alice crossed to the sideboard and began to pour out the tea, conscious of her ragged state and being totally out of place in this elegant drawing room. She handed a cup first to Thomas, and then to James. Inclining her head she said quietly into James Kent's ear, 'My daughter is hardly more than a child and unused to drawing-room talk. Please bear that in mind, Mr Kent.'

When he nodded she poured tea for herself and Celia, then handed round the refreshments.

Lottie's eyes rounded with delight when she tasted the cake and she opened her mouth wider for the next bite.

'No,' Celia said, withdrawing it as Lottie made a grab for the rest.

For a moment Alice thought Lottie might kick up a fuss, but James Kent leaned forward and suggested, 'You hold her and I'll feed it to her.'

Alice placed her cup down. 'Perhaps I'd better take over. She might drop bits and pieces on you.'

James spread a napkin over his knees. 'That takes care of that problem. You enjoy your tea, Mrs Laws. We can put Lottie down when the edge is off her appetite.'

'It sounds as though you know something about children. Do you have a family, Mr Kent?'

'Lord no! I've never met a women brave enough to embark on the matrimonial journey with me. I do have a niece and a nephew though ... my sister's children. The girl is about Lottie's age, the boy is still a baby.'

'They've named the girl after me,' Mr Hambert said with pride.

Alice said cautiously, 'Thomas is rather an *odd* name for a girl.'

James huffed with laughter. 'It's Thomasina. The boy is called James, after his favourite uncle.'

The look Thomas gave him was crushing. 'As you can see I'm obliged to put up with my nephew's eternal conceit.'

Celia giggled, her good temper restored when James whispered an apology to her. Alice was relieved that the tension had relaxed.

A little while later the cat came in to investigate the visitors. Lottie clapped her hands. James tied a piece of paper on the end of a length of string and showed her how to tease Frederick with it. Soon, Lottie was running around giggling, with Frederick after her, his initial dignity abandoned.

Alice closed her eyes and felt sadness inside her that such a moment of innocent happiness in a child's life was a rare event instead of everyday normality. James connected well with children; he'd make a good father if he ever married. The cats in the area where they lived were lean, ferocious hunters, and were as numerous as the rodents they lived off. They were not fat pets to be tamed, pampered and entertaining, but flea-bitten, diseased scavengers who'd been known to devour a newborn baby abandoned to the squalor of the gutter, and they sometimes ended up in the cooking pot themselves.

Was that what she'd become as well? A

predator? What would become of her girls if the damp cough on her chest worsened. She'd turned a blind eye to Celia's activities so far, but she'd had very little choice, and had no resources to fall back on. As a mother, had she allowed the girl to sink too low for her to be redeemed?

No, she told herself. Celia had simply learned to survive within her environment. She was still young enough to adapt to another one ... a better one.

Come spring, Celia would be sixteen. If she could earn enough money she would take her children to the country, Alice thought. To start with she could sell that emerald and diamond ring Celia had hidden away. It must have been stolen, but it couldn't be returned, and the girl was unable to wear it in case it was recognized. There were other trinkets hidden behind a loose half-brick where the girl laid her mattress – a silver locket and a brooch in the shape of a butterfly, a pretty thing shimmering with different-coloured stones.

'Another muffin, Mrs Laws?'

Her hunger had already been satisfied by the cake, but she rarely had a good appetite these days. Celia took one, eating it in small quick bites, like a hungry dog scared it might lose its meal to another. When she placed a hand on her arm Celia remembered her manners and slowed down.

James asked, 'Can you play the piano and sing, as well as recite, Celia?'

'I can sing a little, but I don't feel like it at the moment. My mother can play the piano. She learned to when she was a child.'

'That was years ago, Celia. I haven't been able to practise,' Alice protested.

'You can practise today. I've never heard you play the piano, and I'd really like to. Are you sure you can?'

It was typical of Celia to direct the attention away from herself and on to another. Alice softened. 'I'll just play some short pieces then. Some fugues perhaps, and a minuet or two' She gazed at the two men and shrugged. 'I warn you. It's been fifteen years since I touched a keyboard so don't expect too much.'

'We'll take that into account, Mrs Laws. Besides, I don't think the instrument has been tuned in that time, so we'll blame any mistakes that emerge on that.'

He had lied about the piano not being tuned, she realized, as, after a couple of false starts, she warmed up her fingers with the short fugues, enjoying most the slightly plaintive G minor.

The music was sweet and Lottie scrambled down from James' lap and came to where she sat. She clung to her skirt, gazed at her with wide eyes and jiggled about, trying to dance on her skinny legs. Then Alice became absorbed in what she was doing, and although the couple of wrong notes made her wince, she didn't let them bother her too much as she launched into a more lively prelude in C major.

There was silence when the last note died away, then the two men clapped. They were being kind, and she thought it somewhat incongruous that she was seated at the piano in the drawing room of this man, dressed in her rags and listening to polite applause for her poor performance. She wanted to die from the embarrassment of it. Another thought struck her. Would he have invited her to tea if he'd suspected what she sometimes had to do to earn money?

Her smile was almost a grimace when she rose, and she felt the need to escape. Poverty had brought her down in more than one way, and she'd taken her children with her. They deserved more. Her glance fell on dear, innocent Lottie and she thought: It could be worse. Lottie could have floated away on the tide before she'd had a chance to live.

There was a drift of rain misting up the window. Outside, the sky was grey, and although the drizzle wasn't heavy yet, it promised more. They'd get soaked through on the way home if they didn't hurry. Already Alice was wishing she hadn't come. Being in such an elegant home and eating off such pretty and delicate china had made her feel like an outsider.

'We should go before this rain gets worse.'

Thomas nodded. 'It looks miserable outside, as though it's set in for the evening. I can't allow you to walk home. You must accept my offer of your cab fare. I'll go to the corner and tell a cab driver to pick you up in half an hour.'

James stood. 'I'll go, Uncle.'

He returned, his hair dampened into ringlets. 'It's a raw afternoon. Can we not find something warm for them to wear home, Uncle?'

'There were some blankets, but they were

rather thin and Mrs Packer took them home with her.' His forehead wrinkled in a frown. 'No wait! There are two dark-blue ones folded up on the bed in the guest room, waiting their turn to be replaced. If they're of any use, you're welcome to take them with you, Mrs Laws.'

With as much dignity as she could muster, since she couldn't turn down the offer of warmth for her children, Alice answered, 'That's kind of you, Mr Hambert.'

James opened his mouth to say something, but shut it again.

'James, go and hunt them out if you would. They've been washed and aired so are ready to use. They're the last, and the best of the old ones. And ask Mrs Packer to send in a container of some sort, and a basket to carry it in. We'll arrange the remaining food in it so Mrs Laws can take it home for the children. It would be a shame to waste it.'

They'd hardly finished the task when the cab arrived. The driver looked askance at his ragged fares, but when Thomas slid some money into his hand he tipped his cap. A further sum was placed in Alice's own hand. 'Just in case I haven't given him enough.' He stood back with James, sheltered by a large black umbrella and giving them a brief, but warm smile. 'You may proceed, driver.' The man flicked his whip over the horse's head and the animal trudged wearily off with its burden.

When they were round the corner the driver opened a little window. 'Where to, Missus?'

Alice's fingers closed about the coins. She

wasn't going to part with them, since it was enough to cover the rent. 'The tenements.'

'They're not safe at this time of evening, and it's getting dark. It will cost more than the gentleman paid me to risk going in there.'

'And it would then cost you even more if someone was of a mind to steal it from you. There isn't any more money to spare, driver. We'll alight at St Paul's and walk the rest of the way. Celia, help roll the blankets up.'

The blankets were stuffed under their ragged capes, and they pulled their hoods up as they left the carriage and headed north. Alice carried the basket over her arm and Lottie was in her usual position, tucked on to Celia's hip.

They hurried through the alleyways and squares, aware of the speculative eyes following them. Celia kept up a good pace and Alice followed, trusting her daughter's sense of direction.

People littered the pavements, where they sat or squatted, dirty, sullen and unsmiling. Dogs sprang at them and the smell of urine, rotting vegetables and a nearby cellar slaughterhouse almost overwhelmed Alice. She began to feel a familiar tightness in her chest, and her breath came heavily as they turned into the lane that gave space to the cellar they called home.

It was nearly dark now. Here and there a candle sent out a sputtering gleam from the depth of a window. The sky was the colour of pewter, the rain a persistent, heavy and sooty drizzle. An occasional penetration of pale misty moonlight through the clouds silvered down through the rooftops and painted a falsely romantic gleam on the cobbles to please the creative eye of some impoverished artist.

Celia had the door open in a moment and they were soon inside, bolting it securely behind them. A boot to the rotten wood would soon gain somebody entrance if they tried hard enough.

'Wait there, Ma, I'll put a match to the candle.'

A light bloomed in the darkness, reminding her of a beautiful golden tulip that had once grown in her father's garden. He'd paid a fortune for a variety of the bulbs, she remembered, but the yellow one had always been Alice's favourite. She wished she were there now, in that solid and secure old house that she'd grown up in. Perhaps her family had forgiven her after all these years, and would give herself and the children shelter.

Unhappiness engulfed Alice and she began to cry, giving big, heaving sobs at the thought of all that had been lost to her.

'Don't cry, Ma,' Celia said softly. 'I was so proud of you, especially when you played the piano, just like a real lady.'

'It was a lovely afternoon and Mr Hambert and his nephew were such good company. It reminded me of my home, when I was not much older than you and I didn't have a care in the world. I hate coming back here to this stinking hovel. It's sapping the life from me, and it will do the same to you and Lottie.'

'Hush, Ma. At least we're out of the rain, which is more than a lot of people have got. We must be thankful for that. Here, take that wet cape off. We'll have a warm blanket to sleep under tonight.'

'That was a kind and generous gesture. Mr Hambert lied about them being worn out. He just felt sorry for us.'

Celia kissed her cheek. 'Don't you feel sorry for us, too. I'll settle Lottie down, while you get rid of your wet clothes.'

'I've got a trouser seam to finished before I go to bed.'

'And I want to finish my story, so we'll be company for one another. Afterwards, I'll put the food safely away before it attracts the rats. When I've finished that I'll have your bed rolled out and ready. We'll sleep warm tonight.'

They spent an hour at their tasks, but it was cold and their hands became numb before they finished.

As was usual, Lottie had fallen asleep almost instantly, snuggled under the cosy blanket. Celia was looking forward to joining her there before too long.

Turning to the battered lead-lined box that served as a pantry, Celia busied herself, unpacking the basket. 'Who would have thought it?' she said a little later. 'That superior housekeeper of his has put a small bag of tea in the basket, enough for a decent cup or two. And there's some boiled eggs and half a loaf of bread. You didn't eat much for tea, would you like an egg now with some of the bread?'

Alice bit through the thread and placed her work neatly over a chair. 'I'm not hungry.' Alice knew that she'd choke on it. She was finding it hard to breathe after their dash through the alleys and she leaned her head on her arms, trying not to panic. If she concentrated on each breath the tightness would soon go away. But it felt as though there was pressure on her chest and it wouldn't allow air in. She began to cough, and tasted blood. She placed a rag to her mouth, muffling the sound.

Celia said when the bout of coughing subsided, 'Ma, are you ill?'

'It's nothing, Celia. The damp has got at me.'

Her daughter wouldn't be fooled. 'I'll ask the doctor to come and see you tomorrow.'

'We haven't got the money to pay him.'

'Yes we have. You've got that money Mr Hambert gave you in case the cab fare was extra.'

'You don't miss much, do you? I want that for the rent. Besides, I don't need a doctor to tell me that damp weather makes me cough. Neither do I need you telling me what I should do. Now, finish what you're doing then get yourself off to bed.'

'Yes, Ma.'

Ten minutes later Celia said from behind the curtain, 'I love you, Ma. One day, when I'm rich and famous – though I can't make up my mind between becoming a writer or an actress – I'm going to buy you a piano and the most entrancing gown made of blue satin and lace to wear while you're seated at it.'

Alice smiled into the darkness. She'd once had the same dream herself, only the gown she'd dreamed of had been a dark rose and she'd worn pearls in her hair. Still, a blue gown would do nicely.

* * *

71

Alice went out early the next morning, taking the finished trousers to the tailor. Her work earned her three shillings.

'There will be no more work for the time being, Mrs Laws. I'll send the lad out with some next week for you.'

'I'll be grateful to have it. Do you think you could pay me a little more, Mr Goldstein?'

The man spread his hands. 'Times are hard, Mrs Laws. If I sent you some extra trousers, could you work a little faster perhaps?'

'Impossible.' Her eyes were nearly dropping out of her head with fatigue already. She jiggled the ring in her pocket, the one she'd taken from behind the brick when Celia hadn't been looking. It was a risk, but she'd have to sell it.

Alice wasn't aware of anything amiss as she wandered from one dingy pawn shop to the next, though she'd probably get a better deal from a jeweller, she thought.

She was aware that somebody had overtaken her and had disappeared into an alley, but didn't take that much notice until she was grabbed from behind and dragged behind a cart. Something thudded against the base of her skull and her knees turned to jelly. The last thing she saw as she fell was a flash of red.

'I found it,' the lad said to the jeweller a short time later.

The man examined it then he smiled. 'Ah yes, I know of this ring. There's a reward offered for it.'

'How much?' the lad said eagerly, but the

72

jeweller just put a whistle to his mouth and blew it.

The doorway was blocked by a shadow and a heavy hand fell on his shoulder. 'There's no reward in it for you, lad. The ring was stolen. You're going in front of the magistrate.'

He protested, 'I didn't steal it. I took it from one of Bessie's whores, just a minute ago. She came from the tailor shop a little way back. I think she sews for him in her time off.'

Taken by the collar he was pushed along in front of the man. 'Then let's question this whore. Point her out to me, lad.'

'She's in that alley over there.'

When the man shook the woman she flopped about and blood oozed from the back of her skull.

'I only gave her a little tap, honest. She must be drunk,' the lad said uneasily.

The man looked up at him. 'She looks dead to me. You'll probably swing for this, lad.'

Colour fled from his face. 'But I didn't steal the ring. She must've lifted it in the first place, and I just took it from her. I took money from her as well, that she earned sewing for the tailor. It's in my pocket.'

'What do you call that, if it's not stealing?'

He said in desperation, 'You can have the ring and the money if you let me go. I didn't kill her and it was only a little tap. She was drunk, I tell you. I expect she banged her head on the wall when she fell. She's only a whore, and nobody will miss her.'

The lad was taken away in a covered cart with

73

bars on, still protesting his innocence. Alice Laws' body followed on another cart.

'She was one of my best seamstresses, and a decent and honest woman,' the tailor told the constable when he enquired, and he spread his hands. 'She was a good woman who was down on her luck.'

'Does she have any kin to inform?'

'Mrs Laws has two daughters. My lad will show you where they live.'

Five

Alice was buried in Potter's Field, along with other impoverished victims of crime.

Dry-eyed, because she'd exhausted every tear she'd produced for the previous two days, Celia, with Lottie astride her hip, followed after the coffin cart.

Lottie had asked for her mother several times, but was uncomprehending when Celia told her she was dead and wouldn't be coming back. Celia hoped that, as long as she was kept comfortable, and fed, Lottie would soon begin to forget their mother – which was more than she'd be afforded the comfort of doing.

It was a grey dismal morning; the river, and the bridge over it were embraced by the clinging, ghostly blanket of fog still lingering from the previous night. Stripped of leaves, the phantom

74

branches of the trees reached out bony crooked fingers that clawed the grey blanket to them. Ravens circled over the cemetery, cawing harshly.

The roughly made burial boxes were lowered into the grave one on top of the other, the earth shovelled over. Celia didn't know which one held her mother.

One of the gravediggers offered her a sympathetic look. 'Someone you know in there, lass?'

'It's our mother. Somebody hit her on the head and she died. She was gentle and kind, and would never have hurt anybody.'

The man removed his hat. 'Would you like me to say a prayer for her soul seeing as how you've taken the trouble to come and see her off?'

Celia, who'd been going to say her own prayer for her mother, nodded.

'What's your mother's name, lass?'

'Alice Laws.'

'Bert, take your cap off,' he said to the younger man, and they all bowed their heads.

Dear Lord, take the soul of this good woman into your kingdom. Alice Laws was kind and loving, so say her children who are here to pay respect to her passing. Ask my dear departed wife Mary Holloway to take Alice Laws' hand in friendship so she won't be lonely in heaven. As for her children, help them to grow up as good, honest girls, so she can rest easy and be proud of them.

'Amen,' they all said together.

Celia was touched that a stranger would be so

thoughtful. She remembered her manners. 'It was kind of you to say a prayer. It was a lovely prayer and my mother would have liked it. I'm sorry you lost your wife.'

The man shuffled his feet and said gruffly, 'Mary left some time ago, when Bert was just a lad. As for the prayer, I knew you needed one as soon as I saw you, for you look like little lost lambs. It took no effort since it came from inside my heart. A soul that's loved should be sent off right, so the Lord will notice it and give it special attention.'

'Pa wanted to be a preacher,' Bert said proudly.

'He would make a good one,' she said.

'Likely you girls should go home now. You're young and your place is with the living, not with the dead.'

'I want to stay just a little bit longer.'

'Happens you've got something private to say to your ma then, so we'll leave you with it, lass. Come on, Bert, let's get ourselves home.'

When it came down to it Celia couldn't think of one thing to say that hadn't already been said when her mother was still alive. Still, she hoped the little she did say would reassure her.

'Goodbye, Ma. I love you. I'll look after Lottie, and I'll take her to your sisters' house, like you asked. They might give us a home. But first I'll have to earn some money for the journey, and I'll have to take Lottie with me while I'm earning it.' She gazed down at her sister. 'Is that all right with you, Lottie?'

Lottie smiled up at her and nodded. 'Lottie wanna wee,' she said.

Earning enough to keep herself and Lottie alive without her mother's input was hard enough. Earning enough to take the train to the country was impossible.

For a week, Celia moped, feeling lost and alone without her mother. They lived off the food they'd brought home from Thomas Hambert's house and swallowed the last stale morsels. When her stomach began to rattle and Lottie whimpered with hunger and cried out for her mama, Celia realized that she was being selfish by thinking only of her own feelings, and if they were to survive she'd best stop mourning for what had passed and concentrate on the present.

She took to dipping again, using Lottie as a distraction. And she taught the girl how to cup her hands and smile at people as she held them out. Nevertheless, Lottie slowed Celia down, and she couldn't take her out in bad weather in case she caught an infection and became ill. She was aware, too, that together they were unprotected, because she couldn't run fast with Lottie on her hip if someone decided to follow or attack them.

Yet the inevitable happened. One day, when she hadn't been vigilant enough, and was wearily unlocking the door, someone pushed her through it and followed her in – a woman.

Celia grabbed a blunt knife up off the table. 'Get out!'

'Oh, you wouldn't want to use that, my dear, especially with the child getting in the way. Besides, all I have to do is shout and my man will come in.'

A quick glance showed a muscular back block-ing the doorway. The woman pushed the knife aside, calmly seated herself and took Lottie on to her lap. 'My name is Bessie Jones. I have a proposition to put to you, my dear. A young, handsome gentleman has taken a fancy to you. He's offered one hundred pounds for your services for a week.'

One hundred pounds! Celia found it difficult to breathe. She could barely imagine such an amount. 'Services ... what do you mean? Does he need a maid?'

Hard brown eyes came up to hers. 'Don't act stupid. You know exactly what I mean, girl. Tell me ... are you still intact?'

Celia's face flamed red and she stuttered, 'Of course I am.'

'Good, then we can charge him more for being the first. Men like to think they're the first.'

'No ... I promised my mother—'

'Your mother did some whoring when she needed to. She worked in my establishment on a regular basis, two days a week, sometimes three if she had the mind to. I promised her only the best gentlemen ... she was fussy who she went with, you see. They had to be clean. I approached her about this gentleman with regards to you. She said she'd think it over.'

'No she didn't ... She told me about it and made me promise not to take up the profession.'

One hundred pounds! That would keep them sheltered and fed for a long time.

'Take up the profession?' The woman cackled with laughter. 'Dearie me, that's one way of

78

putting it, I suppose. Always acting the lady, your mother was.'

'She *was* a lady. She was down on her luck, that's all.'

'And the little luck she had ran out.' The woman gazed slyly at her. 'This young man will treat you well, and he'll buy you something pretty to wear. I'd give you half of what he pays me, and you can use a private room. Afterwards, you can work for me if you like. We can accommodate the child.' She stroked Lottie's hair. 'My, but you're a pretty one.'

Fear speared through her at the thought of Lottie being at the mercy of this woman. Her sister was too young to be anything but trusting. Lottie's hands went to a brooch pinned to Bessie's bosom and she gave her a wide smile as she gently touched it.

Celia's hands went to her hips. 'When did this man notice me?'

'It was when you lifted his card case from his waistcoat pocket, dear. He followed you home, but then lost you. I knew who you were, though. I've had my eye on you for some time, and you're a good dip, very promising indeed. Have you still got the card case, by the way? The gentleman wants it back.'

Celia darted a look towards the loose brick and automatically lied. 'I didn't steal anything from anyone. You can tell your gentleman I want nothing to do with him, so I'd be obliged if you left.'

'You should be careful of this precious little one,' Bessie murmured, her voice hardening as she placed her down. 'Now, listen to me, girl. I could have snatched you off the street at any time and forced you into this, but I won't at the moment, because I liked your ma and I have a kind heart ... ask any of my girls. This is big money the gentleman is offering, the like of which you'll never see again.'

One hundred pounds! It was more than tempting. Think of what she could do with it? No, don't think of it at all. It wouldn't be a hundred; it would only be fifty if Bessie took half. Bessie would charge for the use of the room, for meals, and for a bath, because the man wouldn't want her if she were dirty.

Oh, what she'd give to sink into a bath of warm water and soak ... herself at one end with Lottie soaking in the other end. The offer was tempting for that alone, but it was meant to be. Once Bessie got her clutches on them, nothing of the kind would eventuate. There would be other men, one every half an hour, she'd heard. Lottie would be exposed to danger, for she'd heard there were men ... but she didn't want to think about it, and she shuddered. They'd have to do what they were told, or be beaten.

Celia didn't allow her fright to show, but her instincts were so attuned to the danger Bessie represented, that her heart pounded and she began to perspire. 'I'll think it over.'

'I'll give you four days, since your gentleman will be out of town for a week. In four days you can come to me and learn what will be expected of you. I'll teach you how to please a man, before your young man comes back. I shouldn't be at all surprised if he becomes a regular after. Some men are faithful to one girl, and he looks the type.'

Celia didn't care what type he was. Dogs were faithful, so were cats ... as long as you gave them what they wanted. And when it came down to it, Bessie would whittle her share of that one hundred pounds down to a couple of shillings. Celia gave a faint smile. If her virginity was worth all that money to the gentleman, then she might as well cut out Bessie, sell it herself, and keep all of the proceeds. But she wasn't going to; at least, not yet ... perhaps one day, if she had no choice.

Bessie's threats had rattled her though, and Celia knew the woman would follow through with them. She couldn't stay here any longer. It wasn't safe.

Before she went to bed she wrote down the story of Bessie's visit.

The last thing she thought before a fitful sleep claimed her, was that she hadn't seen Thomas Hambert for a while. She wondered what he'd think of her story.

The next morning she rolled up one of the blankets and tied it across her back. Cutting a hole in the second one – a hole big enough for her head to go through, she placed her valuables in the pocket under her skirt. The card case she'd lifted from the young gentleman was solid gold, and it had several cards in it.

'Charles Curtis, Hanover Square,' she whisper-ed. 'I'll take it there like I did with Mr Hambert's watch, since the gentleman is out of town.' Only she'd knock at the door and tell them she found it. Nobody could prove any different, after all.

She placed her mother's private box in a sack, which she tied on her shoulders, and slid her precious notebook inside her bodice. Where would she put Lottie? She wouldn't get far like this. She was too bulky and could hardly move. Lottie couldn't walk very far and she would slow her down. A handcart was needed.

Celia found a cart in the market place. The lad selling it was the only person there, though he was cold and shivering, as if he'd been there all night and she'd just woken him. He wore a frayed coat that reached his ankles, and a battered top hat on his head. It came down over his ears, and had a portion of the front cut out so he could see where he was going.'

'How much for the cart?'

He looked hungry. 'Two shillings.'

It would eat into her precious store of money. 'I can only manage sixpence.'

The boy nodded. 'That's better than nothing. I can buy a feed with it. Are you going somewhere then?'

She wasn't going to tell him where, but nodded. 'Just to the country; I won't know where until I get there.'

Sadly he said, 'I've got nowhere to go, and no family now my old man has been transported. Seven years he got for stealing himself a pair of boots off a corpse. Old ones they were, not worth tuppence. You can have the cart for nothing if you let me come with you. It used to be my pa's. I've travelled the road before and I can help you to find the place you're going to, if you like.'

Celia considered it. She didn't really need added responsibility, but he was small and muscular, and looked as though he might be useful. 'What's your name?'

He kicked at a cobble with the scuffed toe of his boot, obviously expecting a rebuff. 'Johnny Archer.'

'How old are you?'

'Fifteen.'

'You don't look it.'

He shrugged at that. 'All right, I'm twelve.'

It wouldn't hurt to take the lad with her, and he might prove to be useful. Having made up her mind, she nodded. 'Come on then.'

A smile sped across his face. 'What do I call you, Miss?'

'Celia ... and this is my sister, Lottie. I'm taking her to be looked after by my relatives in the country. I promised my ma. I should tell you something ... there's a woman after me, who wants me to work for her. I've refused ... but she might send someone after me. I'm hoping to get out of the district before the sun comes up.'

'We'll pretend we don't know each other then. I'll walk behind you a ways and keep an eye open. If anyone tries to get at you I'll thump them.'

She tried not to chuckle.

'You'll see. My dad used to be a boxer, and he taught me a trick or two,' he said fiercely.

'I'm sure he did. Come on then. I planned to be gone by now.'

They went back to the cellar and Celia picked

up one of the threadbare blankets she'd intended leaving behind. Doubling it over and fashioning it into a rough cape, she arranged it around Johnny's shoulders, tying it around his waist. 'There, that's better than nothing.' She laid the other blanket in the bottom of the cart and put the sack in along with Lottie. There was room for the warm blanket, which went over the top of her.

'You'll be nice and cosy under that,' she said to Lottie.

She'd have to leave the sticks of furniture behind, but now had room for the sack which contained her mother's personal items, one that she'd thought she might have to leave behind. There were other bits, too. A knife, hairbrush and matches. The book Mr Hambert had given her, and the cooking pot.

She left the key in the door when they made their escape, just after dawn. There was a feeling of unease about her when they went rattling over the cobbles because she felt so exposed.

When they passed Saint Paul's Cathedral without being waylaid by Bessie's thugs, Johnny caught her up and Celia felt more confident. Then she realized she shouldn't have worried, since Bessie and her girls kept late hours, and didn't rise early because of it.

Bedford Square was beginning to stir.

'My employer is not seeing visitors. He's recovering from a serious illness,' Mrs Packer told Celia.

As if to prove her point there came the sound

of a hacking cough from somewhere upstairs.

'Step inside for a moment,' Mrs Packer bade her, and her eyes went to the blanket that almost enveloped Celia. She sniffed. 'I wondered where those blankets had gone. He's far too generous for his own good.'

'I'll stay here. I want to keep my eye on Lottie.' And on Johnny, in case he took it into his head to dump Lottie and run off with the cart.

'They were his blankets to give, not yours,' Celia pointed out and handed the woman a small package. 'Would you kindly give him this. There's a letter inside. Tell him I'm going to Dorset to visit my relatives.'

'And how will you get to Dorset?'

'We'll walk. I have a friend with me and he has a cart for Lottie to ride in, so we'll manage.'

Her eyes went past her to where the cart was and she almost screeched, 'Walk! Do you know how far it is?'

'It doesn't matter how far. We'll get there eventually. I can't stay in London any longer; it's too dangerous now I've been marked.'

'Marked? I don't understand.' Mrs Packer peered past her. 'May I ask where your mother is?'

'She's buried in Potter's Field. Somebody hit her on the head and stole the wages she'd worked all week for by sewing trousers.'

'Oh, I'm so sorry.' Mrs Packer looked taken aback, and slightly ashamed of herself.

'And will you thank Mr Hambert for inviting us to tea. My mother enjoyed it immensely. It reminded her of her former life, you see.' A tear

85

sped down her face and she dashed it away as she said bitterly, 'At least she had that before she died. It made her happy.'

'Oh, my dear ... wait there a minute. I've just made some fresh bread.' She disappeared into the kitchen and came back with a basket packed with food. 'Here's some cheese, bread and some ham for the journey. And there is some cake in the basket. I've put some money in there too; there should be enough for your train fare. There's a train at eleven from Waterloo Bridge; you can take that and be in Dorset in three hours.'

'Won't Mr Hambert mind?'

'Gracious, no. The dear man leaves money in an old teapot, just in case someone in need knocks at the door. He's a nice man, very charitable. He's taken a real liking to you, and will be sorry to have missed you. I'm sorry, but I can't let you see him. He's very feverish and the doctor said strictly no visitors. He could pass the infection on, you see.'

'Give him my best wishes and tell him I hope he soon recovers. If I ever return to London I'll come and see him. Thank you for your kindness, Mrs Packer.'

Colour seeped under Mrs Packer's skin and she thrust an umbrella on top of the basket. 'Here, take this. It might keep the rain off of your little sister. Safe journey, my dear.'

Their next stop was Hanover Square. There was plenty going on in the square, with vendors setting up their stalls in the middle. And though most people would be at their breakfasts, there were one or two gentlemen going about their business.

She left Johnny guarding the cart, saying, 'I can trust you, can't I?'

'With your bloody life, Miss,' he growled, looking menacingly round him.

'Don't swear in front of Lottie again, unless you want a good clip.'

'I reckon you would, too.' He grinned. 'Sorry ... I won't let you down, I promise.'

And Celia, who rarely trusted anyone, believed him. Placing Lottie on her hip she went down some steps to the basement and knocked at a door, her nose twitching at the smell of bacon frying.

The door opened suddenly and a maid of about the same age as herself stared at her, looking flustered. 'Who are you and what do you want?'

'I want to see Mr Charles Curtis,' she said, secure in the knowledge that Bessie had said he'd left town.

'Hah! Do you now? What for?'

'That's between him and me, Miss Nosey. As it happens, I've found something of his and I want to return it.'

'You can leave it on the hall table then. I'll see that he gets it.'

'No, I'm not going to do that. Someone told me there was a reward.' Her mouth watered as the sound of sizzling meat came to her ears. Pots and pans clanged and a kettle lid rattled with the force of the steam. She and Lottie could live happily off just the smell in this kitchen.

'Ada, shut that door; you're letting the cold in and the oven's cooling down,' someone shouted.

'There's a beggar here, Mrs Smithers. She reckons she's found something that belongs to Mr Curtis.'

'What is it?'

'She didn't say. I reckon she's just trying to get a foot in the door so she can steal something. 'Ere ... How did you know where Mr Curtis lived?'

'His calling card was in it.'

A grey-haired woman appeared, smiling when she saw Lottie. 'You're a pretty one.' She drew them inside. 'Have you found the master's card case? He'll be pleased, and so will his mother, since it was a gift from her for his birthday and she's been chewing his ear off about its loss. She'll want to see you, to thank you and reward you personally, you know. Would you hand the case to me?'

Celia couldn't do anything else but appear willing, though she was loath to part with it. 'I can't stay long, my brother is waiting outside for us.'

The woman went off and came back in a few moments. 'Mrs Curtis will see you now. Leave the child here. Ada will give her some oatmeal and milk. And give the lad in the street a chunk of bread with an egg and some bacon on, Ada, but don't let him in, since he looks like a bit of a villain to me. Make one for the girl to take away with her, too. The master likes us to be charitable to those less fortunate.'

A few minutes later Celia was being shown

into a dining room, where an elegant woman in a grey silk gown was seated at the table. A maid stood by a buffet, waiting to serve her, and a second place was set at the table.

'What's your name, girl?'

She thought fast. 'Lizzie Carter.'

'I believe you found my son's card case.'

'That's the truth of it, My Lady.'

'Where exactly did you find it?'

She wasn't going to tell her that her son was in the slums seeking excitement of the more basic kind, so she picked a more likely spot where a toff might have dropped it. 'It was on Rotten Row in Hyde Park, on the ground.' Her sense of drama came alive, along with the tale. 'I had to dash under the hooves of the horses to rescue it. But when I looked up the man who'd dropped it was gone. That was quite a while ago now.'

'Why didn't you bring it to me sooner?'

Celia lowered her voice, and it wasn't hard to look teary-eyed at the thought she voiced. 'My mother died, and I had her funeral to see to, and my little sister to look after, My Lady.'

'I do not have a title. You should address me as Mrs Curtis.'

'I'm sorry, Mrs Curtis. I was mistaken, because you look and talk like a proper lady to me.'

The woman looked sceptical at first, but then a gracious smile appeared on her face, as though she'd decided to act the part on the strength of the remark. 'I suppose someone in your position might think so. I imagine you are after some recompense, since you haven't got much by the looks of you.'

'A reward would be kind, and most generous.'

'Do stop trying to put ideas in my head, girl; I didn't say it would be generous. Nevertheless, it was an expensive case and you need to be rewarded for your honesty. My son will be down in a minute. I'll leave him to deal with you.'

Her son! 'But I thought—'

The door opened and the young man she'd filched the case from strolled in. His dark eyes riveted on her and he seemed rooted to the spot for a moment. Far from being self-assured a blush blossomed in his cheeks and he stammered, 'What are you doing here?'

His mother stared at him. 'Am I to take it that you know this young woman, Charles?'

'We've never met ... well, we might've done ... not that I've been at the opera lately, but it might have been at the Lord Mayor's dinner,' Celia said quickly, giving him time to recover.

'That's enough of your cheek, girl,' the woman said sharply. 'Charles?'

His elegant nose wrinkled, but there was amusement in his eyes. 'Really, Mother, does she appear to be the type of young woman I'd enjoy a social relationship with? She looks and smells as though she needs a good bath.'

'I imagine not,' Mrs Curtis said drily.

He was quick-minded, Celia thought with a grin. She didn't need a bath since she'd had one two days before in the bucket they kept especially for the purpose. She'd filled the bucket herself from the stand pump in the street, and had washed her hair as well, working up a lather with some lavender soap she'd stolen from a street

90

stall. It smelled lovely, and now and again, when she shook her head, the fragrance of it reached her nostrils.

Mrs Curtis rose. 'Don't be so churlish, Charles. This young woman found your card case on Rotten Row and has kindly returned it. Her honesty deserves rewarding, and I hope her example will teach you to be less careless. After you've suitably recompensed her, you can get on with your breakfast uninterrupted. Don't be too long, dear. I'm going upstairs to ready myself to go out and I need you to accompany me.'

When the door closed after his mother he said, 'Why did you say you found it on Rotten Row, when you know damned well you lifted it from my pocket?'

'I didn't think your mother would approve of where you were when your pocket was picked, or what you were doing there.'

He laughed at that. 'You've got the cheek of the devil, girl. Why did you return it at all?'

'Since I'm leaving London I thought there might be a reward. I don't need a card case, even a fancy gold one, but I do need money.'

He fumbled in his pocket and came out with a guinea, spinning it in the air. 'Here, will this do?'

She caught it. 'Thank you.'

'Why are you leaving town ... Where do you intend to go?'

'It isn't any of your business. Why should what I do matter to you, anyway?'

He shrugged. 'I might want to see you again.'

Her hands went to her hips. 'I don't want to see you. I'm leaving town because I have no choice.

An *unnamed* gentleman has offered a woman of dubious interests and intent one hundred pounds to procure me for him. Was that you?'

He shrugged and nodded at the same time, though it was more of a squirm.

'Before she died, I promised my mother I wouldn't enter that kind of profession. Because of you, Bessie Jones now intends to force me into it if she can. So I'm taking my baby sister to the country to see if my aunts will raise her. Then I'll try and find decent employment so I can support us both. Lottie is in the kitchen if you want me to prove that I have a sister.'

Shame came into his eyes. 'I'm sorry ... I never thought. I liked you, you see, and I thought Bessie Jones would be able to discover where you lived. I meant you no harm.'

Liking for him sneaked reluctantly into her heart and lodged there; not the least because she'd discovered he had a conscience. That, she could work on. 'That wasn't the way Bessie put it to me. She said you offered a large amount of money for me to spend a week with you.'

'I did ... at her prompting. I intended to teach you a lesson for stealing from me.'

'How ... by forcing me to prostitute myself and live in degradation? I only stole to help feed my family. Because I'm poor, that doesn't mean I have loose morals. Besides, I'd never have seen any of the money you were willing to pay Bessie.'

'That wasn't the reason.' His eyes came alight with mischief. 'You know, that was very good, appealing to my conscience like that. To be truthful, I found you attractive, and you have gentle hands. I still find you attractive.' He grinned when she blushed. 'I'm interested in the way you think, too. How large a price would you place on yourself?'

He'd seen right through her and she could have kicked herself. 'I'm not ready to enter into such relationships. I'm not old enough.'

'How old are you?'

'Fifteen ... almost sixteen.' She didn't know why she'd added that last bit, when it sounded more grown up, and when she'd wanted to appear younger.

'And I'm twenty-one. What's your name?'

'Didn't Bessie Jones tell you?'

'If she had I wouldn't be asking.'

Better that she stuck to the lie she'd created. 'Lizzie Carter.' She made the ultimate sacrifice to prove she was decent and reluctantly dropped the coin he'd given her on to the table. 'You can keep this, I must go.'

'Wait, Lizzie, I don't want you to leave here in anger because of my stupidity. I know you need that money.' One of his elegant hands closed around her wrist when she picked the coin up again. The smile he gave her was irresistible. 'Let me put an alternative proposition to you. I'll offer you one hundred pounds right now if you'll allow me to kiss you, just once.'

She gasped, and slid him an unbelieving look. 'That's a fortune.'

'There's a condition. You must promise to come to me still intact when you think you're old enough ... when you're eighteen, perhaps. One

93

hundred pounds, Lizzie Carter.'

Her eyes widened and she gasped. 'Don't be ridiculous.'

He brought a pouch from inside his waistcoat and placed it on the table. 'The money is inside. I won it on the turn of a card. Buy yourself a new gown.'

'You would gamble on such a promise from me?'

'You said you were honest. Prove it to me.'

'I'm also a liar and a dip. I might prove that to you instead. Keep your money, mister. I don't want to carry a broken promise on my conscience.'

'Then don't break it, else I'll be disappointed in you.' He gave a soft chuckle.

Taking a card from the gold case she'd just returned to him, he scribbled something on the back and handed it back to her. 'You can leave a message for me here when you're ready. It's my club.'

She gazed up at him. Only a fool would be willing to part with such a large amount of money. 'What if I don't turn up?'

'Then I've paid one hundred pounds for a kiss, so we'd better make it a good one.'

The female in her said, 'My face is dirty,' and when she wiped her cheeks she simply smeared what was already there, a liberal coating of dirt to help disguise her face, in case she was recognized.

'I know,' and he laughed. 'It makes no difference to me.'

He was feckless where money was concerned!

But if he didn't care about her face being dirty, why should she? She reached out for the pouch.

'I'll have the kiss first,' he said, his hand closing over hers. A diamond on his little finger sent out dizzying beams of light.

She gazed up at him, trying not to allow her inexperience to show as she scoffed. 'Why would you want to kiss me?'

'Have you looked at yourself in a mirror?'

'I haven't got a mirror.'

His eyes engaged hers. 'When you do get one, you'll know why; your mouth is like a ripe peach.' He cupped her chin in his hands and his mouth brushed against hers, as light as a butterfly at first, then as tender as a lamb and as strong as a lion, so her heart began to pound and her breath left her body. Her mouth parted and she tasted an exploring tongue.

There was no fear in her because there was something innately gentle about Charles Curtis. Her body relaxed and she kept perfectly still. Little arrows of pleasure touched her, here and there, inside her skin, as he took his fill. Her mouth responded to his in no uncertain manner.

Just as she decided she enjoyed the caress too much to part with it, the warm, dewy and highly intimate contact became a void as cool air rushed to fill it. After a few seconds to enjoy the last shreds of fading pleasure she opened her eyes to the enigmatic darkness of his, wishing he'd kiss her again because the latent woman inside her had emerged to enjoy several breathtaking moments of desire.

'Remember it,' he whispered.

She tried to control the fine tremor in her limbs. How could she forget, for her first proper kiss was an introduction to sin. 'Certainly, I'll remember it, since it cost you so much. You're not going to have me arrested as soon as I leave the house with the money, are you?'

'No, and I'm willing to wait for you. It will give me something to look forward to while I complete my education.' He smiled like an angel as he folded her fingers over the pouch, and then rang a bell. 'Safe journey; I'll look forward with pleasure to our next encounter, Lizzie Carter.'

A maid appeared. 'Show this young woman to the kitchen, where she can collect her sister before leaving,' he said, and he turned his back on her and left the room without giving her another glance.

Six

Thomas had recovered from his illness, except for the occasional cough, and had been allowed to dress and go downstairs.

Mrs Packer tucked a rug around his knees and Frederick leaped up to purr throatily against his stomach.

'I've made you some nice chicken broth for lunch,' she said.

'Your chicken broth is always excellent, Mrs Packer.'

'Thank you, sir.'

'Has there been any mail while I was sick?'

'The usual bills and invitations.' She hesitated for a moment, then said, 'That young woman came to see you when you were ill. She said her mother had died and she was going to take her young sister to live with some relatives in the country. Dorset, she mentioned, and prattled on, mentioning a boy ... a right rapscallion he looked with a top hat pulled down over his ears, if you ask me.'

He gazed at her in shock. 'You said Mrs Laws had died? How ... Was she ill?'

'She was killed, sir, but they caught the lad who did it. The young woman wrote you a letter; it's in her diary. I'll fetch it for you. And I gave her enough money for her train fare from the teapot, and some food. I thought that's what you'd want me to do.'

'Yes ... yes, I would have ... the poor child.'

James arrived. 'The doctor has allowed you out of bed, has he, Uncle? We were quite worried about you. Could you spare a cup of tea for a thirsty man, Mrs Packer?' Settling himself on a chair round the fire, he opened his paper and began to read.

Thomas slid Celia's letter from the notebook and began to read it, exclaiming,

'Oh, the poor child ... listen to this, James. It's from Celia Laws. Such a tragedy.'

James lowered the paper and gazed over the top at his uncle. 'Must I?'

'James, do please act your age and pay attention.' Thomas ignored his nephew's groan and began to read.

Dear Mr Hambert,
My mother, who never did any harm to anyone, was hit on the head and killed by a ferocious felon, who then stole the wages that she'd worked all week long for.

James huffed with laughter. 'What's that ... one of Celia's stories? It certainly sounds like a dramatic opening ... definitely a tragedy. I believe she might be descended from William Shakespeare.'

'They say that truth is stranger than fiction, James, and this is the truth, according to Mrs Packer. Celia's mother has been killed, the poor woman. The young man who hastened her on her way has been arrested, or so Mrs Packer tells me.'

Gazing sharply at his uncle, James paid more attention to what the older man was saying. 'Mrs Laws is dead?' Although he'd only met her once, she couldn't have been much older than him, and he'd liked her. It was too sudden to take in.

'What of her children?'

His query was answered with his uncle's next breath.

I am leaving London, where I'm no longer safe from the unwanted attention of certain people. My mother's wish was for me to take Lottie to the country to be cared for by her sisters, if they are inclined to be charitable to their destitute nieces.

'Celia is lucky in that she has relatives to fall back on.'
'She will be if they'll take her in.'

Because I wrote these stories for you, I have left them for safekeeping in the notebook you sent me. They number six in all, but they're not very good. Writing stories was harder than I thought it would be. When Lottie is settled I intend to seek out a theatre company and try and earn my living as an actress, so I can support her.

I will write to you when I'm settled, dear Mr Hambert, then you will not have to say to your nephew, 'Do you remember Celia Laws, the girl who snatched my watch then gave it back again? I wonder what happened to her.'

My respects to Mr James Kent.
Yours truly.
Celia Jane Laws.

James smiled at her comment. 'It's a nicely written letter, and I can understand why she intrigued you, but she has slipped through your fingers now. So much for your study and your address to the Anglican Philanthropic Society; you'll have to find another subject.'

'Not entirely, since her writing reveals much.' Thomas fingered through the book, stopping to read now and again, often giving a faint smile or an occasional, 'Hmmm,' or just nodding to himself.

James raised an eyebrow when Thomas looked up at him and growled. 'This arrived over a week ago, and Mrs Packer has only just thought to give it to me. I could have done something to help the girl.'

'You were too sick. Besides, Celia Laws struck me as being a capable young woman with a great deal of independence to her. She reminds me of a cat that always lands on its feet. Had she needed your help, she would have asked for it, or failing that, would have helped herself to it.' He gave a wry grin, remembering that he'd checked every pocket in his clothing after they had last met. 'She's obviously decided not to take up writing, though. I doubt if she's got the scholarship for it, anyway.'

'She has enough, and possesses a fine sense of story and a flair for drama that just needs channelling. Her characters are delightfully depicted, almost caricatures. I was looking forward to educating her a little further.'

'Did she know of your plan?'

Thomas shook his head. 'Teaching doesn't always have to be obvious. Often it's better if it's unobtrusive, because the rigid application of a set text can become a chore to the pupil rather than a pleasure. Celia was interested in everything going on around her, and her curiosity will open her to learning for the rest of her life. I wonder where she is now. It's so cold out and they'll have nowhere to stay.'

'On her way to the country, I imagine. Don't worry, Uncle. You know there is nothing you can do to help, and she said she will write as soon as she's settled. No doubt she will tell you where she is then, so you'll have to be patient. Surely, she doesn't intend to walk all that way?'

'Mrs Packer said she had her sister in a cart and there was a lad with her. The dear woman gave them some money from the teapot for the train, and had the wit to give the girl a basket of food to take with her. She seems to think they were heading for Dorset.'

'Mrs Packer's bark has always been worse than her bite.'

'James, my boy, do try and stop comparing everyone to animals. I'm quite sure your vocabulary extends beyond the idiom, however apt they are to the situation. You should study zoology perhaps.'

James grinned widely at him. 'If you'd been to the Old Bailey lately, you'd realize that it's practically the same thing. I'll be interested to see how the prosecution of the felon who killed Mrs Laws proceeds.'

James attended the trial a week later. The lad was twelve years old. Charged with manslaughter, he was sentenced to death by hanging. He collapsed in the dock, shivering with fright. His family was dead, he said. He'd been cast from his lodging, was starving and had no money. He didn't mean to kill the woman ... she'd broken her head on the wall when she fell over.

It was a tale that the judge had heard many times before. Immune to it, he had no pity to spare. The man made it clear. Hang, the boy would, if *he* had anything to do with it.

Luckily there was a higher power. Half of the crimes by the young were committed out of sheer desperation, and without thinking of consequence. Often it was a case of steal for a living, or die of starvation. James consulted with an acquaintance of his, and one of the reform lawyers took up the lad's case. He applied for a pardon, placing the lad's petition before a sympathetic minister.

Eventually, James was able to report to his uncle that the lad's sentence was rescinded to transportation to Western Australia for life.

Thomas could only feel relieved. Much as he'd liked Mrs Laws and felt sorry for her children, the lad was only a child himself, and the death penalty was harsh. Children deserved a chance to reform and go on to lead a more useful life, he thought, wishing he had some of his own.

Thomas had learned a lot from his association with Celia Laws and her family. Poverty pulled human beings down. The outcome was destitution, prostitution, and the vilest of crimes being committed in the struggle to survive.

He hoped with all his heart that Celia would find her way out of the mire she was in. That night he included her in his prayers, and asked God to protect her and all who travelled with her on her hazardous journey. He thought to add: 'And I'd be appreciative if you'd make your immediate priority a bellyful of food, and a warm roof over their heads.'

It was the coldest of days; the wind threw splatters of stinging sleet at them. Celia's chest had begun to ache with every breath.

She didn't know how long they'd been travelling, many days, but it had been by foot, since the third-class train had already gone by the time they got to the station, and the eleven o'clock one was for first-class passengers only.

The man who sold the tickets looked down his nose at them. 'It's not for the likes of beggars, even if you have got two pounds for the fare, which I doubt, since I can smell you from here. It would also give the company a bad name. Anyway, there'd be no room for the cart, so be off with you. Come for the third class in the morning. It will take a bit longer, about six hours, but it will be cheaper.'

Celia didn't want to linger at the station, where Bessie was almost bound to send her thugs to look for her. The woman had a long memory, and didn't like being thwarted, she'd heard.

She thought that the seven-shilling fare to Southampton was too expensive for third class, and if the trip only took six hours, it wouldn't take much longer if they went by foot ... a day or two at most. She could put the fare money to better use.

However, the six hours that the train would have taken didn't transfer well to the effort they'd spent tramping by foot, and the money she'd saved had been used up buying food. With the cart to push and the night closing in early, they were lucky to go two miles every day, before, they needed to seek food and shelter.

At night they'd slept in barns and cowsheds, sometimes in the open. The night before they'd come across a deserted cottage, and had stayed there for two whole days regaining their strength, despite the wind whistling through a hole in the roof.

Their last meal had been stale bread washed down with water. After London, with its many stalls and markets, she hadn't been prepared to encounter such stretches of empty countryside – and she now wished she hadn't been so miserly, and had spent the money Charles Curtis had given her on a more comfortable mode of travel.

But it had become a symbol to her, that money. She wouldn't feel under an obligation to him unless she spent some of it, and once she'd taken a bite from it she would throw caution to the wind and spend it all. Then she'd think less of herself, as though she'd sunk below some invisible line of decency.

She had the money she'd saved from begging, and the gift from Mrs Packer on Mr Hambert's behalf, dear, generous friend that he was. Then there was the guinea Charles Curtis had spun twinkling through the air, a reward for the return of his card case.

Celia grinned. Honesty had paid off, though in a dishonest sort of way.

She'd spent a small amount of her precious money on a pot of lamb broth at the last inn, and some milk for Lottie, because their mother had said it was good for her bones. She gazed at her sister. Lottie was still shivering, though her eyes were sleepy. Celia tucked the blanket about her head and made sure that Mrs Packer's gift of an umbrella was pointed towards the wind before she stooped to tenderly kiss the girl. The umbrella had proved to be a godsend.

'It's getting dark. We'll have to find shelter before too long,' Johnny said, with a worried look around them. 'We're in the New Forest. There's bound to be a cottage where we can shelter.'

'We might have to sleep in the open tonight, and we'll have to go hungry.' And to think she'd been looking forward to the country fresh air her mother had told her about. Now there was too much, and it was too fresh!

Celia hadn't expected the journey to be so long or hazardous. She hadn't kept count of the days they'd been trudging along, and knew she'd give almost anything to have a cellar to sleep in tonight, except what people wanted her to give. She'd never go back to that life. Not ever! So what was the point of thinking about it?

Johnny pointed. 'There's a bit of a track going into the trees. Let's look there.'

As they entered the canopy of trees the day darkened considerably.

'What's that,' Celia cried out, pointing to a framework of sticks that supported layers of overlapping sod.

'It's a charcoal burner's hut, I reckon. My dad told me a story about one. See, over there is where he makes the charcoal, but it's not burning at the moment.' Nearby, an axe leaned against a woodpile.

There was no answer to their shouts, so they ventured nearer.

The small, earth-smelling cave looked to be a

cosy place in which to hole up. There was a curtain of sacking across the low entrance, which could be tied to pegs to keep the weather outside. Celia wished she had some milk for Lottie as she unpacked the cart. But Lottie didn't even give a whimper. She was used to going hungry.

Exhausted, they curled up together on a platform of wood, which was nailed to stakes to keep the sleeper above the damp ground. It was covered with a pile of sacks for a mattress. Celia took Lottie under her blanket and snuggled her into her body to keep her warm.

The wind came in fitful bursts, but none of them heard it.

Lottie's giggles brought Celia awake. Her eyes opened to the sight of her sister playing with a small terrier. There was a smell of cooking in the air. Johnny was still asleep. His face, usually pinched with worry, was now relaxed. Celia wished he would always look like that.

Her eyes widened as a shadow of a man passed by the opening, and she shook Johnny awake, whispering, 'There's someone out there.'

A voice rasped, 'Don't you youngsters be frighted, now. Old Busby won't hurt you. Likely you'll want to go and wash your faces in the stream before breakfast.'

'Breakast?' Johnny said with some bliss, elbowing her gently in the ribs, and his eyes began to shine. 'I haven't eaten breakfast since the day we left London.'

Neither had she. Celia's stomach grumbled emptily at the thought of being filled.

The charcoal burner was short, with a weathered face. A long grey beard decorated his chin and his eyes were as blue as a summer sky. He jerked his thumb when she emerged from the den with Lottie, and she followed a path to the stream.

Johnny would allow her some privacy and wait until she was finished, she knew. She took herself and Lottie into some dense bush a short way off, where they made themselves comfortable. Breaking through a film of ice coating the surface of the stream they washed their hands and faces and returned, shivering, to the fire. A pot swung back and forth over a tripod. The terrier wagged its tail and gave a couple of yaps.

'Quiet, Tinker, these be friends,' Busby said.

Celia remembered her manners, though they were easy to forget these days, without her mother constantly reminding her. 'I'm Celia Laws and this is my sister, Lottie. Johnny is our friend, and we're travelling together.'

Busby nodded and spooned some porridge into bowls. 'It ain't fancy, but it will stick to your ribs, and there's some eggs, bacon and bread for after. I've only got two spoons, so us men will have to wait.'

'I'll sup it from the bowl,' Johnny said, his rattling stomach telling them all he was not prepared to wait. But at her bidding, he went off to wash the previous day's dirt from his hands and face.

'I'll share my sister's spoon. Are you sure you can spare this?' Celia asked Busby politely, and even though berating herself for being a miser, she added, 'We can't afford to pay you.'

'I wouldn't be offering it if I couldn't. You're welcome to it.'

Lottie opened her mouth for a spoonful, and tried to grab the spoon. She wanted to eat her meals by herself, but if Celia allowed it, half of the oatmeal would be wasted on her clothes, and she was determined that Lottie was going to swallow every scrap of the nourishment on offer.

Johnny came back, his face glowing with the cold. His eyes lit on the food.

Busby indicated a seat on a log and said as he dished it up, 'Travelling far, Miss?'

'To Hanbury Cross village in Dorset,' Johnny said, and Celia nudged him with her boot and gave him a warning look.

'The road is dangerous these days. Where's your folks?'

She shrugged, saying briefly, 'Up ahead ... I daresay our kin are waiting for us at the next inn. It's just ... it got dark ... and it was cold and we got left behind, so we thought we'd better shelter here for the night. Besides, we've got nothing to steal apart from a few coins.' A lie, since she had a fortune in cash hidden under her skirt.

Busby gave a faint grin. 'I believe you, but felons aren't always after goods, girl. I reckon you be old enough to know that.'

Celia remembered Charles Curtis with a faint blush and some amusement. Her fingers strayed to her mouth. Fancy him handing all that money over for a kiss. He was certainly adept at getting his own way, and she frowned at the thought. He'd been much too generous. Did he really think she'd go back to him and become his whore for a week? The most he'd get from her was his money refunded. After that, she would no longer be under an obligation to him.

She attacked her oatmeal before it got cold. She'd never tasted anything quite so blissfully delicious, except what followed after it – bread fried crisp in the bacon fat with an egg on top. They ate like there was no tomorrow, washing it down with hot tea.

Flakes of snow began to drift down from the sky and Celia eyed the low, heavy cloud doubtfully. She hadn't considered it might snow.

'Dorset's a fair step, and the snow is going to settle. The sky is full of it. You'll be stuck when the wind piles it into drifts, and you won't know which way is left and which is right.'

'We have to go on ... we have no food and shelter.'

'What about your relatives?'

She shrugged. 'There are none with us.'

'Aye, but I didn't think there were, since me and my missus own the place, and I've just come from there. Best you come back home with me.'

'Can't we stay here?'

Busby shook his head. 'Once I've adjusted the kiln and sealed it I won't be back here for several days, when it's cooled down. There's no food, and nothing to hunt this time of year. Besides, my woman would give me an earful if I left you here by yourselves, especially if you freeze solid. Now that would be a thing!'

The thought that Busby had a wife went a long way to settle Celia's unease of going off with a stranger. She remembered Charles Curtis and her fingers strayed to her mouth. She couldn't trust herself to a man who made her feel... She didn't dwell on how he'd made her feel, but moved on to Thomas Hambert, who'd been so kind to them. Not all people were bad, and Busby seemed to be kind-hearted.

'I told the good woman about you when I went back to get something to feed you with. They're as thin as a trio of sparrows thrown out of the nest, I told her.

'Now you feed them up real good, Busby, she says, and you bring them back here so I can look them over. Maybe they can help us round the place until spring stretches its feathers, then they can safely move on. Fact is, missy ... I don't want to come back and find you frozen to death ... that I don't. It would put me to too much trouble explaining it to the authorities and weigh too heavily on my conscience.'

'That's kind of you and your wife, Busby. I think we could all do with a warm bed for a while, and I don't mind working for it.'

'Neither do I,' Johnny chipped in.

'Good lad.' Busby patted Johnny on the shoulder. 'Now you've got some breakfast inside you, how do you feel about giving me a hand with the burner, lad?'

Johnny nodded. 'What do I have to do?'

'See that pile of wood there? We have to pack it nice and tight so no air gets inside to make the wood burn too fast. Then I'll set a fire in the middle and put the lid on. When things get nice and hot we'll seal the kiln with those sods of earth there. It will take a week or so for it to cool down.'

Celia tidied up the camp while Busby and Johnny set about fixing the kiln, and the scene was imprinted on her mind, so she began to weave a story about it. It wasn't long before the two males were covered in dirty streaks. She wished she hadn't left her notebook with Mr Hambert, and decided to buy one at the next town they passed through. In the meantime, the story would grow in her mind without too much effort, just like a mushroom.

Before too long the mound was covered in the sods that man and boy had pitchforked into place, which prevented them from coming loose. Busby grunted, placed his hands on his back and stretched. She grinned when Johnny did the same, leaving two dirty handprints on his waist.

'Ready, lass?' Busby said, grinning at her through a face streaked with charcoal ash.

'No, Mr Busby, we're not ready. Johnny, you look like a chimney sweep. You can brush the dust from your clothes with a leafy twig and wash your face and hands in the stream if you want to make a good first impression on Mrs Busby.'

'My Aggie does have a bit of a sharp edge to her tongue if somebody carries the muck indoors after she's cleaned the floors,' Busby thought to advise.

As she tucked Lottie into the cart, Celia decided she could trust him, even if they didn't have much choice. 'Then you'd best tidy yourself up too, Mr Busby ... then we will be ready.'

He chuckled as he trundled off after Johnny. 'Damn me if you ain't as bossy as my Aggie,' he said.

Seven

Foul weather meant that there was little traffic on the road, so few people required bed and board.

'The railway has taken away some of our regular traffic,' Busby said. 'Still, it's not too big a place to manage, and the sale of charcoal will keep us going.'

The sky was so low it nearly touched the earth. It snowed heavily, not the sooty slush that had fallen on London now and again, but a thick coating of white that rolled over the countryside like a blanket, piled up on the hedges and merged into the horizon. There, the sky met the land without trace of a seam. Icicles hung from the thatch, and from the apple and pear trees in the yard, and their breath, and that of the animals, steamed the air where they walked.

Celia could only imagine what would have happened to them if they hadn't been persuaded to stay.

The silence pressed against their ears until Tinker went leaping through the snow, disappearing under with each landing, only to leap out again and disappear under again. The animal's antics made Lottie laugh. But the little dog had

112

attached itself to Johnny, and slept on his bed.

Celia didn't want to be beholden to anyone, so she helped Mrs Busby in the inn, doing the cleaning jobs and making the beds of the occasional traveller. The woman was a fine cook, and she made a big fuss of Lottie.

'The poor little thing,' she said on occasion. 'It's a wicked world out there if you've got nobody to look after you.'

In case the woman took too much of a liking to Lottie, Celia said firmly, 'Lottie has got me.'

'Aye, and you're a capable girl, no doubt, and no mistake. But you're young and you haven't got much to your name.' She dragged out a trunk and unearthed a couple of serviceable grey skirts from its depths, followed by a bodice of blue velvet and another of green. 'Here, lass, they'll be a bit big round the waist but we can put a couple of tucks into them. You'll grow into the bodices in a year or so, no doubt. I don't know why I was keeping them, since I'll never fit into them again.'

'I like you a bit on the buxom size,' Busby said with a grin, and gave her a smacking kiss on the cheek.

His wife blushed. 'You watch what you say when the children are present, Busby. Get about your business now.'

She pulled out a flannel nightdress after he'd gone, muttering as she shook it out of its folds, 'I don't know what's come over Busby, that I don't. I reckon we can make some smocks out of this, for young Lottie.'

They spent the dark evenings in company with

each other in front of the fire. Busby sucked on his pipe and gazed into the firelight. Mrs Busby sewed. It reminded Celia of evenings spent with her mother stitching trouser seams – except they were now well fed and warm – so she had to swallow hard to keep back the tears. Johnny whittled on a piece of wood and seemed contented, and no wonder, for the Busbys made a real fuss over him.

With the firelight creating grotesquely dancing shadows on the walls, Celia told them the stories her mother had told her when she was growing up, or recited poems with her usual dramatic embellishment.

'Just like a real theatre,' Mrs Busby said, after one spirited performance, wiping the tears from her eyes.

The icicles began to drip, the snow melted. Frozen wheel ruts in the mud patches gradually became mire. The sturdy forest ponies shed their winter coats, and buds appeared on the trees.

Celia was restless and said to Johnny, 'It's spring, we must leave soon.'

He begged, 'Just another week or so, Celia. Let's allow March to pass.'

As it was, they had no choice because Mrs Busby sprained her wrist just when there was a trickle of travellers. Celia couldn't do any less than help the woman out, in view of her kindness to them. Johnny helped Busby tend the charcoal burner.

Then Lottie came down with a fever. Celia woke one morning to discover that her sister had taken ill. Lottie gazed at her through fever-bright eyes and gave a little whimper. Rosy patches adorned her cheeks; her nose was thick and clogged and her appetite gone.

'You'll soon be better,' Celia tried to reassure Lottie, though she was far from convinced herself. She called Mrs Busby.

'I reckon we'll have to wait and see what develops,' Mrs Busby said.

For three days Lottie was a lethargic and grizzly creature who shook and shivered even while her temperature raged, and it was hard put even to get her to swallow liquid.

'She's not going to die, is she?' Celia said to her host, so desperate that she burst into tears.

Mrs Busby took her in a comforting hug. 'There, there, my love. I can't say she will and I can't say she won't, but there's a strong feeling inside me that she will survive, and when she does I'll eat young Johnny's top hat in celebration.'

The thought of which made Celia giggle.

'That's better,' Mrs Busby said. 'That Lottie of yours is a strong little girl, and she'll get better ... you'll see.'

On the fourth morning Lottie was covered in spots.

'Measles, I reckon. She would have caught it from that traveller a couple of weeks ago. He had spots on his face, though I didn't think nothing of it at the time. Now the spots are out she'll soon get better.'

And Lottie did, but she'd lost the weight she'd gained at the inn.

'We must go soon, Johnny,' Celia said one day,

when Lottie seemed stronger.

She sensed the reluctance in Johnny to leave. He found excuses ... He needed to clean the windows, or he went back and forth with Mr Busby, with whom he'd formed an attachment ... making himself useful.

The days passed and the trees in the orchard were covered in pastel blossoms that attracted an industrious army of bees to the pollens.

Busby sensed the need in her to move on, and returned one day with Johnny, who was wearing a new set of warm clothes. 'His trousers were so old his arse was hanging out and freezing in the wind,' Busby said, 'and the buttons on his shirt didn't do up. I thought he needed something more hard-wearing to travel in. I bought them from Ellie Green in the village. They belonged to her lad who went off to war and never came back.'

'And right smart he looks too. You should have bought him a new hat; he looks like an undertaker in that'n,' Mrs Busby said with a sigh.

Still they lingered on, like hibernating squirrels. It was almost the end of April before they left, when Celia took it upon herself to pack their belongings in the cart.

They had tears in their eyes as they hugged each other.

'You've been so kind to us, thank you,' Celia told them.

Busby gazed at his wife, and when she nodded he cleared his throat. 'Mrs Busby and I have been thinking. We were once blessed with a son and he'd be about Johnny's age now if the good

Lord hadn't taken him for his own. It doesn't seem right, you youngsters being on your own in the world.'

'I have kin, and I promised my mother that I'd seek them out,' Celia told them, even though those kin were strangers to her. The stepmother had already denied Alice Laws and her daughter a home. Would she welcome that young girl back? Celia doubted it. And what of the aunts? They were probably both married and with children of their own to look after. They might not even live in the family house any more.

Mrs Busby took over, as though she'd picked up on Celia's thoughts. 'It's only right that you'd want to be with your kin, but we've got room if you feel the need to settle, or if you're not wanted when you get to where you're going. Johnny could help Busby and the lad could learn a trade from him. And later, when his pa has served his sentence, we could help them find each other. As for you, lass, you could help me in the inn. We rub along quite nicely and could look after the bonny little one between us.'

It was a generous offer, but as much as Celia liked the couple who had offered them a home, she reluctantly refused. They would have been comfortable living at the inn, but the stink of the London slums was still in her nostrils and the further away from it she was, the better she'd like it. Lottie needed to be educated, and Celia intended to set her aim higher for her sister.

Johnny had the need to settle in him, though, she could see it in his eyes. As for their hosts ... they were simple, open-hearted country folk

117

with a vacant place by their hearth and a need to replace the son they'd lost.

When they said their goodbyes and were barely on their way, Johnny kept gazing back at the couple with a wistful look.

Tinker began to wriggle and yelp as Busby held him fast, lest he followed after Johnny. Mrs Busby had one hand clutching her shawl around her, the other holding a handkerchief to her eyes. Busby was comforting her as best he could, awkwardly patting her back. She could hear the rumble of his voice on the wind. 'There ... there ... don't take on so, Aggie love.'

Celia brought them to a halt. Johnny wasn't really her responsibility. She had no right to make up his mind for him, or tell him what he must do. She wondered if he might be acting out of loyalty to her. 'Johnny, you're free to stay if you want to, you know. The Busbys would be grateful for your help, I imagine, and you'd have a comfortable home at the inn. In fact, they'd treat you like a grandson. They're nice people and you couldn't find better.'

Hope came into the lad's eyes. 'What about you and Lottie? I promised to help you.'

'I'll manage by myself, like I was going to in the first place.' Though she wondered now if she wouldn't have been better off taking a train all the way in the first place. But as her mother had once told her, it was no good worrying about mistakes of the past; much better to just learn something from them.

'Busby told me that it's not much further to go ... t'other side of Poole,' she mimicked. 'We're in Hampshire now, and it's about eighteen miles to the Dorset border. Hanbury Cross village will take me a bit longer. He drew me a map so I know how to get there without getting lost.'

It crossed her mind that if Johnny stayed with the Busbys it would be one less problem for her. Celia had been wondering what to do with him when they got to her destination. She might be able to get away with Lottie if she appealed to their consciences by pouring on the pathos. She doubted if her relatives would feel obliged to take in a lad and feed him. They might turn herself and Lottie away, but at least she would find a home with the Busbys if need be.

Busby chose that moment to release Tinker. He came hurtling down the road and leapt into Johnny's arms, squirming and yelping and licking his face.

Celia smiled encouragingly at him, knowing Busby had released the dog deliberately to help the boy make up his mind. She sent Busby a smile. 'Go if you're going, Johnny; I don't want to stand here all day.'

He grinned and picked up his bundle. 'Are you sure you won't stay with me?'

'I'm sure.' She fumbled in her pocket and pulled out two shillings. 'I haven't paid you for the cart. Here, take that with you. Good luck, Johnny boy; thanks for your company.' She turned him round and gave him a gentle push.

He hesitated, then flipped the money back to her. 'It cost you more than that for my food on the way, and you might need it.' He took a few hesitant steps, then began to run back up the road to where the couple stood.

Celia watched with tears in her eyes when Mrs Busby gave Johnny a hug, and Busby placed a secure, fatherly hand on his shoulder. The three of them waved at her, then turned and went into the inn together.

Just like a family? Envy tore through her and a lump grew in her throat to nearly choke her, as she experienced a lonely feeling of being cut adrift.

Tears blinding her eyes she trudged on without looking back, the capricious puffs of the wind thrusting at her back and the rain clouds scudding overhead.

'Stop feeling sorry for yourself,' she said loudly when the inn was out of sight and earshot.

Lottie's bottom lip quivered, and Celia stooped to kiss her. 'Not you, my love. I was talking to myself.' Lottie giggled when she tickled her, and Celia's spirits brightened.

Around her the countryside was coming awake. The air was full of birdsong, daffodils shook out their brilliant golden skirts and a scattering of violets turned butterfly faces to the sun. She knew very little about plants or animals, so gazed with wonder at the secrets nature revealed to her.

For a fleeting moment she wished she'd returned to the inn with Johnny. But the feeling that time had passed the place by still persisted, and a stronger instinct surfaced. Johnny needed all of the security and affection the Busbys offered, but ahead of Celia, she sensed that destiny had something different waiting.

Celia wanted to embrace the life she'd been given, not hide herself away. She looked down at Lottie's dark head and smiled as she composed a snatch of a prayer. 'Listen to this and take heed, Lottie love.' She struck a pose, folded her hands together and said into the wind, trying to look as holy as she knew how,

May the unknown incite my passion,
Your strength allow mine to renew.
Heart of my heart, take courage.
Arise, and dare ... and do!

When Lottie clapped her hands and giggled on cue, even though she didn't know what Celia was talking about, Celia bowed. 'Thank you, Lady Charlotte, you're indeed an appreciative audience. I just hope it falls into the right pair of ears. Now, we'd better get on our way, because it will be a while yet before we reach our destination.'

Eight

Harriet Price lingered in the grounds of Hanbury Church after the congregation had scattered, loosening the crop of spring weeds from the graves of her sister and mother. After over a year of occupancy the memorial tablets had gradually lost their stark whiteness, and now resembled the colour of bones. Mother and daughter had been carried off painfully from diphtheria within hours of each other.

For reasons unknown, Harriet had been spared the same fate. She often wondered why, when she'd been the sickly child, the frail, youngest one of the two sisters, who'd caught a cold easily as a child, and was often ill.

Harriet had always taken longer to recover from illness than the robust Jane. So even while she'd tried to make Jane and their mother comfortable during their illness, she'd fully expected to catch the disease and die with them.

'You had it when you were a youngster, I expect,' Millie Smith, the housekeeper, had told her. 'You were always being ill, and nobody expected you to survive childhood. They say that if you can recover from a childhood illness, you'll never suffer from it a second time.'

Harriet missed her elder sister. Not so much

her mother, who'd been tediously disagreeable for most of the time, though she hadn't realized it until peace had descended on the house, she thought guiltily. Her mother had been pleasant to people, but had gossiped and made unkind remarks about them when they were no longer in earshot, and she'd been demanding and quarrelsome at home.

Harriet stood, a petite woman of exactly thirty-three years, elegant in the modest grey gown that she'd replaced the drab black of mourning with. Brushing crumbs of dark earth from her skirt and hands she thrust them into already-soiled gloves and headed out of the churchyard with short, rapid steps. Being out of mourning made her feel more alive ... like spring itself. There was a feeling in the air, as if there was going to be change in her life, and for the better.

It was the beginning of May. There had been a shower of rain. It had been heavy enough to soak the ground and wash the flowers and leaves, so they now sparkled in the sunshine. A short lane led from the church to the village.

Hanbury Cross consisted of a main street that contained four small shops. A haberdashery sold everything a woman needed for sewing, including ribbons and laces, as well as an assortment of gloves, hosiery and handkerchiefs. The proprietor also advertised her skills as a dressmaker, though should the ladies of the village need something special to wear they'd take their business to the nearest bigger towns of either Dorchester or Poole. Then there was a baker, a butcher, and a shop that sold everything for the house from soap and beeswax, through to pots and pans, stationery and ink.

Behind, and beyond the main street was a straggle of neat cottages, mostly built from brick and cob, the roofs thatched with reeds.

The larger homes – built beyond the village and usually standing in ample gardens to offer their occupiers privacy as well as the illusion of being landed gentry – were roofed in grey slate, as was the home Harriet grew up in, and now owned. She could just see the sooty tops of the brown glazed chimney pots beyond the copse, where there was a slight rise. It was an empty house, which the laughter of children had long since deserted.

Although Harriet loved her home, she felt lonely living there by herself with only the maid to keep her company. She couldn't leave, not now, while there was still hope that her half-sister, Alice, and her young daughter – Celia, she recalled that that was her niece's name – might return.

There was a duck pond in the village, fed by a trickle of a stream that trickled through many villages, and was inclined to flood across the road and into the cottages in the winter unless the debris was cleared from it regularly.

A strong smell of pigs saw Harriet hold a handkerchief to her nose, for most people kept a pigsty. Chickens and ducks clucked and quacked, and waddled out of her way. She stopped to briefly pat the nose of the farmer's big shaggy carthorse and it whuffled moistly into her hand.

'Sorry, Nellie, but you had your ration of sugar

on my way out.' Harriet hummed a little tune to herself as she continued on towards her home, skirting the puddles, for the showers had intruded into May, keeping the land moist.

She kept her mind occupied with her own thoughts, though she waved and said a pleasant good day to any villager she saw. Arthur Avery, who'd been her mother's legal representative, as well as being engaged to marry her late sister, intended to call on her this afternoon to discuss her inheritance. She found the widower tedious in his quest to acquire Chaffinch House.

Today was Harriet's birthday. Not that anyone would remember it, except Millie perhaps. However, she hoped to hear some good news from Mr Avery regarding a trust fund that her mother had left for her.

She stopped to gaze at the warm brick facade of her home. Apart from wanting to be here in case Alice returned, for many reasons she didn't want to leave the place. She loved the garden with its secret places, made even more secretive now the gardener could no longer be afforded, and the growth had been left untamed. Harriet harboured a notion that, if it was left to grow, the grass would envelop the house and nobody would know she existed.

Except one day a handsome man riding by on a black horse would find his way through the clutter to her door, and fall instantly in love with her.

She laughed at the notion, saying out loud, 'Stop that nonsense, Harriet. Your spinsterhood is now entrenched, and I thought you'd given up on that particular dream.'

The only horse to arrive that day belonged to Arthur Avery, and it was a rather superior-looking chestnut gelding, attached to a rig.

Harriet watched Arthur descend from the rig. He was a heavily built man of about fifty years, with a fulsome moustache and a balding head under his top hat. Not that he could help his baldness, she thought, since most men seemed to succumb to the condition eventually. As he turned to retrieve a satchel of papers the cloth strained under his arms, revealing a beefy back.

Harriet couldn't imagine Jane being married to the lawyer. But then, Arthur Avery was the only offer Jane had received. Her sister had indicated that having Arthur as a husband was better than not being married at all. It was a sentiment Harriet disagreed with, although she didn't say so at the time, for Jane would have accused her of being jealous because Arthur hadn't proposed to her instead.

'After all,' Jane had said, sounding as though she was trying to convince herself as well as Harriet, 'he's quite wealthy, and he hasn't got any relatives to leave his money to. He does want a child, which would be quite worthwhile. Mother said one must put up with the creation of it first, which is distasteful, and you must try and think of something else while that's going on.'

Arthur Avery had wanted to buy the house, and their mother had been considering it, because it was expensive to maintain. He had some good qualities, Harriet supposed, as she waited in the drawing room for Millie to announce him. He was intelligent and hard-working, she imagined. He was also boring and pompous, she reminded herself.

'Miss Price,' he said, bowing over her hand and sweeping it with his moustache, which, for all intents and purposes, resembled the head of a broom. He left a dewy patch, which she managed to wipe off across her skirt as she retrieved her hand. The lawyer was perspiring quite heavily, though the day itself wasn't particularly warm.

'Are you quite well, Mr Avery?'

Taking out a handkerchief he mopped his brow. 'I'm rarely ill, Miss Price.'

Harriet gazed at Millie. 'We'll have some tea, and some cake if there is any.'

'There is, Miss Price. I made one when you were at church ... It was going to be a surprise for your birthday.'

'It's a wonderful surprise, Millie. Thank you.'

When Millie had shuffled off, Arthur tut-tutted. 'That woman is too familiar now your mother and sister have gone.' He ran a gloved finger along the mantelpiece, bringing it down covered in dust. His lips pursed. 'She's far too old to do her work properly, and you should get rid of her.'

'Millie has nowhere to go ... besides, she's company for me.'

'Which brings me to the point of my visit, Miss Price.'

'Does it?' She allowed her astonishment to show. 'I wouldn't have thought that Millie was of any importance to you. I thought you were coming to talk to me about finances.'

'Oh, dear me no, Miss Price. Your mother's

will has yet to go through probate, and there are debts. In the meantime, your monthly allowance should be sufficient to see you through.' He mopped more perspiration from his forehead. 'Miss Price, I have something to say to you. Kindly sit down and listen without interruption. Perhaps it will turn out to be a happy surprise for your birthday.'

'Good Lord, you're as agitated as a man about to propose marriage,' she said helpfully, and wondered if Arthur was being completely honest with her about the will. It was taking a long time to be sorted out.

'Quite,' he said, and fumbled in his pocket. 'Now your sister and mother have gone it has occurred to me that you must be lonely living in this big house by yourself.'

She opened her mouth to speak, shutting it again when he held up a hand for her to keep quiet.

'My dear Harriet, I'm a man of considerable means. All I lack in life is a wife to see to my comfort, and an heir or two. Your mother had come to an agreement with me, that were I to marry Jane, then your mother's own portion of the house as well as Jane's would come into the marriage with her.'

So, her mother had been going to sacrifice Harriet's own portion to buy Jane a husband. 'And what of my entitlement?'

'You would have been recompensed, and, of course, would have always enjoyed a secure home with us. You are now in the happy position of owning Chaffinch House outright, which is much less complicated for me, and also along with a moderate amount of money, which will provide for you, without any serious expense on my part.'

'Mr Avery, I must tell you I was not being serious when I suggested you looked like a man with marriage on his mind. You are *not*, in fact, seriously proposing a marriage between us, are you?'

'Why, yes, am I not making the situation clear? Now Jane has gone, I'm offering myself to you. Of course, your manner is a little more spirited than I'd look for in a wife. That comes from being a long time without having a father to correct you. But once we were wed I'm sure you'd respond to my guidance, and according to my calculations, you are still of childbearing age, and I am, as you know, in need of an heir.'

One to leave my property and estate to, she thought. Pompous fool! Harriet slid her hands into her cuffs in case they took on a strength and a mind of their own – and strangled him! She allowed her gaze to drop demurely to her lap. 'Thank you, Mr Avery; it was kind of you to think of my welfare. However, I have no intention of marrying.'

'Miss Price, allow me to be frank. You're a spinster lady with very little chance of meeting eligible men or making a better match. Due to that unfortunate business with your father and your half-sister, the family name is not as well regarded as it once was.'

'Ah ... poor Alice. It wasn't her fault.' The sigh she gave was heartfelt. 'All she did was fall in love with Jackaby Laws. I wonder what happened to my sister.'

'Nothing good, I imagine.'

'Why should you imagine that, when father told me there was a legacy for Alice from her mother, enough to live modestly on if need be?'

She felt like laughing when his face mottled red and he began to splutter. 'Unfortunately, there was nowhere to send it, and on your mother's advice it was used to maintain the house ... since it would go a long way towards repayment of the debt Alice Laws' husband owed to the estate.'

'Are you telling me that my mother spent money that belonged to Alice?'

He shrugged. 'That's so.'

'That money had belonged to Alice since she was a child, and came through her maternal grandmother. Alice was not responsible for payment of her husband's debts. And since my mother was no kin to Alice Laws, but her stepmother, surely she had no right to authorize it to be spent in such a manner. Can that be legal?'

'Dear Miss Price, I would suggest that your knowledge of legal matters is sadly lacking and you shouldn't test your brain with such assumptions.' He gave her an effusive smile and loosened his collar by running his finger around it. 'But we've strayed from the matter in hand, have we not? I'm a man with a mission,' he said with awkward gallantry.

'Then let us come back to it by all means.' She stood, obliging him to do the same. 'Mr Avery, I'm afraid that I must refuse your proposal, and since you've insulted me at every turn, I therefore must conclude that I'm unworthy to become your wife. There, your mission is no longer valid, sir. We shall put it behind us, and allow our acquaintanceship to remain on a business level. As soon as possible, Mr Avery, I will require an accounting of the worth of my estate, since I need to know exactly where I stand.'

He looked bewildered. 'You can dismiss my petition just like that? But why?'

'You have made it quite obvious that I'm not worthy to hold such a position as your wife. Jane may have been satisfied with that, but I'm not. Besides, Mr Avery, because you've been so very persistent, I might as well tell you that I do not admire you enough to marry you.'

'Your money will not be able to maintain this house indefinitely. Will you allow me to buy it from you? There's a nice little cottage in the next village that would suit a spinster in your position admirably.'

'I do not intend to move at the moment, Mr Avery. My sister Alice may return. In fact, I'm thinking of having a search made for her.' She'd thought no such thing until this moment, but now it seemed like a good idea. She'd been thinking a lot about Alice and her child since her own mother and sister had died.

An expression of extreme uneasiness crossed his face and she leaned forward. 'Why Mr Avery, you look quite put out. Is there something you're not telling me?'

Gathering his things together the solicitor stood, saying in great huff, 'Only that you do not

131

have the resources to hire a man to carry out the search. The house will deteriorate and my next offer will not be so generous. However, if you married me I could attend to the matter for you.'

She drew herself up. 'You have already had my answer on that. The next time you visit I'd be obliged if you would confine yourself only to business matters. You have my instructions. I'll expect a full accounting of my affairs within the month...' something she suspected – correctly as it turned out – that wouldn't happen.

Hearing Millie with the tea things Harriet opened the door and said, 'Mr Avery is just leaving, Millie. Take the tea back to the kitchen and I'll join you in a few minutes.'

As Arthur Avery was on the way home he passed a beggar girl pushing a cart with a child seated inside. She was coming in the opposite direction, limping. Her hair was in a tangle and she looked fatigued.

She waved him to a halt and asked, 'Can you direct me to Hanbury Cross, sir?'

He jerked his thumb over his shoulder. 'It's three miles back that way. You take a right-hand turn. It's signposted, so you can't miss it. But don't expect any handouts from the villagers. We don't take kindly to wanderers in these parts.'

'I'm not a wanderer. I have kin living there.'

Some of the field labourers, he supposed sourly. The peasants didn't seem to mind crowded conditions, and they crammed as many relatives as they could into their cottages.

If Arthur had stopped to think, he would have

known it was an unfair assumption, since the residents of Hanbury Cross did no such thing. Their cottages were well maintained, clean and tidy, and definitely not overcrowded ... which was the very reason Arthur had set his sights on living there, in Chaffinch House.

'Is there a farmhouse hereabouts? We haven't eaten since yesterday.'

The child stared hungrily at him and held out her cupped hands, making him feel guilty and aware of his own corpulence. She was thin, though not emaciated, and her eyes were bright. It wouldn't hurt the child to miss a meal.

Arthur was in a bad mood after his meeting with Harriet Price. The woman was troublesome. She was a shrew, and her tongue too sharp and to the point for comfort. No wonder nobody had ever offered for her hand.

Arthur was glad Harriet hadn't accepted him. She was too astute and capable a woman for his liking. Jane had been more biddable, though, more like her mother, who'd responded to flattery. Now he'd have to find all the receipts and get the ledgers in order, and he'd just dismissed his clerk. It was selfish of Harriet Price to want everything to be in order within the month.

He tried to ignore the child, but she was making persistent little pleading noises. They started begging young so they didn't have to work for a living, he thought. It was easy money, and thank goodness they didn't all take up begging to earn a living.

Wearily the older girl murmured, 'Thank you for the directions, sir. God willing, I should make it by nightfall.'

Hadn't the reverend preached about charity the previous Sunday? He'd said that generosity towards the poor would be returned twofold.

'If you take the next turn to the right there's a cowshed, and the herd was being milked when I came past. This should buy you a cup of milk.' Fishing thruppence from his pocket he spun it through the air and she deftly caught it.

'You're most kind, sir.'

At least she had good manners, he thought, and clicking his tongue he urged his horse forward, glowing inside from his generous gesture.

Despite her sore feet and tiredness, Celia grinned. There was nothing like a mention of the Lord to bring out the good in people.

Nine

Dusk was nearly overtaken by night when Celia took the turn-off to Hanbury Cross.

She'd nearly missed the sign, a weathered plank of wood nailed to an ivy-covered wall that had the name of the village carved on it.

The countryside sloped down in a gentle incline, then up again. Celia could see the village in the distance, the windows just beginning to glow as darkness fell. Beyond it was a copse, and behind it was the rooftop of a house. It was the one she'd been looking for. Chaffinch House.

The village still seemed a long way away, but at least it was downhill at the moment. It had taken her longer than she'd expected to get here, and she'd missed Johnny's help in pushing the cart. She'd lost her direction many times over the past two days. Now it seemed as though the end of the journey was finally within her grasp.

Her mother had told her the house was one of the larger ones. It was called Chaffinch House and set a little way apart from the village.

Filled to the brim with milk straight from the cow, Lottie had fallen asleep. Her body was quite relaxed, for she was used to the movement of the cart as it jolted through the potholes.

Celia trudged on into the darkness. The lane beneath her feet was covered in loose stones, and her torn and blistered feet were an agony with each automatic step. She'd lost track of time. When darkness fell, she and Lottie usually slept in some corner of a field, a haystack or a barn. She slept like the dead, with Lottie tied to her wrist by a strip of rag, in case the child wandered off in the dark.

The air was cool, but soft. It smelled of cow dung, hawthorn flowers, bruised bluebells and cut grass – an odd combination.

The wheel of her little cart had worked loose, and it wobbled back and forth. She hoped it would last the journey. It had to, because she did not have the strength to carry Lottie. In fact, she was too fatigued to carry herself much further.

She looked into the infinity of the sky, where the scattered stars winked and twinkled. There were such wonders in heaven and on earth to enjoy, she thought. A glow on the horizon signalled the appearance of the moon.

She whispered a little rhyme that came instantly to her. *Oh, glowing moon that shines so bright, lead us to Chaffinch House this night, and may we find some welcome kin to invite such weary travellers in.*

An unwelcome thought eroded her confidence. What if her family no longer lived there?

'Then you'll go to that church and you'll swallow your pride and throw yourself on the mercy of the rector,' she said out loud.

The moon appeared, rising up from behind a stand of trees with a fierce incandescent glow. It was a good omen to light her path to the village.

It was a friendly place with its twinkling windows, and the moonlight shining on the water of a pond. But dogs began to bark at her passing, and she was glad she hadn't walked through the village during the day, for even though it was dark she saw the curtains twitch and sensed curious eyes on her.

Celia walked on, and the copse was a dark rustling place on either side of her. But ahead was a light, and she saw the house. It seemed familiar, as though it had burned into her memory from her fleeting visit here when she was but a child. A welcoming light burned in the window.

'Chaffinch House,' she whispered, and the weight of the past journey hit her so hard that she wondered if she'd be able to reach the front door.

The gate squeaked as she pushed it open. Her trembling legs could hardly hold her upright and she had to support herself on the cart. The porch was a dark space ahead of her. One dragging step took her closer ... then another. It took all of her will to place one foot in front of the other, to get herself up the path. The wheel came off the cart and went spinning off into a flower bed.

She reached the tiled entrance and fell to her knees, crawling the rest of the way to scrabble at the door with her fingers.

Lottie woke, shouting out her name in alarm. 'Celia!'

'I'm here, Lottie.'

Climbing from the cart Lottie came to where she lay and cuddled close to her. 'I was afraid.'

'There's nothing to fear. Bang on the door, Lottie.'

'Are we there?'

'We will have to be, for I can't go a step further.'

A gleam of yellow light spilled across them as the door opened to Lottie's thumping. A woman gazed down at them. She held an oil lamp in one hand and had a poker held aloft in the other.

There was another woman behind her, and her hand flew to her chest when she saw them. 'Oh, my goodness, it's a young woman and a child. She looks to be at the end of her tether. Help me to get them inside, Millie.'

'You be careful it isn't a trick, Miss Price.'

'Are you Jane Price?' Celia croaked.

'Gracious ... no ... I'm Harriet Price, Jane's sister.' The woman's arms came round her. 'Can you stand, my dear?'

Celia managed it, and with Lottie clutching at

her skirt tottered into the nearest room, where she sank on to a sofa. The lamp was set on the table, another one lit.

A circle of light framed the woman's face. It was a kind one, and there was the look of Celia's own mother about her.

'Mama,' Lottie whispered uncertainly, and pressed against her.

Celia placed an arm around her. 'The lady looks a little like mama, but it's not her. Mama has gone to live in heaven.'

'What's your name, dear?'

'Celia Laws.'

Shock and recognition came and went in Harriet's expression, and questions tripped from her tongue one after the other. 'Celia Laws? Are you my sister Alice's daughter ... yes, you must be ... has Alice passed away? She must have, for where else would you go? We're kin, after all, though Alice swore she'd never come back while she had a breath in her body. How odd that I was thinking of you today, as though it was meant to be. Your poor feet, they're all cut and blistered. Have you travelled far?'

Celia managed to get a word or two in. 'From London.'

Harriet gasped. 'All that way ... Millie, go and put the kettle on, and make up a bed for them. Use Alice's old room, because her things are still there. The child can sleep in the same room, on the daybed, so she won't feel alone. We must see what we can do for them. Are you hungry, dear?'

'We've only had a cup of milk and a chunk of bread each in two days.'

On cue, Lottie cupped her hands and held them out to the woman. 'I'm hungry, missus.'

'This is Charlotte, my little sister. Don't beg, Lottie darling. However hard life was for us, mama wouldn't have approved of it,' Celia said, feeling like the biggest hypocrite on earth for playing on this woman's emotions.

Harriet burst into tears. 'Oh, my dear, I'll warm you some broth. Then when you've eaten it you can rest.'

'My cart ... the wheel's broken.'

'We'll drag it into the porch, in case it rains. Nobody will steal anything from it here. Goodness ... imagine walking all this way from London. How brave of you ... your poor, poor feet.'

Celia wanted to cry too, mostly because of her aunt's kindness, but she couldn't give in now she'd achieved what she'd set out to do. Her tattered feet were placed in a bowl and gently soaped and bathed in blissfully warm water. A soothing salve was applied to her blisters and they were bandaged with strips of clean linen.

The two women fussed around, trying to do everything at once, tripping over each other. Somehow it all got done. Lottie lapped up her broth then fell asleep against Celia's shoulder, her dirty little face so innocent and sweet in sleep that Celia nearly cried out with the wave of love she felt for her. She gently kissed her cheek, hoping the journey was finally over and they'd be offered a home here.

Harriet bent to the sleeping child. 'I'll carry her upstairs. Do you think you can manage alone?'

Celia nodded. She was warming to this

woman, who'd welcomed a complete stranger into her home, accepting her for what she was without asking questions.

She followed her up two flights of stairs, hobbling with each torturous step. They turned into a room where a night light burned in a saucer of water.

'We're both dirty,' she said when she saw the crisp, white sheets.

'As I see. I can also see that you're fatigued beyond measure, and that must take precedence.' She slid Lottie's ill-fitting boots from her feet and removed her clothing, leaving the child in the flannel smock Mrs Busby had fashioned for her. Lottie was tucked into her bed.

'There, that will do her for tonight. Tomorrow you'll both take a bath and we'll talk. You must tell me about Charlotte and the circumstances you find yourselves in. Millie has put a nightgown and robe out for you to wear. Things will look better tomorrow, I promise.'

'You're very kind, Miss Price.'

'Aunt Harriet,' she said firmly, and gently kissed her on the forehead. 'Goodnight, Celia dear. Wake me if you need anything during the night. My room is opposite.'

It would indeed be a good night, Celia thought as she sank into the feathery depths of the mattress and kept on sinking.

Celia vaguely remembered hearing a cockerel crow earlier, something she'd managed to ignore. Now she was woken from sleep by a beam of sunshine shining through a crack in the curtains, determined to single her out for attention.

She was reluctant to leave her warm and comfortable nest. Lottie's little bed was empty. Swinging her legs out of bed she winced as she gingerly put her weight on her feet, and called out, 'Lottie, where are you?'

Footsteps came pattering up the stairs, and a knock at the door was followed by the appearance of Harriet, wearing a smile. 'The child is downstairs, and Millie is going to take her into the garden to collect the eggs after breakfast. She's been bathed in the laundry sink and I took the liberty of looking in your cart for a clean smock. I hope you don't mind.'

'No, I don't mind. Both her smocks are dirty.'

'So I noticed. I've washed the spare one, and it should soon dry in the wind. You are quite the pair of ragamuffins, but it can't be helped, I suppose.'

It was said so kindly that Celia couldn't feel angry.

'Put on your robe, my dear. We've filled the bathtub, but it's downstairs in the laundry room. There's a clean gown for you to wear afterwards; it used to belong to my sister, Jane, but she has no use for it now. You can wash your hair first. There's a mirror and a hairbrush on the table to use. I'll see to your feet afterwards and you will soon be comfortable.'

Celia's glance darted with some alarm to the dirty skirt she'd laid over the back of the chair. She was relieved to find it still there, for the pocket contained all her money. Before she went down, creeping on her sore feet, she removed the money and slid it under her mattress.

The laundry room was large, and had a stove in the corner on which to heat the water, so it was pleasantly warm. The soap smelled of lavender, reminding her of the soap she'd stolen from the stall in London, which had been a rare treat. Celia stayed in the tub until the water grew cool then dried herself. As well as sore feet, her muscles ached. She groaned as she stepped out of the tub.

The gown her aunt had left was blue checked, with a little lace collar. There was also a cotton petticoat. Celia felt shiny and new in the clothes, as though she'd just been born.

Her aunt came in and doctored her feet before handing her a pair of cotton stockings and some shoes of soft leather. 'These might fit you; they used to belong to Jane.'

'What happened to your sister?'

'She and our mother died within days of each other a year ago from a throat infection.'

'I'm so sorry... I shouldn't have babbled on about my own troubles when you had your own loss to bear.'

They left the bath water running into the garden, using a hose attached to a small tap near the bottom of the bath.

Harriet came to stand in front of her, gazing into her eyes. 'You weren't to know, and look what has come of it. We've been brought together, and perhaps that was meant to be. Now, come and have your breakfast.'

Wearing a milky moustache, Lottie smiled at

her when she entered the kitchen. 'Mrs Millie has a cat called Moggins. Can we stay here always?'

'I don't know. That rather depends on Aunt Harriet.'

A dish of oatmeal was placed in front of her and there was toast with gooseberry conserve and tea. Celia hadn't felt so full since she'd left the inn, and she couldn't remember how long ago that had been. The hardships of the long trek seemed somehow remote from her. If it wasn't for her sore feet... Spoon suspended in mid-air she wondered how Johnny was getting along.

Millie took Lottie outside, leaving her alone with Harriet.

'Tell me about Charlotte; is Alice her mother? I cannot see a family resemblance.'

Celia was tempted to lie. If she did that would put her mother in a bad light, for she'd used the Laws' name up until the very end. She decided that the truth wouldn't hurt anyone. Whatever came of it, she'd never desert Lottie.

'No, she isn't. We found Lottie on the banks of the River Thames. She was newly born, and had been left there for the stray dogs to make a meal of, or for the tide to carry her away ... whichever came about first.'

When Harriet sucked in a deep, scandalized breath a knot of resentment surfaced. What did this woman in her fancy house know about poverty?

She laid it on thicker. 'Oh, we could have taken Lottie to the workhouse and forgotten she existed. She wouldn't have lasted long there, but would have died of some disease or neglect before she was a month old, and without ever knowing love. We didn't have much. My mother worked long hours sewing seams in trousers to pay the rent. I begged on the street or recited poetry to the crowds for coins.'

Tears glistened in Harriet's eyes.

'I was teaching Lottie to beg when our mother was killed. I could have earned a living, doing some work where I could take her, for she's too young to be left alone.' She shrugged, knowing it would be wiser not to say what that living would have been. 'The work was ... *unsuitable* for someone my age.'

'Oh, my dear. Is that why Charlotte cups her hands like that when she sees food on the table, because she had to beg?'

Celia nodded. 'At first we were tempted to leave her on the mud and pretend she didn't exist, because we hardly had enough money to feed ourselves with. But when she began to cry, my mother couldn't bring herself to ignore her.'

'So you don't know who her parents are?'

'She was born with no name, so my mother gave her ours, and called her Charlotte because she thought it was a name with some substance to it if she survived. So she became my sister.'

Harriet had a dubious look in her eyes. 'Are you telling me the truth about the child?'

'What would be the point of lying about her? Lottie thinks I'm her sister, and doesn't know any different. If you cannot find room in your heart to accept Lottie, I must go too. I don't want us to be a burden to you.'

144

'Where would you go if I turned you away?'

'There's an inn in the forest where we were offered a home by a generous-hearted couple. Our travelling companion took advantage of the opportunity, and I'm given to believe we'll be welcome there. Do you intend to turn us away? My mother told me to beg on my knees if I needed to – but I won't do that.'

'Celia, my dear, you don't need to beg. I wouldn't dream of closing my door to either of you. In fact, I told my legal adviser that I intended to instigate a search for you and my sister.' She screwed up her nose. 'I shall consult with him. There was a legacy for Alice, but he said it had been spent on house maintenance. I suspect we're not very well off because the money we had may have been mismanaged. Father was such a fool when it came to trusting people, and my mother was a spendthrift. I'll try and find out if any is owing to Alice from the estate. Arthur Avery will require proof that you're who you say you are, though.'

'I have my mother's box containing her private papers in the cart. And I have some money ... lent to me by a *friend*, in case I needed it for the journey,' she said with some difficulty, for she hated lying to this kind and generous woman. It was odd, too, how reluctant she felt about parting with, or spending the money she'd gained from the bargain she'd made with Charles Curtis. She'd never had so much money, and wondered if he'd been sent by the devil to tempt her.

'It can't be much, so you keep that, dear, for if

it's a loan you'll need to pay it back. I'll let you know if we're ever desperate enough to need to draw on it. I do feel sad that Alice has died, and I've thought of her often. She was badly treated by the man she married, as well as the family. I'm pleased she told you to come to Chaffinch House.'

'You are the one who's too trusting, Aunt Harriet. I could be an imposter.'

Harriet smiled at that. 'Are you one?'

'No.'

'Neither am I. I'm definitely your Aunt Harriet.'

Celia giggled at that. 'I've vowed to take revenge on Jackaby Laws for what he did to my mother, you know.'

'Oh ... and how do you intend to go about that?'

Celia hadn't planned her revenge past the uttered threat stage. 'I ... I don't know yet. I might put an advertisement in the paper and offer a reward for his whereabouts.'

'And then?'

She shrugged. 'I've learned to act and recite. When I'm a little older I intend to join a travelling theatre company to earn my living. With a name like his, if he's still connected to the theatre I'm bound to come across him, sooner or later.'

A faint smile touched Harriet's lips. 'You sounded so much like your mother then. Alice dreamed of going on the stage. Then she fell in love and forgot about it.'

'My mother never forgot her dream. She joined

146

a theatre group called The Wentworth Players and we toured with them for a while.'

'Then what happened?'

'The owner's wife didn't like my mother because she was a lady, as well as being a better actress. She complained to her husband and caused trouble, accusing him of flirting with her. My mother was dismissed from the company when we returned to London.' After a moment of reflection she said, 'A good thing really, I suppose.'

'How could it have been a good thing?'

'If she hadn't been dismissed we wouldn't have been on the river bank at that particular time and Lottie wouldn't be alive today.'

'Ah yes; do you think our destiny is controlled by fate then?'

'The famous Russian mystic, Sophia de Lyle, does.'

Aunt Harriet raised an eyebrow. 'Who?'

Celia giggled at her aunt's astonished expression. 'Sophia de Lyle travelled with the Wentworth Players and told fortunes with a crystal ball. When I was eight she told me I was going to marry a handsome prince and live happily ever after. She told my mother she was going to live a ... *long life*.'

After a short silence when they looked at each other and shared the same moment of sadness, Harriet said lightly, 'Goodness, you've met some interesting people. I must say, though, her name doesn't sound very Russian and her prediction in your mother's case was sadly inaccurate.'

'Sophia de Lyle's real name was Ellen

Higgins.'

She *had* met interesting people, and intended to write about every one of them. Life here would probably feel all the slower, for she admitted that her past now seemed rather dramatic and colourful. She wouldn't have to beg or steal, or look over her shoulder here.

'I wrote a story about Sophia de Lyle for my friend, Mr Thomas Hambert. He had lots of books. He bought me *Robinson Crusoe* as a gift. It's in my cart.'

'That was kind of him. You must unpack your cart, then we'll drag it to the barn, though it doesn't look to be of much use after its travels, except perhaps for firewood.'

Millie came in with Lottie, who carefully carried four brown speckled eggs in a small basket over her arm. She was wearing a big smile on her face. 'Mrs Millie gave me a chicken of my very own. She makes funny noises.' Lottie awkwardly clucked her tongue a couple of times, trying to mimic the hen. 'Her name is Ginger and she's got shiny red feathers and is my friend. She laid an egg for my breakfast. And there's a donkey in the barn called Major and he pulls the cart. He allowed me to sit on his back.'

The pleasure Lottie got from such a simple act made Celia want to weep. Lottie had never had a garden to play in, let alone an animal to fuss over. 'I'm sure Ginger lays beautiful eggs.'

Lottie's clothes were still dirty, but her hair was a halo of soft curls decorated with a ribbon. Tears welled into Celia's eyes.

Harriet also became teary-eyed. 'I must buy

148

Charlotte something to wear; we'll go into Dorchester this afternoon and buy her what's necessary, something serviceable to wear to church school – sailor suits are popular for children, I understand. And we must get her some boots with a little more room in them, else her feet won't grow properly. There are several gowns and some night attire that used to belong to my mother. We'll use the fabric from one of those to make her some pretty smocks, and some bodices. And I'll enrol her at the church school when she's ready.'

'She can nearly write her name already. My ma taught her, and she can write the letters of the alphabet on a chalk board.'

'Alice was a good teacher. Charlotte is very thin and we must build up her strength a little first.' She kissed Celia gently on the cheek. 'We must build up yours too, my dear; you've had a hard time of it. Now, we must get your luggage unpacked.'

Celia was ashamed as she pulled out the soiled blankets and ragged cloaks. 'Mr Hambert gave mother these blue blankets when we were in need of warmth. I should like to keep them.'

Harriet took one look at them and made a face. 'I think not, Celia. They're past redemption. Everything you have is. We have plenty of blankets, and as for clothing, we can do better than what you have from my sister's wardrobe. Whatever the future brings, we must try and keep up standards, and improve on them. If the worst comes to the worst I can always sell this house. Let's make a bonfire out of them later; it will be like burning certain aspects of your past.'

'I need to write some letters before we go to Dorchester. I didn't say goodbye to a friend because he was sick, and I'd like him to know I reached my destination safely, otherwise he will wonder, and fret about us.'

'Is that the Mr Hambert you mentioned?'

And Celia had thought she hadn't been listening. 'Yes. I also need to thank Busby and Mrs Busby for their hospitality. Without their help I think we might have perished.'

'This third party you were travelling with; how old was he?'

'Johnny Archer?' Celia shrugged. 'He was about twelve and had nobody. The cart was his, and he was trying to sell it so he could buy something to eat. He asked if he could come with me, so he could find work. He'll grow up to be a good man with the Busby family. I must write to him too, because I know he felt guilty about following his heart and staying behind. He will worry about what happened to us, too. I don't want him to think he was unimportant.'

Harriet bestowed a smile on her. 'I'm pleased you are charitable as well as having such good manners, my dear. I'll find you paper, pen and ink.'

In a short while Celia was settled at the writing desk in the study. She gazed into the air for a moment, then dipped the pen in the inkwell and began to write.

Dear Mr Hambert, things are greatly looking up...

Ten

In September, Charles Curtis was celebrating his twenty-fifth birthday with a dinner at his house in Hanover Square. The dinner was hosted by his mother, and several acquaintances and friends were in attendance.

Charles had completed his education, graduating from Cambridge with honours. He'd spent the past year touring the continent with a group of several young men, taking in the sights, visiting the art galleries and learning about the antiquities as well as socializing.

His mother had invited a collection of pretty and eligible young ladies to dinner, but although they were lovely, he had no intention of marrying until he was firmly established in his career, nor falling into the trap of leading any young society woman astray. A forced, or loveless marriage was not for him. There were other types of women more than eager to fill a man's needs, and they didn't require a promise or a ring on their finger.

Abandoning her widowhood, his mother had married again before Charles had gone on tour. Joshua Harris was an insurance broker, and Charles got on well with him.

To his surprise, his mother had produced a daughter while he was away, so he now had a baby sister as well. Adelaide was a delightful child, affording Charles much amusement as she cooed, smiled and dribbled her way into his heart. Flirting was a female art from an early age, he concluded.

Before dinner Joshua asked to talk privately to him, and they went into the book-lined study. 'I know a barrister who's keen to take you into his law practice if you intend to follow in your late father's footsteps,' he said.

'I'd thought that I might. My father would certainly have expected me to become a barrister, had he lived.'

'There might be a partnership in it eventually, if the pair of you suit each other. He's well thought of, and is building up a good practice. It will mean living in Poole or surrounding areas, and travelling around the district. I doubt if you'd mind that, since you've often talked about moving to the country. You must be prepared to sign articles. In return, he promises that you'll be offered plenty of court experience, much of it unpaid to start with.'

'I would expect to sign articles, and I can easily support myself, as you know.'

'On another matter altogether, I'd be prepared to buy this house from you, if you want to sell it. I don't feel happy about living here free of charge.'

'It's a good address and I really don't want to sell. As it always has been, it's still my mother's home as far as I'm concerned. I'd rather you both lived here than lease it out to strangers. Does having me come and go bother you?'

'If you'll forgive my frankness, Chas, I do get the impression that you're looked on as the master when you're here, which is a little galling. At least allow me to establish myself by paying the expenses and the household bills.'

'You can pick up the servants' bill if that will make you feel better; a gentleman's agreement will suffice. I'll inform my accountant to present the accounts to you from now on.' They shook hands on it. 'If having me here is a bit of an imposition, I might as well tell you that I'd intended to move into bachelor rooms now mother has you to look after her. I find living at home to be a little restrictive after the freedom of my travels. If I move to the country there will be no need.'

Joshua grinned. 'I imagine it would be restrictive. After all, a young man must sow his wild oats before he settles.'

'There speaks a veteran. I'm pleased that my mother married you, Joshua. She was too young to be left on her own. I must admit that I thought you were a dedicated bachelor, so the fact that you were seeing my mother worried me ... and the marriage surprised me.'

'I was a dedicated bachelor until I met Imogene. It was love at first sight as far as I was concerned, and she was worth waiting for. Now we have Adelaide, and that was something neither of us had really counted on.'

To which comment, Charles smiled. 'I couldn't have had a nicer gift to come home to. However, putting my baby sister to one side, I confess I'm interested in the offer you mentioned. If I decide to pursue it I can quite easily move to Dorset. Does this barrister have a name?'

'James Kent. He's a fairly young man, still in his thirties I should imagine. He is ambitious, but represents the poor on a regular basis.'

Interest came into Charles' eyes. 'My father was an advocate for the poor.'

'So I'm given to understand. James Kent is the nephew of the poet and philanthropist, the Reverend Thomas Hambert, who tutored your father at Cambridge. He has been retired for some time now.'

'Ah, yes ... I do vaguely remember him. The last time I saw him was at my father's funeral. It's been remiss of me to overlook him since then. I must call on him, especially if I decide to join his nephew in the practice of law. When can I meet James Kent?'

'At the weekend, if you wish. He's in London for a week, and I've invited him to dinner. His uncle cannot attend unfortunately; he has a prior engagement.'

'A pity,' Charles murmured.

'You're lucky to be in a privileged position where you don't need to add to your existing wealth, which is why I thought this position might suit you. However, don't be too hasty about it, and please think it over.'

Chas liked Dorset and was quite prepared to establish a modest country home there if he decided to move to the county. Although never without a coin, he wasn't obvious about his

154

wealth. He gambled in small amounts, settled his accounts promptly, and no longer allowed his waistcoat to swing open when he was slumming it. That had been a lesson well learned!

He grinned as the thought hit him, which it often did. The cheek of that blue-eyed ragamuffin girl, coming to his house to claim a reward for a card case she'd lifted from him. It had been an expensive kiss, but well worth it. He wondered where she was now; and was she still innocent? He doubted it, and he doubted if he'd ever set eyes on her, or his money, again. Still, that had been easy come, easy go.

He remembered how large her eyes had become when she'd set them on the cash. Remembered how soft her mouth had been. After she'd gone he'd experienced shame at the way he'd treated her, demanding a kiss ... ashamed that he'd been the cause of her leaving her home by involving Bessie Jones, who ran the whorehouse. What if she'd been forced into that life, along with her young sister? A sick feeling yawned inside him at the thought. If he ever met her again he must try and make it up to her.

Dinner was a social occasion to be relished. The conversation was witty, the laughter spontaneous. Charles and his friends flirted lightheartedly with the ladies. He hadn't enjoyed himself quite so well for a long time. His mother was proud of him. He'd never seen her so happy, and he had Joshua to thank for that.

When the ladies retired, heading for the drawing room in a swish of multi-coloured silk and lace, feathering eyelashes and fluttering fans, his stepfather ushered the men towards the games room, where they could talk freely.

Talk mostly settled on the Crimean war, which had started with the sinking of several Turkish boats by the Russians. The French and English had become allies, and in the battle for Alma had beaten the Russians back.

That was followed by concern over the month-long cholera outbreak.

'I've heard that the source is one of the street pumps in Broad Street,' somebody said morosely. 'The handle has been removed so it can't be used any longer.'

'I heard that the pump was blocked by a decomposing eel, and that caused the outbreak.'

Joshua handed round brandy and cigars. 'Then again, it could be the system of pumping sewage into the Thames that caused the sporadic outbreaks in the past. The staff have been instructed to boil all the water.'

'Oh, it seems as though the outbreak is just about over though. Luckily it hasn't affected this part of London.'

Another brandy and the talk turned to lighter subjects – the latest music hall acts, then, inevitably, on to women.'

Someone said with a guffaw of laughter, 'Did Chas ever tell you about the time he paid one hundred pounds advance to a young woman, on a promise?'

All eyes turned his way.

He shrugged, then chuckled, for it all seemed so stupid now. 'It's true. Because she was a beggar, I also assumed that she was a street-girl, and I offered to buy her services from a madam. As a result, she had to run for her life, with her baby sister in tow. The girl came to return my card case, which she said she'd *found*,' and his arched eyebrow brought laughter. 'She asked me if she could claim a reward. The long and the short of it is, when I saw her up close she was—'

'An old hag?' Joshua suggested.

'On the contrary. She was on the brink of womanhood, but she was an exquisitely beautiful creature under her dirt, with the most amazing eyes. The thing was, she recognized me. She said that if I'd paid the madam, then she would not have seen a penny of it, and besides, she was still intact and had promised her mother she'd be a good girl.'

'And we all know that Chas Curtis likes his girls on the wicked side,' Ernest Edwards said drily.

Barnaby Dean laughed. 'So Chas gave her the hundred pounds he'd won from me the night before at the gambling table.'

Charles shrugged. 'I felt responsible for her plight, and I told her to come back when she was eighteen with her virginity intact. In fact, I was quite taken by her. Unfortunately, she took the money, and I haven't seen her since. That was over three years ago.'

The butler came in while they were still laughing at Charles' expense. When the man caught his eyes he nodded towards his stepfather to re-direct him.

Joshua didn't miss the gesture and he grinned

157

as the butler whispered something in his ear. Joshua announced, 'Gentlemen, you'd better don your parlour manners again. It's time to join the ladies for the entertainment.'

'I hope Mrs Robothan doesn't do any of her caterwauling tonight,' Ernest said under his breath as they made their way back to the drawing room.

Thomas Hambert's work in London was finished. His paper on the London poor had been read to a meeting of the Anglican Philanthropic Society, earning a standing ovation. The paper had also been presented to the House of Lords by a titled gentleman of Thomas' acquaintance.

Following that, *The Times* newspaper printed it in full, which attracted lively discussion through readers' letters, and donations of a gratifying amount of money to the society, to benefit the poor. Afterwards, printed into pamphlet form it was distributed through the clubs and coffee houses to anyone who wished to read a copy.

Pleased with the results of his research, Thomas had gone back to more pleasurable writing pursuits, perfecting some poems he'd written. Barely back from a visit to the printer's establishment he partly owned, he received an invitation from his sister to visit for Christmas, and to stay as long as he wished.

Thomas accepted, and began to plan his journey. He was looking forward to seeing James again. And he intended to surprise Miss Celia Laws if James could discover her whereabouts, for her letter had omitted her address. It had said they were safe, and living in Hanbury Cross, in Dorset, with her aunt Miss Harriet Price. She had thanked him for the friendship he'd offered to herself and her family, and hoped they would meet again one day.

Thomas had been mightily relieved to receive the first letter from Celia, but she hadn't followed it up with a second one. Celia was a resourceful young woman, and it was obvious she wouldn't presume on their friendship – one Thomas intended to retain if he could, since her future welfare, and that of Lottie, interested him.

After all this time Celia would be quite the young woman, he thought, and he hoped she'd not given in to the impulse to go on the stage, especially since he had a surprise for her ... if it were ready in time.

Although his housekeeper would drop in from time to time to keep the place dusted, he would leave a key with his adjoining neighbour. As for Frederick, it would be unthinkable to leave him behind. His cat had travelled by train before, and, although not enamoured by the process, Frederick put up with his confinement to a wicker basket tolerably well, and without too much complaint. After all, it wasn't a long journey on the train, and he'd sleep for most of the way.

If the trains were running on time and he managed to catch the Southampton to Dorchester connection, James would meet him at the station. If not, he would get a cab.

A month later Thomas set out for Waterloo station. It was one of those odd, unsettled days, that threatened much but did very little but grumble. The wind gusts tumbled rubbish along the gutters. Ladies clung to their skirts with one hand, yet still they afforded more than a glimpse of a petticoat to the discerning eyes of the gentlemen, who clamped their top hats firmly to their heads with one hand. The day had a bite of winter to it.

The air smelled of soot. Waiting at the station, looking important with its funnel stretching tall and the brass-work gleaming, the engine, with carriages at the ready, gave impatient little puffs of steam.

Thomas had made sure Frederick's basket was securely tied, and had settled the dolefully meowing cat in the luggage compartment.

'You'll be all right, Frederick. Just settle down and go to sleep like the last time. I won't forget you and we'll meet at the other end.'

Now seated comfortably in his first-class compartment, he watched the people on the station going about their business. Taking out his notebook and pencil he began to write.

A loud whistle followed by a series of louder steam blasts startled him. With clanking jerks, the train began to move, then settled into a smoother motion. As they made their way out of the station and he sank back into the padded, buttoned seat, Thomas admitted to a flicker of excitement at being able to use such a fast and luxurious mode of travel. Who would have imagined such a thing when he'd been young?

James was indeed waiting for him at the other end. While they took a cab through the port town, James told him, 'I have discovered the whereabouts of Miss Laws for you and we shall pay her a visit as soon as you're settled.'

Lottie had settled in to Chaffinch House, and it seemed to Celia that the child had already forgotten her early years of poverty. She'd been a sweet infant; now she was six, and a child who charmed everyone around her.

At eighteen, Celia had reached her full size. Physically, she'd not changed much over the previous two years, except for becoming slightly fuller in the bosom and hip. She was more mature in her outlook though. She'd learned a lot from copying her aunt, but didn't possess her elegance, a fact she bewailed.

'My dear, we're all different, and you are lovely. Just be yourself,' Harriet told her.

Gradually, the rough edges of Celia's speech had been smoothed away and her voice, always slightly husky, adopted the same inflections and mannerisms of her aunt as she worked at it. An actress must be able to master different voices, she told herself. The watchful distrust that was once a barrier to friendship thinned enough over the months to allow her to take people at face value – though she was aware of the difference between friendship and acquaintance.

As part of the Price family, they'd been accepted into life at Hanbury Cross.

Harriet had been honest with her from the first day they'd met. 'Few of the people living here will remember Alice clearly. The murky nature of her departure wouldn't have been made public by my mother, since it would have reflected badly on her.'

If Harriet knew exactly how murky her sister's life had become at times, she would probably turn Celia out. But she had lived in this big house since birth. Despite having to be careful with her money, she had no concept of real poverty, and neither had she needed to stoop to the level her sister had.

'I shall tell people the truth, that you're my beloved niece, and Charlotte is my late sister's ward.'

When Celia had looked askance at that, Harriet said, 'Charlotte must be told the truth of her birth when she's old enough to understand, in case she has expectations that cannot be fulfilled. It would be upsetting if she learned of her lowly start in life from another ... a friend perhaps ... and was judged by it.'

Feeling troubled, Celia said, 'Surely real friends don't judge you, they accept you for what you are.'

'One would think so, my dear, but it doesn't pay to be too trusting with people, however friendly and supportive they seem – or to offer them confidences which could prove detrimental to either of you in the future.'

Towards the end of November the water in the village pond crackled over with ice and the tree limbs became stark bare bones, except for a fringe of hanging icicles decorating each branch. The land woke each morning covered in a layer of mist that sometimes lasted all day. It smelled better than the London fogs, and was a stark reminder to them all that Christmas was nearly upon them.

There was an air of excitement in Hanbury Cross. Neighbours visited, exchanging recipes for Christmas puddings and fruit tarts, and sampling the port and gossiping. Celia had been invited to read one of the lessons at the Christmas Eve service, and she was looking forward to it.

'I hear there's a company of players coming to Dorchester in time for the January hiring fare,' Mrs Hardy said.

Celia's ears pricked up. 'Do you know who they are?'

'It has a foreign name, Bento or something similar. I heard that it's a variety show with different acts, with a talent show for anyone who wishes to enter. There's a five shilling prize.'

Benito's troupe of jugglers came to mind, his performing dog act and his wife, who walked across a rope stretched between two poles. Celia smiled. 'May we go and see them, Aunt?'

'Perhaps. We'll see what the weather is like. I do hope they're not too vulgar.'

'Oh, they're not, really. That's if it's the Benito I knew in London.'

Mrs Hardy's eyes began to gleam. 'You know him? How interesting. Was he a neighbour?'

'No, he was just somebody I knew, a street player. Sometimes he'd allow me to work for him ... to collect the money, and he'd give me sixpence. I was only a child then.'

'How odd to know an entertainer.'

The woman's superior tone annoyed her. 'Why is it? There's a large world outside of this village, Mrs Hardy, and people are all different. In fact, my mother and I toured with a theatre company once, when I was a child, and my father was an impresario.'

'Ah, yes ... so he was ... an American I recall. My husband invested some money in one of his shows, but we heard no more, and we lost our investment. I recall that Jackaby Laws was a charming man. What ever happened to him?'

Celia wished she knew. Pleased for once that she possessed such a sorry skill, she plucked a lie from the air. 'I imagine he's making his fortune in America with a Wild West—'

Harriet intervened, saying smoothly as she hid her displeasure, 'Perhaps you'd like to fetch a jug of hot water for the tea, Celia. It's a little on the strong side. After that, help Millie in the kitchen, please. Perhaps take Charlotte off Millie's hands.'

'Yes, Aunt.'

'A rather forthright young woman,' Mrs Hardy said with a sigh as Celia walked away, and without bothering to lower her voice. 'She has the look of her father and her mother's manner. Alice was always straightforward. A pity, since Jackaby Laws had so much charm.'

As did most deceivers, Celia thought, scowling. Uneasily, she remembered the snippet of information she'd gleaned from the conversation. Had Jackaby Laws been an American? If so, she might never catch up with him.

Later, her aunt took her to task. 'Celia, you

164

must not deliberately make a guest in our home feel uncomfortable again. Mrs Hardy meant no harm. She was just making conversation.'

'She was looking for something to gossip about.'

'And you gave her plenty of ammunition with all that talk about street players and touring with a theatre company.'

'Oh? I thought it fitted in well, since she knew my father, the great impresario.' She gave a gurgle of laughter. 'Or thought she did.'

'What do you mean by that?'

'From the little I know of him, it's occurred to me on more than one occasion that he might have been a liar and a trickster who went around fooling people to steal their money. Was he from America?'

Harriet sighed. 'He may have been. I was a child, and I can't remember him all that well. I would advise you to leave this well alone.'

'I can't. You don't know what my mother was forced to do to keep me alive. That was his fault.'

'You said she was a seamstress.'

'Yes, she was.' Celia bit down on her bottom lip. 'But sometimes she was forced to ... *entertain* ... otherwise we would have starved.' There, it was said.

'I don't understand; you've already told me that Alice acted on the stage.'

'My mother entertained ... *men*.'

There was a sudden silence, into which a small, choking cry of comprehension dropped. Harriet's eyes widened, and their momentary disbelief was slowly replaced by horror and disgust. 'No,' she whispered, and the anguish in her voice raised pity in Celia.

'I'm sorry; I needed to tell you that. Now you know why I must find him. I need to confront him on her behalf.'

'Yes. God help me ... I do understand. What sort of life must you have led to know of such things?' Harriet had tears in her eyes. 'My dear, I hate to ask you this but are you still ... well, you know?'

'Intact? Physically, yes, but that was placed in jeopardy when mother died because I had nobody to protect me. I've seen too much, know too much. That comes of poverty. Children grow up too quickly with the constant need for survival foremost in their mind. That's why my mother told me to throw myself on your charity.'

'You poor child. I'm so glad you came. It's a pity Alice didn't survive to come with you.'

'My mother would have been too ashamed, and too proud to let you know how low she'd fallen. Now you can understand why she made me promise to come here. She loved me, and she didn't want me to follow in her footsteps.'

Harriet held out her arms and Celia stepped into their protective circle. They hugged each other tight and Celia bathed in the warmth of Harriet's sympathy, and love.

'You will never do that – not while I still have a breath left in my body,' she whispered.

Into the fraught silence, a knock at the door sounded startlingly loud.

Eleven

Millie brought a card in. But instead of giving it to Harriet, Celia found herself the recipient.

Astonished, she gazed at it, a smile spreading across her face. She hadn't known Thomas Hambert was a church official; if she had she would probably have run in the opposite direction rather than allow him into her life. But it couldn't be anyone else with the name *Reverend Thomas Hambert.*

Harriet gazed at her. 'Who has called on you, dear?'

'It's a gentleman friend of mine from London. May I invite him to join us?'

'There's two of them,' Millie said. 'One's a right handsome gent who said his name is James Kent.'

Celia's smile encompassed the room as she said with great enthusiasm, 'How wonderful.'

Harriet looked worried. 'Do you think we will be safe? They won't breathe fire and set light to the house, or do acrobatics or anything.'

She giggled at the thought of the portly Thomas Hambert doing acrobatics. 'I do hope not.'

'They look perfectly normal to me,' Millie said. 'I'd better get back to the kitchen. I'm

167

teaching Miss Charlotte to make scones and she's up to her eyebrows in flour.'

Celia chuckled. 'I'll vouch for them, Aunt. Millie, on your way out would you tell them to come in please? And ask Lottie to join us when she's finished.'

Thomas came in first, dressed in black, and followed by the taller James, whose eyes widened at the sight of her. They laid their capes and hats on a vacant chair and removed their gloves.

'I hardly recognize you, Celia,' James said, stepping forward to kiss her cheek.

'I told you there was a lovely young woman waiting to emerge from inside our little heathen,' Thomas murmured, doing likewise. 'Though I must admit to being amazed by the transformation myself.'

'May I introduce you to my aunt, Miss Harriet Price. Aunt, this is...' She grinned as she gazed at his card before meeting his eyes. 'My friend; *Reverend* Thomas Hambert, who has turned out to be a dark horse, after all. This gentleman with him is his nephew, Mr James Kent, who is a lawyer.'

'Soon to be a magistrate.'

'Stop showing off.' Celia grinned at James, and at Harriet's bewilderment over her guests. 'I shall have to behave myself from now on, then, I suppose.'

Aunt Harriet looked even more bewildered by that, for Celia had never told her the details of her former profession. 'My aunt was worried because she thought you might be fire-eaters or acrobats from a travelling show, so you must prove that you're respectable.'

James kissed Harriet's hand and smiled. 'You'll be relieved to hear that I have yet to master the art of flame throwing, and if I tried acrobatics of any type I would probably do myself an injury. But how nice to meet you, Miss Price. I do hope you don't mind us coming unannounced. I had some business over this way, and my uncle had a gift he wished to deliver to Celia.'

And indeed, he had a book-shaped parcel tied with string in his hand.

'You're welcome, Mr Kent, and you also, Mr Hambert. Goodness, I had no idea that Celia was so well connected.'

Thomas made a humming sound in his throat. 'Thank you, Miss Price. I'm pleased that my little ragamuffin friend has found herself a good home.' He gazed around him. 'Is Lottie not here with you, Celia? Is she well? I have a gift for her too.'

'She's in the kitchen helping to make some scones. I'll fetch her. Would you like some refreshment?'

'We can't stay long, with the afternoons drawing in so early. However, a cup of tea before we return to Poole would be welcome.'

A little while later, Lottie was handing round scones with plum jam to spread on top, a smile on her face because, although she didn't remember the guests, they had taken an interest in her. There had been a gift, a jigsaw puzzle of a map of the world. She'd never played with a jigsaw before and Aunt Harriet had said she'd help her and tell her the names of all the countries on it.

Celia grandly poured the tea and played the part of hostess to perfection, though she caught a grin being exchanged between her gentlemen callers now and again.

'My uncle has been worried about you,' James said, when they were seated.

Celia sent a smile towards her former mentor. 'You shouldn't have worried, Mr ... *Reverend* Hambert. Didn't you receive my letter?'

'I did, but that arrived a long time ago. You omitted to inform me of your new address. I knew it was Dorset, and James tracked you down on my behalf. Are you still writing?'

'I've written several stories, plus an account of my escape from London, and events rising from it.'

'Good; then you've given up thoughts of being an entertainer.'

Celia sent a swift glance towards her aunt, who was conversing with James and wore a delicate pink blush on her face. She lowered her voice, gazed at the parcel again and knew she could wait no more. 'Not entirely, but I do have Lottie to consider, and she's settled and happy here. What's in the parcel? Is it for me?'

'Aha! I wondered when your curiosity would be aroused. I had a wager with James on how long it would take you to try and ferret it out of me. He now owes me a shilling.'

An imp of mischief rose in Celia. 'I see you have tied it with literal string.'

He laughed as he handed it to her. 'And I see you have learned the meaning of the word in the meantime.'

'You should have corrected me at the time.'

'It would have been mean to do. Besides, I knew you would figure it out eventually, and I enjoyed your puzzlement. Half the fun of knowledge is in the method used to gain it. The joy in the journey of discovery can never be underestimated.' He clapped his hands, drawing attention to them. 'Everyone, please pay attention while Celia opens my gift to her, since it's a moment not to be missed.'

She teased at the knots with her fingernails, loosening them, aware of all eyes on her. She glanced up after she pulled the string free. James wore a secretive smile. Her aunt's face was puzzled, and Thomas Hambert looked like a cat who'd swallowed the cream. She wanted to giggle, because he was enjoying this little scene as much as she.

Lottie was running a finger over her own gift with a pleased smile on her face. She was enjoying her time at school, and although she was an average student, she was quiet and well behaved.

Celia lifted the paper off and uncovered three leather-bound books. The breath she drew in was a gasp of delight. On the ruby cover impressed in gold lettering was written, *Famous Fictional Tales of the London Slums, written by T. Hambert & C. Laws.*

Tears welled to her eyes and she felt choked up, a feeling swiftly overturned by elation. 'I don't know what to say, Mr ... *Reverend* Hambert,' and she found herself laughing and crying at the same time. 'See what you've done ... mixed me up, and I don't know what to call you now.' She threw her arms around him and hugged him, knocking his spectacles sideways on his nose. 'You're so kind and thoughtful, and I wish you were my uncle instead of belonging to James. Thank you! Thank you! Thank you!'

'Dear me ... dear me ... this is most unseemly, Celia my dear,' he said, and extricated himself in a flurry of embarrassment from her embrace.

'That's the first time I've seen my uncle in such a pother,' James informed them, his laughter ringing out. Thomas straightened himself up, his efforts to hide his grin at her display woefully inadequate.

She hugged the books against her. 'It's such a lovely surprise; I'll treasure them always.'

Thomas Hambert vigorously polished his spectacles, and placed them back on his nose again. 'The leather-bound ones are limited special editions. I thought you might like one for yourself and another two to sign and gift to someone special. The bulk of the volumes are cloth bound, which makes them more affordable to the public.'

Tears in her eyes Celia ran a fingertip over the lettering. 'My own stories in print; how wonderful a surprise this is. I can't wait to read them, and yours, of course.'

'I'm better known for my poetry, which is what I contributed to this volume.'

'I'm so proud that you considered my work good enough to share a book with yours.'

Thomas cleared his throat. 'We've already earned a small amount of royalties from sales, and can expect more in time. I've placed it in an envelope inside the book with the accounting so far. Some readings have been arranged. My sister Abigail ... James' mother, that is, is hosting a social dinner and evening on Saturday. I thought you might like to come and read some of your work. I have a friend passing through, who will collect you, bring you to Poole and return you home the next morning.'

Celia gazed at her aunt, who seemed quite bemused by the turn of events. The thought of reading to Thomas Hambert's friends was awe inspiring, though thrilling; they were bound to be serious-minded and learned people.

'Am I good enough to read my work, or are you just being kind to me? I don't want to make a fool of myself.'

'You're every bit good enough, Celia. They are just people, and you should have more faith in yourself, and in my judgement.'

It was just the boost she needed in her moment of doubt, and she turned to her aunt. 'May I?'

'Of course you may accept the invitation, Celia. I consider the reverend to be an excellent chaperone.'

James smiled broadly at Harriet. 'Perhaps you'd like to attend as well, Miss Price. You will be my guest.'

'Are you sure your mother won't mind?'

'I'm quite certain she would enjoy meeting you.'

Harriet appeared pleased by the invitation. 'Well yes, I could come. Millie will look after Charlotte. She's a sweet child and they get along so well together.'

Thomas turned to James. 'I've forgotten something ... what is it James?'

'Richard Parkinson.'

'Ah yes ... Celia, I know a gentleman who edits a London magazine. He's eager to publish some tales of the London slums, such as those you've written for our book; a dozen in all, since the magazine is a monthly one. Or if you prefer you could write a serial – one continuous story in twelve sections. I'll leave a copy of the magazine so you can read it for yourself. They have their own artist to illustrate it, and you will be paid a fee – one I negotiated myself, so you can be assured you will receive a fair recompense for your efforts.'

Celia felt dubious, even though eager to accept. She was filled with awe that someone liked her writing enough to actually buy it.

'Everything seems to be happening at once. Having my name on a book is one thing, but writing tales for a magazine is another. There are things I'd rather not write about because it wouldn't be *seemly*, and the truth might reflect badly on me, or my *family*.' Her eyes slid towards Harriet, who now knew a lot more about her previous life, but not everything.

James leaned forward. 'They needn't be the actual truth, but rather the truth as seen and recorded through the eyes of a fictional person.'

'I'm not a professional writer, Mr Kent, and I'm sure Reverend Hambert must have heavily edited my work for the book.'

'Ah yes.' Cocking his head to one side Thomas gazed at her with bird-bright eyes. 'Your writing

174

actually needed very *little* editing, as a matter of fact, and the moment you were paid for your work you became a professional author. You could, of course, write the stories under a pseudonym.'

'A pen name?' She shrugged. 'I wouldn't know what to call myself. How can it be true tales if I make the stories up and use a false name?'

Thomas gazed with approval upon her. 'I see you haven't neglected your education, or your need to query everything. Your mind reaches out in all directions. The truth is often exaggerated or sacrificed in publishing, as the title of our book was. Famous, the stories were not.'

'But they will be when everybody buys our book, won't they?'

Thomas laughed. 'Exactly, and people will buy the books because they're given to understand that the stories are famous. But Celia, we have had this conversation before. The magazine publishes original fiction, therefore the stories must appear in fictional form.'

Celia grinned and tut-tutted. 'You mean the editor tells lies. I'm surprised you would condone such a concept, Reverend.'

'I doubt if anything would surprise you, young lady.'

'You certainly have. Why didn't you tell me about your profession?'

'Celia!' Harriet admonished faintly.

Hearing her, James, who was examining the contents of the jigsaw box with Lottie pressed against his knee, whispered from the corner of his mouth, 'It's obvious you haven't observed the two of them argue the point before, Miss Price. I'll be interested to see who wins this round. My money is on my uncle.'

'If I had any money to waste it would be on my niece,' she came back with.

'You never asked me what my profession was,' Thomas reminded Celia. 'Let's get back to the point. To be offered a contract for twelve stories is a testament to your talent. If you turn it down it will be an opportunity wasted, and most likely it will never be offered again.'

The truth of that statement filled her with confidence. 'That's true, but I never had any intention of refusing, and I shall accept with my aunt's permission.' Not that she needed it, but her aunt liked the niceties of life to be observed, and it was a courtesy.

'Checkmate,' Harriet whispered, and when James grinned at her she turned to Celia. 'You must decide for yourself, Celia.'

'What shall I use as a pen name?'

'Lightfingers?' James suggested without thinking, barely able to hide his chuckle.

Harriet gazed at James, puzzled. 'What a very odd name.'

His brow furrowed in a frown when Celia sent him a warning look, for she hadn't revealed that part of her life to Harriet. There were so many secrets to keep hidden, and she had to be careful not to allow them to escape, lest they scandalize people.

'Ah yes, but your niece is an odd person, and she has a fine sense of humour.'

And indeed, Celia was laughing inside, firstly

because the name was so apt, but mostly because of the interest James was taking in her aunt. He seemed to be intrigued by her.

After tea, he stood, as tall and straight as an arrow. He was soberly dressed in grey trousers, a darker grey jacket and a blue waistcoat of satin brocade. Celia watched him bow over her aunt's hand, then look directly up at her with a quirky smile. 'Thank you for your hospitality, Miss Price; I so enjoyed meeting you.'

Once again, a delicate blush suffused her aunt's cheeks. Goodness, Celia thought, grinning. A relationship between them might be worth encouraging.

James' head slanted to one side. 'Celia, I'm glad to see you looking so well, and so grown-up. I've enjoyed your company.' He slanted a smile towards Harriet. 'I'm sorry we can't stay longer and I look forward to seeing you on Saturday.'

'Please visit any time you're passing,' Celia dared to say. 'I'm sure my aunt won't mind.' Celia kissed James' cheek, then Thomas Hambert's. 'I'm so pleased to see you both again. Thank you for coming, and for the gift, Reverend. I'll treasure it.'

'The gift is inside it, Celia, in our words and thoughts, and for all to share.' Thomas gazed at her for a moment, suspicion filling his eyes. When he patted his pockets she offered him her most cherubic smile and shook her head in a gentle reproof. 'How could you think such an awful thing of me?'

Behind her, James slanted Harriet a look and

laughed. 'Match to Celia, I believe,' a remark that left her looking puzzled.

After their guests had gone, Harriet looked her directly in the eyes. 'Explain, *Lightfingers* to me.'

'Ah, yes, I imagined you'd ask. Brace yourself, Aunt, because you are not going to like this. As well as beg, I used to pick pockets in London. I stole Reverend Hambert's watch. Then I returned it to him. That's how we met.'

Harriet gasped. 'Is there anything illegal you haven't done?'

'Yes there is, Aunt, and it's because you gave me shelter and unconditional friendship when I needed it ... otherwise I'd be lost now. Reverend Hambert was kind to me and we became friends. If he'd had me arrested, which was his right, I would have been transported, or worse. He's more than I deserve.'

'He certainly is,' she said tartly. 'While he was visiting I remembered who he was. The man is a respected poet, and well known in reform circles.'

'Then he must have reformed me, for I've done hardly anything illegal since I met him, and you have my promise that I never will, if it can be avoided.'

She turned her mind to the one hundred pounds she'd taken from somebody on false pretences ... though it wasn't really false pretences, since she'd given Charles Curtis the kiss he'd paid for. The imprint of it was still on her mouth, to remind her at odd times of the debt she still

178

owed. She still had the money hidden away, and one day she'd hand it back to him – the man who'd tried to buy the use of her body to satisfy his lust.

She turned her aunt's mind aside with, 'I've never been to a social dinner. What will we wear?'

'Oh Lord, it's been years ... It will be dinner suits and evening gowns with lace or frills. Let's go upstairs and see what we can find in the wardrobes. Luckily, my sister and mother were fashion conscious.'

When Saturday came Harriet looked elegant in a dark-rose taffeta gown that had belonged to her mother and had never been worn.

Celia's gown was the colour of bluebells. They'd shopped in Dorchester, buying a layered lace collar and matching trim for the sleeves. Celia paid for it herself, with the royalty money that had been left by Thomas. She bought some matching ribbons for her hair.

Between them they dressed each other's hair in the fashionable style, parted in the middle and drawn into the side, giggling like children all the while, in case they singed each other's ringlets with the curling tongs.

Lottie smiled when she saw them. 'You both look so pretty, like princesses.'

'Thank you, my dove,' Harriet said. 'I certainly feel like a princess.'

Celia bent to kiss her sister when she heard the carriage. It was late afternoon, the shadows long when they left. Evening would soon be upon them. But it promised to be a clear night with a three-quarter moon to light their way. 'Be good for Millie. We'll be home tomorrow, and I'll tell you all about it.'

Cloaks around them, for it was going to be a cold night, Celia picked up the bag that contained their overnight necessities. She'd been reading out loud all week, and was word perfect, though she admitted she was a little nervous.

They were handed into the carriage, where an elderly man and his wife were comfortably ensconced. A blanket was tucked over their knees for warmth, something they were grateful for. The couple introduced themselves as Reverend and Mrs Emery. After a few pleasantries they promptly fell asleep, one in each corner, and began to snore.

Soon the daylight faded and they were passing through the busy town of Poole. The quay was crowded with seamen and labourers going about their business in the dusky light, and the dark, tangled, swaying masts of the ships were outlined against the darkening sky. Seagulls shrieked overhead as they headed back to their nests.

Abigail Kent's house was situated halfway up a hill, with a fine view over the harbour. Their companions woke with a start when the carriage stopped, yawning behind their hands.

Some of the guests had already arrived. Thomas called his sister over. After introductions, a maid showed Celia and Harriet to a dimly lit room on the second floor, where two beds waited. A fire burned in the grate and shadows danced upon the walls. The maid turned the gaslights up, revealing a room prettily decorated with wallpaper of delicate blue stripes on cream, and colourful patchwork quilts.

There was a note on one of the beds.

Dear Harriet ... You will not mind if I call you by your given name, I hope. I was detained, so late arriving home. Only now am I dressing for dinner ... now being 6.45p.m. My abject apologies for not being there to greet you on arrival, as planned. I promise to escort you both down at 7.15 on the dot, so you can properly meet the other guests before dinner. Sincerely, James.

'James Kent is a fine gentleman,' Harriet said with a faint smile.

'I think he's attracted to you, too,' Celia teased, which earned her a reproving look.

'I did not say I was attracted to him, Celia.'

'But you are, aren't you?'

'I refuse to answer that.' Harriet laughed and threw a cushion at her.

The three of them went down together, and James introduced them. There were magistrates and churchmen present, including a bishop. And there was a younger man – a man who made Celia's heart thud with sudden alarm.

'This is my partner, Charles Curtis. Chas, may I introduce Miss Harriet Price and Miss Celia Laws from Hanbury Cross.'

'My pleasure, ladies.'

Charles Curtis was tall, taller than Celia remembered, and more handsome. The youthfulness he'd displayed the last time they'd met had been honed into an interestingly angled, and manly face. His eyes were still as black as night, his hair a dark torrent and his mouth ... her own tingled and flamed into life as the kiss was remembered in all its glory to crowd into her senses. How could the effects of a kiss, even one so potent as the one they'd exchanged, last such an annoyingly long time?

She felt herself fall apart. The effect he had on her was catastrophic, especially when she gazed into his eyes. The least of that problem was that he might recognize her. She was a crumble of shards ... a small pile of rubble at his feet, waiting to be rebuilt.

Then she remembered she'd used the name of Lizzie Carter and began to breathe easier.

'Ah...' he said, as though he'd just tasted something that had given him much pleasure, and his smile became, all at once, ironic. 'I understand you're to be part of the entertainment for the evening, Miss Laws. A little romantic story for our delight, no doubt.'

How patronizing of him to assume such a thing. 'Please feel free to leave if something as mundane as romance displeases you, but preferably not when I'm reading. If you do I shall take off my shoe and throw it at your retreating back.'

He chuckled at that. 'I shall make a point of staying if it will make you happy.'

'I shall try to contain my delirium at the notion.'

His eyes suddenly impaled her. 'Have we met before, Miss Laws? I feel as though I should know you.'

He didn't recognize her! She drew her defences around her. She would get through this with as much coolness as she could muster. Her nerves cemented themselves together again and she said, 'We may have, though I can't remember you.'

He raised an eyebrow and chuckled. 'How crushing it is not to be remembered ... or is this a defensive stance you're taking because we danced together at Mrs Maybury's summer ball and I trod all over your toes?'

A huff of spontaneous laughter escaped her. Although fascinating, he had a streak of arrogance that pleased her. 'Yes, I agree, it is crushing not to be remembered. As for Mrs Maybury's ball ... now let me see,' she teased, and took a moment to appear to think about it. 'No, I didn't attend it, so it must have been another unfortunate woman's toes you stomped on.'

He wouldn't be put off. 'Still, I'm sure we've met before. London comes to mind, a social gathering of some sort. There can't be another woman on earth who has eyes of such a deep and beguiling blue.'

She blinkered them with her eyelids and gazed at the toes of his highly polished black evening shoes. 'I haven't been to London for some time.'

'Neither have I. Don't sound piqued because I can't quite remember you, Miss Laws. It will come to me eventually.'

Celia hoped not, but she felt relieved rather than miffed, and hoped he'd never recall the occasion. Enough people knew her secret, and if he did remember she'd have to lie her way out of it ... and just as she was making a habit of being honest! Damn him for turning up again in her life. 'I'm not at all piqued.'

'I don't mind you admiring my guests, Chas, but your approach is embarrassing to Celia, I believe.'

'So speaks a man who hasn't courted a woman in years.'

'All that could change,' and James turned his smile on Harriet, who promptly blushed.

Celia raised an eyebrow as she exchanged a glance with Charles Curtis, who grinned. 'Ah ... so that's the way the wind blows, is it?' He shrugged, and a smile spread across his face, altogether warm and genuine as he kissed Harriet's hand. 'Well, I can only admire your taste, James. What do you expect from me when you bring two perfectly exquisite females to dinner and keep them both for yourself? You would have more than your share with only one of them on your arm.'

While Celia was admiring a small scimitar of dark hair that curled against Charles' ear, his glance unexpectedly shifted back to her, something she wasn't quick enough to avoid. 'I'm looking forward to hearing you read your work, Miss Laws. Forgive me if I embarrassed you in any way.' He inclined his head as they moved away.

Her breath exhaled in an exasperated rush, something that drew a smile from James. 'He's a disarming young man, isn't he? And very good at his profession.'

Harriet appeared a little flustered as they moved on to the next person, and so she should, Celia thought with a grin, for James had made his intentions towards her perfectly clear.

Thank goodness she wasn't seated next to Charles, Celia thought a little later, giving the bishop – who had been seated next to her – a beaming smile.

'Has Reverend Hambert seated us together so you can keep me in order, my Lord Bishop,' she whispered to him.

'I do believe it might be the other way round. He thinks very highly of you.'

'Then I'll be sure to keep a close eye on you.'

They dined at a long table set with polished silver and decorated with flower arrangements. The candlelight sparkled on the crystal glasses. Charles was close enough to send her a smile now and again.

If only you could see me now, Ma, she thought, but knew deep in her heart that she'd swap everything and go back to famine and rags if that would bring her mother back. To be brought down so low after being raised in such a comfortable environment must have been hard to endure.

They moved to the drawing room, where three rows of chairs were set out. One of the women played the piano and sang a duet with her husband. When they had finished, Thomas recited a poem about the River Thames. It had several verses, and she admired his stillness, the emotion coming from his quiet reading of it, which had just enough rise and fall to keep the audience interested.

He beckoned to her afterwards, and she took her place next to him when he introduced her. Beyond the circle of light she saw Charles Curtis. Seated on the back of a couch, one long leg dangling, he had a damnable superior smile on his face.

So, Charles was expecting a romance, was he? There *was* one in the book, a tragic love story, where the soldier hero returned from war to discover his true love married to his enemy. That was not the story she was going to read tonight, though.

She picked up her book, opening it to where the red ribbon marked it. This one is for you, Ma, she thought as she drew in a calming breath. Be proud of me.

She was well rehearsed. Harriet had listened to her read the story over and over, advising her on where to pause, and helping her to modify her tendency to talk too fast or overdramatize. She waited until her audience settled, then gazed around at their expectant faces in the moment it took her to get into her narrative role.

The child couldn't have been more than four years. Her name was Sarah. Barefoot, covered in sores, and with only a flannel smock to cover her shivering body, she wandered the filthy alley-ways, calling out fitfully, 'Mamma, where are you? I'm hungry!'

A muffled sob came from somewhere in the audience, then another as the story progressed.

The story ended up in the same river Thomas had written about, unhappily, as most true stories about the London slums did. She admired Thomas Hambert for drawing attention to the plight of the poor there, even knowing improvement wouldn't happen in his own lifetime.

When she finished there were a few moments of silence, in which she looked over the heads of the audience to where Charles was seated alone. His enigmatic smile was now laced with wryness at the discovery of his own mistaken assumption. The women were dabbing at their eyes with lace-edged handkerchiefs, trying to compose themselves. Men spoke gruffly in case emotion got the better of them; a couple applied handkerchiefs to their noses and honked like geese.

Charles' eyes shone with moisture. He smiled ruefully at her and blew her a kiss. Then he began to clap. Others joined in and there were shouts of 'Well read, Miss Laws,' and 'Encore.'

Celia stood there while the applause circled around her like a storm, certain she was grinning inanely and not quite knowing whether to take her seat or stay where she was.

Thomas joined her. Beaming a proud smile all round, he said, 'I'm sorry ladies and gentlemen, no encore. We can only offer you a small taste, otherwise you won't buy the book. I do happen to have a few leather special editions for sale amongst the cloth-bound ones tonight.'

'How fortunate, Thomas, since most of us collect leather-bound first editions,' the Bishop said drily.

'I hadn't realized, my Lord,' Thomas said,

looking so innocent that everyone laughed. 'As you all know, a proportion of each sale will go to a good cause. After the concert, Miss Laws, or myself, or both, will personally sign each copy bought tonight.'

'No doubt,' James said softly.

To more applause, Thomas presented her with a posy of flowers and led her back to her seat.

It wasn't until Harriet took her hand and gently squeezed it, that Celia discovered she was trembling all over.

Twelve

The next morning, beyond Brownsea Island, where the horizon of dark, foam-lashed water met the pale sky, a thick scribble of charcoal clouds had begun to gather.

Mrs Emery displayed agitation at the sight, and her husband declared their intention to leave earlier than they'd intended, lest it rain and the road became a mire.

A breakfast of oatmeal was quickly consumed and Harriet and Celia readied themselves for the journey.

Saying goodbye to Thomas Hambert, Abigail Kent and James, who expressed his disappointment that they were leaving so early, they were soon on the road, the pair of horses clip-clopping along at a steady pace.

There had been no sign of Charles Curtis at breakfast. 'He rose early to return to his lodgings,' James told them. 'He begged me to pass on that he enjoyed the short time he spent with you ladies, and he hopes to renew the acquaintance at the earliest opportunity.'

The thought of meeting him again aroused a tug of annoyance in Celia, but mixed in with it was a strong thrust of anticipation. She would have to be careful of what she said around him.

'Do you have far to travel after you drop us off?' Harriet asked the Emerys.

'Only to Blandford,' Reverend Emery told them, and he smiled benevolently at Harriet. 'We so enjoyed your performance, Miss Laws. Your voice carries clearly and well, doesn't it, Annie.'

'Indeed. I was quite enthralled by the performance. How clever of you to write those stories. You have such a lively imagination, and we wouldn't have missed it for the world.'

Celia was about to tell her that they were true stories when Harriet's fingers squeezed hers. 'Thank you, Mrs Emery,' she said instead.

'It must be wonderful to have a natural talent for reading aloud, so the characters' voices come easily to the tongue. They sounded so real. I'm afraid that I frequently stumble over words when I read aloud.'

Celia exchanged a rueful smile with Harriet, both of them remembering the hours of practice she'd put in.

'I'm sure you are being too modest, Mrs Emery. My niece is going to read the lesson of the three wise men at the Christmas Day morning service at Hanbury Cross church. I'm so looking forward to it.'

'Indeed ... then we must attend the service, if the weather is clement.'

'Do you have a family?' Harriet asked them.

Where the Emery couple had been as silent as the grave on the way in, now they were as voluble as a couple of gobbling geese as they talked of their seven children and their growing number of grandchildren.

'It's so jolly at Christmastide when we're all together. There always seems to be an extra one each year. This year it is dear Bernard, who is three months old.'

By the time they reached Chaffinch House Celia seemed to have a thousand Emery names and occupations buzzing around her head, as though it were a hive of honey bees.

'Oh, are we here already?' Mrs Emery said with some disappointment. 'I was just about to tell you about the Peircy family, who are part of the maternal side. I was one of twelve children, you know.'

'Oh, I'm so sorry we haven't more time to spend together then,' Celia said, keeping a straight face. 'I found your relatives so interesting.'

'Another time perhaps, Miss Laws.' She gazed out of the window, a frown appearing on her face. 'I do hope we miss that storm. I'm sure it was just behind us.'

'Nonsense, dear, we have plenty of time in which to get home,' her husband said, as the coachman helped his guests out of the carriage.

They'd hardly waved the pair goodbye when Lottie came hurtling down the path, a big smile on her face. 'Major escaped from the stable. I chased after him and got his bridle on, but he wouldn't move. Mr Hardy came out of his house. He said it was the time of the full moon, and Major was having one of his moments. He stung him with a twig,' Lottie said with a giggle, 'and that made Major move. He gave a loud hee-haw and trotted all the way home by himself.'

Harriet smiled. 'Perhaps the coming storm has unsettled him. We must make sure his stable is secure.'

'Mr Hardy said the gate had dropped and needed a new hinge. He sent Jed round to fix it for you, and Millie paid him sixpence.'

'That was nice of him.'

A scatter of dried leaves rattled along the road, pushed by a gust of wind.

'I'll see to Major.' Celia hoped Reverend Emery and his wife arrived home safely before the storm broke as she made her way round to the stable. They'd been a nice couple and good company on the whole.

She filled Major's oat box and his water trough and picked up the brush, as she did most afternoons. She'd discovered that brushing him relaxed the donkey when he was in a fractious mood.

'I understand you misbehaved in our absence, Major.'

Major whuffled and closed his eyes as the brush smoothed long strokes over him.

'You know, Major ... you're such a handsome

donkey with that pale muzzle and pretty mane.'

Celia drifted off into her thoughts as she continued brushing – and those thoughts inevitably went to Charles Curtis. There was something about him that made her feel aware of herself.

'Do you know what it feels like to be in love, Major?' Then she giggled as she remembered the donkey had been gelded. 'Of course you don't. But then ... perhaps love and lust isn't the same thing.'

Charles Curtis had felt lust towards her the first time they'd met. He'd been willing to pay a fortune to satisfy that lust, even though she'd been dirty and ragged.

What was worse, he'd made her feel the same way. She'd never forgotten the kiss he'd demanded of her. She touched a finger against her mouth. How would his kiss feel against her mouth, now he was fully a man – and an experienced one at that, she thought?

She jumped when rain splattered against the roof of the stable. It was a solid building, built of stone that had withstood the onslaught of many storms. She made sure that the windows were secure and the doors were bolted on the way out.

Her dress flattened against her body as she pushed into the wind to make her way back to the house. The sky was dark, almost as black as night, and the house was filled with gloom.

In the drawing room a fire burned. Shadow dancers leaped on the wall. There was a tray of tea on the table ... slices of cake to eat. She felt safe in this house, reassured that nothing would ever go wrong for herself and Lottie again. She could no longer imagine cold and hunger, the feeling of having to look over her shoulder all the time like a hunted creature.

Lightning flashed and thunder rumbled. Lottie came to where she sat. 'Storms make me feel scared, Celia.'

Sliding her arm around the girl Celia held her close. 'The storm will soon pass over, my love.'

'You smell like Major. Tell me about the social evening. You said you would. Did you get to dance with the handsome prince, like Cinderella did in my book of fairy tales?'

'It wasn't a ball. It was dinner and a social performance. I didn't meet a prince ... well not a real one, but there were some nice people there, don't you think so, Aunt Harriet?'

But Harriet was staring into space with a soft smile.

Celia laughed. 'It looks as though Aunt Harriet met a handsome prince though.'

'Yes ... James is handsome, isn't he?' Her eyes came back to the present, and sharpened. 'What were we talking about?'

'Lottie and I were discussing Cinderella and her handsome prince, and you were discussing ... James Kent.'

'Oh.' Harriet grinned self-consciously, then said again, *'Oh!'* and a blush touched her cheeks as she busied herself with the teapot.

'What do you think of Celia Laws now, James?' Thomas asked his nephew the following day.

'The girl has turned my original opinion of her on its head. She is still outspoken, but interestingly so. She's also quick to learn. She worries me though.'

'Why, James, when you can see for yourself that she told the truth and her background is sound?'

'I think Chas Curtis is taking an interest in her.'

Gazing at him, Thomas said, 'Is that such a bad thing? Celia has grown into a beautiful and lively young woman, and her aunt has turned her into a lady. The difference is remarkable.'

'She's a young woman who spent most of her childhood in the London slums picking up bad habits and earning her living by trickery. Chas is a lawyer ... an association with a parvenu could harm his future.'

'There for the grace of God, go I,' Thomas murmured. 'I would never have imagined you'd turn into a stiff-neck, James. Only a few people close to Celia know of her background and rise to fortune – if you can call it that, for she still seems to have precious little to brag about. How would Charles learn of her unfortunate background pray; from you?'

'Things have a way of getting out. Besides ... it's not right to deceive a man.'

'You surely don't expect her to expose her past on first acquaintance, do you? Charles Curtis strikes me as being a resourceful man – old enough to run his own life. Let the relationship run its course without interference.'

James sighed. 'Of course he is. I'm being stupid, you're right ... I'm being stiff-necked.'

'You're worrying needlessly, James. They've only met each other once. If the time ever came when Charles needed to know, I'm certain that Celia would reveal all to him. In the meantime, she's not going to risk her background becoming common gossip by confessing to all and sundry. If that's deceit, so be it.' He looked James straight in the eyes. 'You know, James, you're showing signs of becoming a pompous ass. It's about time you married and produced some children.'

James grinned. 'Yes ... You are quite right, Uncle. I've been thinking along the same lines, myself.'

Thomas gazed at him with more than some interest. 'Who must I thank for this metamorphosis, Miss Harriet Price?'

James smiled. 'What was that you were saying about interfering in the lives of others? How did you know it was her?'

'You looked quite dazzled by her. I heard that Miss Price was approached by Arthur Avery once or twice – he was engaged to Harriet's sister before she and her mother sickened and died last year.'

'Arthur Avery? Good Lord; he's old enough to be her father. Who told you such a thing?'

'Your mother did. Much as I love my sister, I'd be the first to say that Abigail is a busybody who makes it her business to know everyone else's business. But she's usually correct about things. Avery is Harriet's financial, as well as legal adviser, by the way.'

James' smile slowly faded. 'There are rumours about him.'

'According to my sister, Harriet firmly rejected

Avery, but he thinks it's only a matter of time, since her father's estate is almost bankrupt and she now has Celia and young Lottie to support, as well as the family house to maintain. He offered to buy it, but she refused him that too. Apparently, he told her she wouldn't be able to afford the maintenance much longer, and his next offer would be considerably smaller.'

'That sounds like a threat.'

'Doesn't it? So take my advice, James. If you intend to marry the woman, you'd better start courting her. Invite them for New Year.'

James headed for the door and Frederick slipped through it in the opposite direction. When Thomas stretched his legs out towards the fire, the cat jumped on his lap and began to knead and purr. Thomas felt warm and contented, and smiled at the thought that he'd spurred James into action.

'You're pulling threads in my trousers,' Thomas murmured to Frederick, not that he cared much, since they were an old pair. 'You know, Freddie, perhaps we'll settle down here, after all.'

Abigail came in with a tray of tea and some fruit scones to go with it. She was a small, neat woman, ten years younger than him, but there was a likeness between them. She took the seat opposite, and, handing him a plate supporting two buttered scones, began to pour the tea from a china pot. 'Well, Thomas?'

'It seems that James has taken a liking to Harriet Price.'

'I had noticed him paying attention to her. I

thought her to be a nice young woman with a sensible head on her shoulders. I'd almost given up on James marrying. Do you think anything will come of it?'

'He's just the right age, my dear, and is now established professionally. Harriet Price does appear to have a sensible head on her shoulders, as you say.'

'That girl you've taken under your wing ... Celia Laws. Is that Alice Price's daughter?'

'It is. They fell on hard times and her mother recently died.'

'I hear she has a child to raise.'

'The child is no blood relative, but a foundling who was taken into the family by her mother. She's named Charlotte, and Celia regards her as a sister.' He wondered if he was making a mistake in confiding in his sister and gazed at her. 'Abigail ... everything I have told you about Celia Laws must remain confidential. Celia is a dear girl who deserves a better chance in life than she's previously been obliged to endure.'

'I know you think I'm a gossip, but when it's close to home I can be the soul of discretion.' His sister gazed at him with genuine concern in her eyes. 'The girl is so young, and I'm not entirely comfortable with what I know of her background. You won't do anything silly will you?'

'Silly! What on earth are you talking about, Abigail?'

'Well, you know ... marriage. You wouldn't be the first older gentleman to be taken in by a pretty face, and anyone can see how fond you are of the girl.'

'She reminds me of my own, dear daughter, whose name she bears, and who would have been much the same age now. Marriage?' He chuckled. 'I would have absolutely nothing to offer a girl of that age.'

'You have money and property, and it's clear she worships the ground you walk on. Such attention is flattering for a man of *mature* years.'

'It might be for some. Celia wants neither money nor property from me, and if she admires me, it's because I trust her and I give her confidence in herself. Celia has few pretensions, but her expectations in her own ability are high.'

Thomas' hand jerked when his sister said, 'I thought I saw her father the last time I was in London. He was in the theatre, and I heard him being referred to as the American tenor, Daniel Laws. Although the man had greying hair, he seemed about the same age as Jackaby Laws would be now. Eighteen years have passed, so he could quite easily be the same man. Apart from his name, even his speaking voice was the same.'

'You've met Celia's father then?'

'It was a long time ago, and only briefly. Jackaby Laws was handsome, charming and distinguished-looking. My husband invested some money in his theatre show ... only a small amount, thank goodness, so we didn't lose much.

'But then, perhaps it wasn't Jackaby Laws, because I've since been told he is dead.'

Thomas allowed that snippet to take root in his mind. Alice Laws had indicated to him that her husband had deserted her. Had she known he'd died? Indeed, *had* he died, or had he just changed his name? Celia seemed convinced that he was still alive, and a confidence trickster. Thomas had been left with no doubt that she intended to seek him out and take him to task.

'Can you remember who told you of his demise?'

'Really, Thomas, can you remember who you had conversations with eighteen years ago? The subject just came up, as it has now. He was one of those men with presence, who it was hard to forget. No wonder Alice Price fell hard for him. I vaguely remember it said that he was taken ill, and had died on the ship taking him back to America.'

Which was a plausible rumour to put about if the man had wished to change his identity and leave his past behind.

'Alice was shunted off to Scotland to look after some relative or another, but when her father died her stepmother sent her packing.'

'I don't suppose you know what happened to Jackaby Laws' estate?'

Abigail snorted. 'All I know is that we didn't get our investment money back. Neither did anyone else. There was talk over the years ... that Alice kept it ... that their marriage was a sham right from the beginning. Some said that Jackaby had deserted Alice and the child, and finally, that he'd actually died. All the same, Daniel Laws reminded me so much of him that I began to wonder again what the truth of it actually was.'

Thomas' curiosity was now thoroughly aroused. He'd always disliked a story without a satisfactory ending.

Thirteen

There was a crash during the night that woke them all. Candles lit, they inspected the house and the attics to discover there was a hole in the roof. The storm had blown one of the chimney pots off, which in turn had cracked some tiles, allowing room for the rain to seep through. Luckily the room was unoccupied, so the fire wasn't alight to cause a hazard.

They placed a bucket under the drip and went back to bed, hoping that the rain wouldn't get any heavier to worsen the damage.

A shivering Lottie held on tightly to Celia's nightgown. Her sister had her own room now, adjoining Celia's. Now, she said quietly, 'Can I sleep with you tonight?'

There wasn't much of the night left, for the long clock in the hall had chimed three just a few moments ago. She smiled at Lottie. 'Come on then.'

There was a warm lump under the quilt where Moggins had sought safety from the storm. He set up a loud purr.

'You're supposed to sleep in the kitchen,' she scolded, but Celia couldn't be bothered to go out into the cold again, and the three of them snuggled down together, despite the crash, bash, and blustering fury of the storm outside.

It had blown itself out by morning, leaving a beaten-down and sodden garden in its wake. A few more tiles had been lost to the storm, others loosened.

But it was a fine, if cold, day, and when Major was turned out he trotted around the paddock, his tail frisking, and hee-hawing loudly, as if he was pleased to have survived the night.

A couple of the chickens had escaped through a hole in their run, but came running out of the hedge at the urgent clucking of those left behind when Millie dished out their mash.

'The chimney and roof cannot be repaired,' Arthur Avery said on his next two-monthly visit. 'You have very little money left. In fact, Miss Price, it's my duty to tell you that in a month or two there will be no money left in the account at all. Then what will you do? I did warn you.'

'So you did, Mr Avery. What you didn't do was provide me with a list of our monetary assets and an accounting of what the money has been spent on. I demand that you do so, and as soon as possible.'

'To do that I'd have to hire the services of an accountant, and his fee would be beyond your means.'

He was being evasive.

'Very well, Mr Avery; then what would you suggest that I do? We can't leave the chimney damaged and a hole in the roof. The sparks might get inside and set fire to the house.' Not that it was likely to happen, since that side of the house was rarely used. 'If there's another storm the damage will only worsen.'

He sighed. 'If you'd taken my advice, sold the house and bought something smaller, then you wouldn't be in this position now.'

'Perhaps I should have, but I didn't, and that's because I grew up here in this house, and I love it. It's my family home.'

Leaning forward he took her hands in his. 'My dear Miss Price ... my offer is still open. If you married me then you could stay here. I have a great deal of money with which to refurbish the place.'

'I thought I'd made my position on that perfectly clear, Mr Avery. I will not marry you. I don't want to. Perhaps you could kindly furnish me with a loan.'

'May I ask how you would repay that loan?'

Harriet didn't know. Perhaps it *was* time she found something smaller to live in – a house in Poole perhaps. 'You offered to buy the house before. How much would you be prepared to pay for it?'

He smiled gently at her, but his eyes were sharp and astute. 'Considerably less than my last offer since I'd need to pay for the storm damage to be repaired, and refurbish the house to make it habitable and more to my taste.'

She supposed it had become a bit shabby, but that had never bothered her. 'I see,' and she smiled. 'Half of this house belongs to Celia, you know. I can't sell it without her approval.'

'Of course you can, Miss Price. The girl is not named in any will, and has no expectations.'

'But her mother was ... and that legacy has been spent. When my mother and sister died you personally assured me that the annuity I inherited would last me for the rest of my life.'

'It would have, except the money was invested. Market forces, my dear. One can rarely predict them with any great accuracy. Unfortunately, they sometimes don't behave as expected. And there was my professional fee to take into account, of course.'

'Of course; you certainly believe in taking advantage of your clients. Exactly what were your fees, Mr Avery? I don't think you ever discussed them.'

'I'm running a business, not a charity, my dear. A man must be cautious, and one must take the opportunity to better oneself and grow his fortune. My dear, will you please reconsider my proposal. I don't want to see you out on the street, or, God forbid, in the workhouse.'

Neither did Harriet, especially after reading some of Celia's tales. And neither did she want to be hung on the gallows at Newgate, but she was definitely thinking of murdering this man, and in the most painful way possible! 'I'll think on it, and I'll let you know in due course, Mr Avery.'

'Don't leave it too long, my dear. I'm not exactly short of admirers and your position is getting desperate and so is mine. I do need an heir or two before I'm much older.'

After the lawyer left, Celia heard the sound of weeping. She abandoned her writing and went downstairs.

Looking forlorn, Harriet had the written estimate for the repairs spread out on the table.

'Don't cry ... we'll think of something,' Celia said, and kissed her cheek.

'Mr Avery tells me we no longer have any money,' Harriet said, hurriedly scrubbing her eyes with a handkerchief. 'We can't even pay for the chimney to be repaired. I'm very much afraid that I'll have to wed him ... but I so despise the man.'

'Then you mustn't marry him.' Celia's arms went round her aunt and she held her tight. She hesitated; loath to spend the money Charles Curtis had given her. If she didn't repay the actual money the price she'd have to pay to cover the debt would be too high.

She remembered the one or two pieces of jewellery she still had, the butterfly brooch and the silver locket. It wasn't as if she'd ever be able to return them to the original owners, and she was too ashamed to wear them now she realized that most people were kind and decent. Best she got rid of them so they were no longer on her conscience. 'I've got a couple of pieces of jewellery I can sell. It will tide us over until I'm paid for my first story.'

Harriet gazed at her, her eyes red from weeping, but hopeful. 'And there's some jewellery that belonged to my mother that could be sold.'

Harriet raced around the house, finding other articles they no longer needed ... bits and pieces of solid silver, a christening cup or two, a tea service, so heavy with silver that it was almost impossible to lift.

'We can't carry all that. We'll sell the jewellery to a pawnbroker by itself. It should cover the repairs to the house with some left over. Just make a list of the silver you don't want.'

'I'll polish everything so it sparkles.'

'There's no need to. Nobody will want to buy a christening cup with an inscription on it, so a silversmith will buy it for the silver and melt it down. We will take one mug as an example of quality, and can get an estimate of what it's worth from a silversmith. If they're interested they'll say so. And we don't want to appear desperate.'

'We *are* desperate.'

Harriet had no real notion of what desperation was, so Celia argued, 'No we're not ... I still have some money left and the garden has some winter vegetables, and we have chickens that lay eggs. We also have a roof over our heads, and I can go and clean people's houses for money, or ... or we could take in paying guests.'

Harriet sniffed. 'Oh, dear, that would be too undignified, and everyone would know that we were practically destitute.' Her eyes rounded in horror. 'How will we afford a goose for Christmas?'

Hooting with laughter, for that was the least of their worries, Celia gave her aunt an extra squeeze. 'If the worst comes to the worst I'll wring the neck of one of those fancy ducks on the pond. And if I can work out how to fire that rifle in the rack, I can go to the woods and shoot a pigeon or two out of the sky. There are trout in the pond, as well.'

Gasping, her aunt said, 'They belong to the squire.'

'What does he need so many fish for? He won't miss an occasional one. Besides, we won't be the only villagers who poach them. Mr Hardy had a couple of lively ones wriggling in his sack when I saw him the other day, though he tried to keep them still. We'll show Arthur Avery that he can't force you into marriage.'

'I think he's been cheating me, Celia. He's never given me any accounting, even though I've asked and asked. I don't know what to do.'

'Ask James Kent to help you. We'll go into Poole tomorrow. While you ask for his advice I'll haggle with a pawnbroker for the best price for our goods.'

'What if Mr Kent charges a fee for his advice?'

'He won't, I promise. Just flutter your eyelashes at him and look helpless. He won't be able to resist you, and he'll swoon, and fall over with his legs in the air.'

'I wouldn't dare do that,' and Harriet looked so shocked that Celia giggled.

Harriet was halfway through her interview with James when there came a knock at the door and Charles Curtis came in. He stood within the still quality he possessed; his eyes going speculatively from one to another before he smiled. 'How nice to see you again, Miss Price. I'm sorry to disturb you, James; I had no idea you were entertaining. I just wanted to tell you that I'm off to the bank, so will be out of the office for a short time.'

'Harriet ... Miss Price ... is here for my advice, Chas.'

'I see; then I won't take up your time any further. My pardon, Miss Price.' He hesitated for a mere second before saying, 'Did you travel to Poole by yourself, Miss Price?'

'Celia accompanied me.'

'Ah ... yes, Celia ... I had almost forgotten her.' James rolled his eyes.

'I imagine she's shopping then.'

'No ... she had some business to conduct. She's looking for a pawn ... a silversmith. Oh dear!' She brought her hand to her mouth. 'I meant ... yes, I imagine she is shopping with Christmas so near.' She shrugged and gazed at James, unaware of the appeal in her eyes, or the melting effect it had on him.

'With your permission I'd like to entrust my partner with your problem a little later, Harriet,' he said. 'I guarantee that he is discreet and trustworthy, and he can be quite the terrier when called upon.'

When his partner raised an elegant eyebrow, chuckled and stated, 'I'd rather be compared to a greyhound,' Harriet nodded.

'The description does suit you much better, Mr Curtis. Greyhounds are so hungry-looking though. You should eat more.'

Now it was James' turn to raise an eyebrow. 'Before you tuck into a rabbit or two, Chas, perhaps you'd chase Celia down and bring her back here.'

'It will be my pleasure,' he said, and his smile

207

told them that he meant it.

Harriet's hand flew to her mouth and she gave a nervous laugh. 'That was awful of me. I'm so sorry.'

James patted her hand. 'Nonsense, Harriet. It was totally apt.'

After Charles had gone, James said, 'You do realize that I cannot charge Mr Avery with the misuse of your funds without proof, don't you? However, if you employ my company to handle what remains of them, I can insist on a proper audit. Do you have copies of your mother's will; also your father's if that's possible, since you have given me to understand there were some trust funds, and Celia might have been entitled to anything that was due to her mother. And I must ask you to sign a request form, giving me permission to access your accounts.'

'That will be the less painful option than becoming Arthur Avery's wife.' She opened her bag and removed a wad of paper. 'Here are copies of the wills. Mr Avery has the originals.' Her eyes met his and she grinned, mainly because his were filled with amusement. 'Now, I must ask you how much this will cost, James.'

'A penny,' he said.

She laughed. 'Celia said you wouldn't charge me for your advice, and I must flutter my eyelashes at you if you do. She said you'd probably swoon and fall over with your legs kicking in the air.'

'Celia has a fine sense of melodrama, I'm afraid. Are you too sensible to flirt with me, Harriet, my dear? I'll waive the penny fee if you do.'

She fluttered them, laughing. 'There, will that do?'

'Will you marry me?' he said, and her eyes widened and she couldn't prevent a blush from creeping into her cheeks.

'But we've only just met.'

'Does that matter? This might sound conceited, but I do think I'd be an improvement on Arthur Avery.'

Head to one side she regarded him with the beginnings of a smile. 'No, James, I suppose it doesn't matter, and yes, you'd definitely be an improvement on Mr Avery.'

'Then?'

'You're acting on impulse, so I'll overlook your odd behaviour. You must take time to consider this course of action. If your sentiments remain constant and you are in the same mind in the future, then you may ask me again.'

'My cautious little mouse; I fell in love with you the moment I set eyes on you. You must all come and spend Christmas and Boxing Day with us. I'll propose marriage to you with proper decorum, and you can give me your answer then.'

'Thank goodness,' she cried out. 'Celia is making plans to steal a duck from the pond and strangle it to cook for Christmas dinner.'

'I surrender my freedom to you, and all you can think of is food?' James burst out laughing. 'Surely your finances haven't reached the stage where you're obliged to hunt down your Christmas dinner.'

'According to Mr Avery, I'm very much afraid

they have,' she said soberly. 'Celia is such a practical girl, and says we'll manage.'

How they would manage he could only imagine ... would Lady Lightfingers be forced to fall back on her specialized skills? 'She's certainly inventive ... a duck from the pond? Good grief!' Leaning across his desk he took her face between his palms and tenderly kissed her.

It was Harriet's first kiss, and was special because the man who'd given it to her had declared that he loved her. Harriet forgot Celia and her Christmas duck when joy swept through her.

Charles ran Celia to earth just after she'd exited the pawnbroker's shop. There had been no questions asked. She'd done her best, but she'd been unable to push the broker up in price.

She gazed at the money in her hand with some dismay, hoping she could do better with the christening mug and the silversmith – if she could find one.

'Ah ... the lovely and talented Miss Laws, there you are,' somebody said against her ear, and she jumped backwards. A shilling fell from her hand and rolled towards the road. The toe of Charles' soft leather boot came down on it. Picking it up he flipped it, spinning through the air, exactly like the time when he'd given her the one guinea reward, followed by offering her the one hundred pounds. Exactly like the last time, she plucked the coin safely from the air. Habit made her swiftly slide the coin with one smooth motion into the pocket inside her skirt.

'You have a good eye and quick reflexes.'

'Thank you, Mr Curtis.'

'You can call me Charles if you wish, and I shall call you Celia from now on, if you'd permit.'

She *would* wish, and she *would* permit, but her aunt might think it too familiar on such a short acquaintance. He'd kissed her on a shorter one, she reflected, and when a tease of a grin flirted around his mouth, she wished he'd kiss her again.

Her gaze moved to the satchel he was carrying. 'If you have business to conduct, please don't allow me to detain you.'

'I've already conducted it. What about you, Celia?'

She was pleased he hadn't sought to embarrass her by saying he saw her emerge from the pawnbroker. Did it matter that they were not well off? Did she mind if he knew that? She gazed at the wrapped mug in her hand. It didn't, because she'd been poor since she could remember. 'I was looking for a silversmith to discover what this object might be worth.'

'May I see it?'

Unwrapping the item he gazed at the inscription and gazed from under his dark brows, an enquiry in his eyes. 'Jane Price?'

'Harriet's deceased sister. You see, a chimney fell down in the storm and damaged the roof, and her lawyer said ... well, I shouldn't disclose Harriet's business, but she needed advice, so I suggested she consult with James. We couldn't afford the repairs just at the moment. Harriet didn't know how to go about selling things to a pawnbroker, and I thought a silversmith might be better, if I could find one.' Her eyes widened. 'I didn't steal the mug ... Is that what you think?'

He nodded, trying not to laugh and thinking to himself, so this was what Harriet Price was all about, cosily closeted with James. 'I don't recall thinking that you'd stolen it?'

Her grin had a shamefaced feel to it because she'd misjudged him. 'You gave me a sort of legal-looking frown that suggested it was a possibility.'

He frowned at her. 'Like this?'

'No, it was more like this.' She lowered her chin, screwed up her face and looked up at him.

He chuckled. 'That's how my horse looks when he's got the gripe. Actually, I was thinking how lovely a young woman you are. Stop glowering at once, else I shall change my mind.' He held out his arm to her. 'Shall we walk?'

He was an elegant man in a suit of dark grey with seamed cuffs. Under it was a light-grey brocade waistcoat displaying twinkling ruby-coloured buttons.

Tucking her hand into the warm crook of his elbow, she said, 'I must find a silversmith, else we won't be able to pay for the roof repairs. Do you know of one?'

'Not in Poole, or on the quay, which is not an entirely safe place for a young woman to be unaccompanied.'

'I've been in worse places.' Indeed, she found the quay to be an interesting place with the ships swaying in the harbour, the cockle and eel sellers and people with carts coming and going.

'The place is full of thieves. It's a wonder you haven't had your pocket picked, or been abducted and taken on board one of the ships.'

She slanted him a glance, wondering if his mention of picking pockets meant he'd remembered who she was, and had a barb attached. But no, the expression on his face told her he was oblivious to any connection. 'That is a hideous suggestion. For what reason would anyone take me on board a ship?'

The next moment she could have bitten her tongue off, for he gave an entirely wicked grin. She blushed.

Gently he changed the subject. 'If you'd like to leave the mug with me, I'll be going to London to visit for the New Year and I'll see what I can do. I could advance you a sum to cover the repairs if you like.'

Her heart squeezed at the thought of owing him more money, when she had the one hundred pounds he'd given her safely tucked away. They'd have to be desperate before she gave in to spending any of it though, for then she'd have to repay it in kind, something that was now a more attractive proposition than she liked to admit. The more she saw of Charles, the more she liked him and wanted him to think well of her.

The money had become the price of her downfall, and she'd labelled Charles as the devil himself for advancing it to her on such a promise. She smiled to herself. How odd then, that despite half of her not wanting to disappoint him by

213

becoming what he'd wanted then – his whore – the other half of her wantonly craved such attention from him, as she imagined it would be.

She'd reached a fork in the road of her life on that day of the loan. Taking it had been the first step on a downward path. She had since decided to give the money back to him. Until she could do so, whilst still remaining undetected, the money mocked her, tempting her to use it.

'The house belongs to my aunt, and I can't incur a debt on her behalf.'

'Then allow me to give you an advance on the sale of the silver, which I'll sell to a dealer in London, one who I know will pay a fair price for it.'

'It may embarrass my aunt to know what I've done.'

'Embarrassment is a small loss of pride when compared to the pains of hunger. Don't worry, I'll make sure she doesn't see it.'

'Thank you, Charles.' When she handed him the mug, he took a note from an inside pocket and placed it in her hand. 'This is too much.'

'Since when have you been an expert on the value of silver?'

'Never ... when have you?'

He laughed. 'Stop arguing.'

Her eyes slanted to him as he escorted her back along to the town hall and beyond to the High Street, where, halfway along, the suite of offices Charles shared with James was situated. How handsome and confident he looked. He certainly drew the eyes of women and Celia felt proud to be paraded on his arm.

His eyes met hers, dark and unfathomable. She was absorbed into the liquid of them, and saw herself reflected there. 'You have a pretty mouth, Celia. Like a ripe peach. I'd like to kiss you until you went crazy from it.'

He'd said before that her mouth was like a peach – before he'd kissed her that last time. Her mouth began to tingle and her knees felt weak, as if her body was falling apart like grains of sugar melting into sweet rivulets of honey.

'Charles, please don't talk to me like that,' she whispered, wanting to lean into the strength of his firm body and be consumed by it.

'Oh, don't worry, Celia my little innocent, I won't kiss you here in the street with the world looking on. But before too long, I'll find the opportunity.'

Celia knew she'd die from the pleasure of it if he did. She dragged in a deep, ragged breath as Charles held open the door to the offices for her to pass through, and he said against her ear as he followed her through, his voice as delicate as a strand of golden silk, 'That's a promise.'

She couldn't allow it, because it couldn't be. They couldn't be. Charles was a fine man. He was sensitive to the needs of others, honest, and he represented the law of the land.

The day would come when she'd have to tell him of her background – of the way she'd deceived him. No matter that she'd shed her rags and now knew which fork and spoon to use, she was a child of the London slums – one who'd stolen from him, and who would steal again to keep herself and Lottie alive if it became necessary.

Women with her background might attract professional gentlemen, but professional gentlemen didn't marry them. And she craved Charles' admiration, his respect and his attention. She was damned if she confessed her past, and damned if she didn't, because secrets had a way of getting out once they'd become the property of another.

Because of that she could never become a companion of any sort to Charles Curtis, no matter how much money he offered her.

So let this meeting be the end of it, she thought, feeling the warmth of him at her back as he closed the door behind them. He took off his top hat, placed the mug inside it and laid it on the hallstand with his gloves over the top, to conceal it from the sight of Harriet.

The secretive smile he winged her way endeared him to her.

Fourteen

It seemed to Celia that everyone turned up for the Christmas morning service.

The church was decorated with holly and mistletoe, and they sang carols. Celia had read the nativity lesson about the three wise men, her voice suitably hushed as the miracle of Christmas was revealed – and the congregation equally

216

hushed because word had spread about her literary alliance with the famous poet Thomas Hambert, and he now smiled at her from the second pew, despite some of the villagers having thought it was one of Celia Laws' highly un-likely tales.

After Celia introduced him to the presiding reverend, a rather serious younger man, they left the church and walked to the carriage through a line of curious people.

Mrs Hardy was overheard to say softly to her neighbour when Celia was in range, 'I don't know what she's got to be so fancy about, when her father was a rogue. Where is he, that's what I want to know?'

'I heard he'd died; and there's no smoke with-out fire.'

'I told you that. But the girl tells me he's coming back. I wouldn't be surprised since I saw him in London; he was working under the name of Daniel Laws. There can't be another man on this earth who looks and sounds like him, can there? And Alice Price was too proud of him as she walked down the aisle. There was something fishy about that marriage right from the start. Nobody can say any different.'

'My Rob said that Celia Laws stole into the village after dark, as though she didn't want to be seen. He said she was dressed in rags and pushing a cart with that small girl in, just like a beggar.'

'And how did he see that in the dark?'

'He thought she was a robber, and he followed her to see what she were up to. Miss Price and her servant opened the door, and Miss Price let her in. Rob tried to see what were going on through the windows, but the curtains were drawn across.'

'I'd better make sure I keep mine closed from now on then if your Rob is prone to sneaking round the village at night peering through windows at folks. Where did that small girl come from, that's what I'd like to know.'

No doubt she would, Celia thought, but she wasn't going to satisfy her curiosity. A quick glance revealed that the second woman had turned away in affront at the disparaging remark aimed at her Rob's nocturnal activity.

Not by a flicker of an eyebrow did Celia reveal that she'd overheard the spiteful remarks, though flags of red flew into her cheeks and her fists bunched. She would have liked to snatch the silly pink feather from Mrs Hardy's even sillier bonnet – which had more decorations than a Christmas tree – and snap it in half under her nose.

But although the woman didn't know it, her comments had done Celia a favour by giving cause to reawaken her almost dormant desire, which was to confront her father. It was all right settling cosily here like a hen on a nest, but there were issues from her past she had to resolve, and finding out about her father was only one of them.

All the same, she thought ruefully, managing with great effort to keep her temper under control, it was easier to hide in the crowd in London. Here in the village of Hanbury Cross, anything out of the ordinary attracted comment and rumour – and Celia knew she was out of the ordinary, even after all this time.

Harriet gave no indication that she'd heard anything amiss, but offered her a sympathetic smile when she was assisted into the carriage. The hood was up, a fur rug spread over their knees to keep them warm. James took a place on top with the coachman, and they were off.

They spent pleasant Christmas and Boxing days with Thomas, Abigail and James. Patricia, the daughter of the Kent household, was blue-eyed and fair-haired. Her quiet husband and two boisterous children were introduced. Even Millie had been invited to the festivities.

Celia had half-hoped that Charles Curtis would be there, but he'd gone to London to spend some time with his family.

'He's left a gift for you under the tree,' Thomas told her.

The gift was a prettily enamelled bird in a cage of silver gilt, which whistled a tune when it was wound up. How pretty it was, and she wished she had something to give him in return. But for his own sake he mustn't be encouraged.

After dinner, Thomas drowsed in the chair in front of the library fire, while the women helped the servants – who'd dined with them on this special day – to clear the dishes from the dining room and wash them up.

When James took Harriet by the hand and led her into the drawing room, Celia and Abigail gazed at each other and smiled expectantly. Thomas disappeared into his lair in the library.

A little later Thomas came into the drawing room with a wide smile on his face. He busied himself setting out champagne, kept cold in a bucket of ice for the expected announcement, and glasses.

'Well?' Abigail said.

'Be patient, my dear.'

'I do hope you haven't been listening at the keyhole, Thomas. You used to when you were a disagreeable boy. Father caught you doing it once and gave you a good thrashing.' It was an accusation that made everyone present laugh.

'I had a good excuse; I was trying to find out which school I was going to be sent to.'

'What is going on? Pray tell me at once, since I'm dying of curiosity.'

Thomas gave a great huff of laughter. 'My dear Abigail, considering you've talked of nothing else for the past few days, I'm surprised that you profess to be so unaware of the situation.'

James and Harriet came in. James was smiling proudly, and Harriet had a shy and pretty pink glow to her face. Celia had never seen her look so beautiful as she was in her dark-rose gown with its pink velvet bodice.

Thomas gazed round at them all, now armed with a glass of champagne. He cleared his throat. 'It's my pleasure to announce that my dearest nephew, James, has asked for the hand in marriage of Miss Harriet Price ... to which proposal, Harriet has very bravely agreed to take him off of our hands.'

Glasses were raised and toasts drunk, laughter and congratulations rang out. Harriet showed off the love token that would bind her promise to James, an elegant band of rose gold set with three perfect diamonds that flashed and winked in the gaslight.

'You're now looking at the happiest man alive,' James said, his affection towards Harriet plainly inscribed in the glance he gave his intended.

The couple's happiness gave extra sparkle to the house party, as they sang carols around the piano and played charades. The children played happily together, and Celia was glad that Lottie had some company of her own age.

The next day Thomas said to her, 'I have a couple of engagements in London next month. Would you care to accompany me and do a reading, Celia?'

She looked towards Harriet, who nodded. 'Millie and I will be happy to look after Charlotte for you. We're so proud of you, you know.'

It would be an opportunity to sort out the issue of her father. The theatre was a small world, one she'd longed to belong to. But that dream had faded now. She realized while working on her serial for the magazine that it had been her mother's dream to act on the stage – and her mother had gone.

Celia couldn't live her mother's dream for her, but must live her own. Somebody must know about Jackaby Laws though – know what had happened to him. All these years later had he resurrected himself under the name of Daniel Laws, as Mrs Hardy had once suggested? If she could meet him, she'd ask him outright, for surely he wouldn't deny his own child.

'I'd hoped to visit Johnny Archer and the Busby family at their inn near Lymington. They were good to me when I needed them, and I'd like to satisfy myself that Johnny is happy and well cared for.'

'How old is the boy?'

When she answered him with, 'He must be fifteen years old by now,' Thomas smiled.

'He's almost a man, then?'

'Yes ... I suppose he is, but he was small for his age.'

'Then we shall go there in the carriage and stay the night at the inn so you can satisfy your mothering instinct. William can take us on to the train station in Southampton before returning home with the carriage. I should like to meet the Busbys.'

'I'm sure you'll like them.'

Celia, though, was surprised at the change in Johnny Archer. Though still slim and hard-muscled, he'd grown considerably upwards.

He hadn't recognized her at first, and she concealed herself behind Thomas when he called out, 'Ma ... we have guests.'

Aggie Busby came bustling through, a warm smile on her face for Thomas. 'Good day, sir ... madam. Will you be staying?'

'Two rooms and accommodation for my coachman and horse for the night.'

'Take their bags up to the front rooms, Johnny—'

'The rooms warmed by the chimney,' Celia

said, and she stepped forward with a smile on her face. 'Have you both forgotten me already then?'

'I'll be blown down by the wind,' Johnny said, an expression used by Busby himself, Celia recalled.

She gave the woman a hug while Johnny stood grinning warily at her. 'I'm not a hugging sort of man, so keep your hands off me, Celia,' he said.

She poked him in the stomach, instead. 'I can see that Mrs Busby's been fattening you up.'

Aggie looked behind Celia. 'Isn't young Lottie with you?'

'She stayed behind with my aunt. Reverend Thomas and I are going to London on business, so thought we'd visit you first.'

'Well, I'm surprised; for I can't say I've given anyone cause to visit us before, especially for social. We don't know anyone, that's why.' She gave a throaty laugh. 'Take them bags up then, Johnny boy, then go and see to the horses. The coachman will want to know where the stable is.'

'If he can't see it for himself he must be blind, Ma.'

She snapped a serving cloth at him. 'Don't you give me none of your blessed cheek now, else I'll put you over my knee.'

Johnny flipped her a grin. 'It's you who needs putting over someone's knee. I'll have a word with Busby about it.' He sauntered off, hands in pockets and whistling.

Aggie's smile encompassed them both. 'Busby will be with his charcoal burner. He'll be home before dark for his dinner. You look like a proper young lady now, Miss Celia.'

Which reminded Celia of her manners. 'May I introduce you to Reverend Thomas Hambert? Reverend, this is Mrs Aggie Busby.'

'Ah, yes, Celia has spoken often about you.' Thomas bowed over her hand. 'I understand you were kind to Celia and Lottie in their time of need.'

'Well I never,' Aggie said again, turning pink. 'I never expected no thanks for doing the decent thing for folks, that I didn't.'

'No doubt the Lord will reward you.'

'As for that, I reckon he already has by bringing young Johnny to our doorstep.'

Celia kissed her on the cheek. 'I've brought you a gift,' and she handed Aggie the soft creamy shawl she was carrying. It was made from the softest wool by a village woman, who spun her wool from her own sheep to fashion shawls from. It hadn't been very expensive. 'This is for you, and there's some best pipe tobacco for Busby.'

Aggie placed the shawl around her shoulders and rubbed her cheek against it. 'That's beautiful and soft. Thank you, my love, that's right kind of you.'

A bed was found for the coachman, who joined them for the evening, for it would never have occurred to the Busbys to treat William any other than an equal.

They spent a pleasant evening together, with Busby peering into the fire puffing on his pipe and making the occasional comment, and Aggie bustling around, making sure they were all comfortable.

The men talked about what men talk about – horses, charcoal, politics, war. Aggie was impressed when Thomas told her he'd seen the Queen in person.

'Is she grand?'

'Very grand. She was riding in her carriage with Prince Albert by her side, surrounded by soldiers in uniform.'

'A good breeder is Victoria, she does her duty for England,' Busby commented, nodding in agreement with his own words.

Celia and Aggie looked at one another and giggled.

Early the next morning, after eating a hearty breakfast, they were ready for off. It was a crisp bright morning. The horses' breath steamed from their nostrils and they stamped their feet and gave shrill whinnies, eager to be off.

Celia thanked the Busbys for their hospitality and gave them a hug, for they wouldn't take a penny piece from Thomas.

'I was glad to have the company of a woman for once,' Aggie said, 'and this is a bad time of year for passing traffic. Were it summer you'd have had to sleep in the stable with the horses.'

'If it was good enough for our Lord, then I'm sure it would have sufficed for us poor sinners,' Thomas murmured, his eyes twinkling, because he and Celia often had lively discussions on the subject of what the Lord was about.

Unexpectedly, it was Busby who offered Thomas the challenge. 'I never heard no mention of horses at the birth of Jesus, just camels and a sheep or two ... though there might have been a donkey, now I come to think on it,' Busby said.

Thomas shook Busby's hand. 'I'm sure you're right, Mr Busby.'

'Thanks for coming, Celia,' Johnny said with a smile, and he was so self-assured that she laughed.

'I don't know why I was worried about you.'

'Were you worried about me, or just curious? Besides, you wouldn't have known what to do with me once you got to that village of yours. Your aunt wouldn't have wanted to house and feed a lolloping great lad like me, as well as the two of you.'

'You look happy here.'

'I *am* happy. The Busbys treat me well, like I was their own lad, and I'm grateful for it. They've had me at school for the past two years, and I've learned to keep the books for Ma. I can read a real treat, too, though not as good as you. Busby likes me to read to him every evening. They were pleased to get your letter, and so was I.'

'Good, because I've got this for you,' she said, placing a leather-bound copy of *Famous Tales from the London Slums* in his hands. Give them to someone special, Thomas had said, and the other one had gone to her aunt. 'Perhaps you'd read this to Busby sometimes.'

Johnny gazed at the name on the spine, then smiled. 'You were always one to spout a bit of poetry and make up tales. I thought you intended to go on the stage.'

'I've changed my mind. We've signed the book

for you.'

Opening it he read slowly, *'To Johnny Archer. Wherever the wind blows, may you always land on your feet. Best wishes. C.J. Laws & Thomas Hambert.'*

Although he'd stated he wasn't a hugging man, Johnny hugged her anyway, a quick, brief squeeze. 'I'll read it to him. Goodbye, Celia ... Reverend Hambert it was a pleasure to meet you. William, call in on your way back and you can have a bowl of ma's stew to warm you on your way.'

'Keep in touch,' she said, her voice beginning to crack, and Johnny helped her into the carriage and she took her seat next to Thomas. 'Now don't you start bawling,' he said.

'And a letter now and again would be appreciated,' she flung at him.

'I reckon it would, at that. Can't say I'm much into letter writing though.'

There were tears in Celia's eyes as Johnny stepped back. 'I have the feeling that this is the last time I'll see him. Time has almost made us strangers, and I might never come this way again.'

Thomas placed his hand over hers as the carriage began to move, saying gently, 'You're right. Do you remember me telling you that if you and your mother had ignored Lottie's cries she would have perished?'

She nodded.

'Where would Johnny be now if you'd left him behind in London? You have a compassionate nature, Celia. Your selfless act set him on a different course than the one he was already on. He's found his home, and it was one you led him to.'

'And what of *my* home?'

He didn't mistake the physical for the spiritual in her. 'Your heart will tell you when it's found a place to reside.'

'And I'll have you to thank for that.' She gave a light laugh, teasing him. 'I do believe you were fishing for a compliment, Reverend Hambert.'

His eyes reflected his smile and he sighed. 'Ah, the vanity of man ... I do believe I was.'

The house in Bedford Square was quiet when they arrived. Celia settled herself in the bedroom the Reverend had offered for her use, and she placed the satchel containing the one hundred pounds under her mattress.

Mrs Packer had kept the house clean, but it had an air of waiting about it. She had not been expecting him, for there was no fresh food in the larder, and the potatoes had grown eyes and shoots while waiting to be eaten. There were some preserved fruits and conserves though, and some oatmeal.

'I hate coming home to an empty house,' he said. 'It's always too quiet, and that makes me feel lonely. I keep expecting Frederick to come out from under the chair.'

'Then you should take your sister up on her offer. James will be moving out when he and Harriet wed, I expect.' Though she had not discussed with her aunt whether James would move into Chaffinch House, and if he did, where would she and Lottie go? 'Mrs Kent will be lonely too, then. If you lived with her you'd see more of Patricia and her children, as well as James. I'd visit you, too, just to remind you of your folly in taking an interest in me.'

She laughed when he gave a heartfelt groan. 'You know you don't mean that, Thomas Hambert.'

'No ... I certainly do not, because I enjoy your company. I've been seriously thinking about moving, which is why I left Frederick with my sister. He dislikes travelling.'

'So would I, were I a cat.' She placed a basket in his hands. 'We must go to the market, else we won't have anything to eat.'

'I usually leave that to Mrs Packer.'

'Mrs Packer isn't here. You must have forgotten to tell her when you'd be returning, else she would have filled the larder.' She scooped up a second basket. 'Unless you want oatmeal for dinner, come on ... it won't take long if we hurry. We'll buy enough for today and tomorrow. If I roast a chicken it should last us for two days.'

They also bought eggs, bread, butter, lard, and some bacon and ham, as well as winter vegetables such as cabbage, potatoes, beans and turnips.

Thomas carefully carried a jug of milk home, spilling only a third of the contents. 'I'll put the jug out for the milk carter to fill in the morning,' he said.

Both the kitchen range and the fireplaces were laid. Celia put a match to the kindling and watched it crackle into life. The brass coal-scuttles were full. Soon the house had warmed up and felt more welcoming.

Mrs Packer was an efficient worker, Celia thought, and indeed, it wasn't long before she came to investigate the smoke coming from the chimney.

'It's you is it, Reverend? I thought it must be,' she said and her nose sniffed at the air before pointing at Celia, the brow branching over it furrowed. 'I know you. You're that little beggar girl Reverend Thomas took under his wing. You're back in London, then.'

'It's just for a short time, Mrs Packer. Thank you for being so helpful to me on that day I came here to say goodbye. I was a child then, but the kindness of people helped me through.'

Mrs Packer turned pink from being complimented. 'How is your sister?'

'Lottie is well and happy, and amongst people who care for her.'

'It was a long way you intended to take her, Miss. I prayed for your safety.'

'It must have worked, for we got there ... eventually,' she said gently.

'Who would have thought to see you again, and you looking such the lady.'

Thomas tut-tutted. 'Miss Laws is my guest, Mrs Packer. She's no longer a beggar, but is being cared for by her aunt, who is a very respectable lady, and who has just become engaged to my nephew. So let us put talk of her past life behind so she can enjoy the present one. We are to do some readings together while we are here.'

Mrs Packer took no notice of his gentle remonstration. 'So, Mr Kent is to wed? That's good news. Give him my heartfelt congratulations if you would.' Her glance fell on Celia again. 'I must say you've grown into a pretty young woman, Miss Laws.'

'Thank you, Mrs Packer.'

'What is it you're cooking, Miss?'

'A chicken and some roast vegetables. I thought it would serve for tomorrow, as well.'

She nodded, as though satisfied with the answer. 'Don't let the oven get too hot, else it will burn. There's a clean apron in the bottom drawer to protect your clothes. Oh yes ... and *please* clear up any crumbs, since they encourage the mice. The dirty creatures leave their droppings everywhere if they get a hold. Not that Frederick doesn't do a good job chasing them off when he's not visiting folks in the country.' More abruptly, she said, 'Do you want me to make your bed up before I go, Miss?'

'That's kind of you, but I can manage it.'

'I daresay you can, a young girl like you, not that you haven't got some nice manners though. Despite her situation your mother taught you well.' She gave them both a bit of a smile, one that softened the planes of her face. 'I'll be off now I know you have everything for your immediate needs. I'll be in tomorrow, as usual. Reverend, your letters and calling cards are on the hallstand.'

'Thank you, Mrs Packer.' When the door gently closed behind the woman Thomas chuckled rather apologetically. 'One grows used to Mrs

231

Packer's ways after a while.'

'I like her. She's very conscientious and she doesn't bow and scrape. She'd fit well into the village of Hanbury Cross.'

A thoughtful expression crossed Thomas' face, at that.

The office was closed until the end of February, except for a clerk who would take appointments, issue receipts for payment of accounts, and inform him should anything that needed his urgent attention arise.

When James took up his magisterial work, a new solicitor would be employed at the legal offices of *Kent & Curtis*. In the meantime he was about to ruin the day, and perhaps the career of another solicitor, but as quietly as possible. James made his way to Dorchester, left his rig to be minded by a lad, and cornered Arthur Avery at his club.

After introducing himself he handed the man a paper. 'This is a formal notice from Miss Harriet Price of Hanbury Cross terminating your services.'

'The devil it is,' the man spluttered. 'We'll see about this. I've been the family solicitor since before she was born, and was affianced to Jane Price. Indeed, since Jane's death I've offered Harriet marriage. I'm still awaiting her answer.'

'I understand that her answer was negative in that respect on more than one occasion. I'm also aware of what your reaction to that refusal was. Miss Price has some concerns about the way you've been handling the estates of her relations,

232

and of the manner in which you conduct business. After examining those concerns and the evidence presented by several business houses, my partner, Charles Curtis, and I concur with those concerns. You have until the end of March to present documents to support your claims that no fraudulent charges have been levelled against the Price estate, and it is indeed bankrupt – or offer suitable settlement as recompense.'

'Damn the woman, what evidence has she got? All she can charge me with is incompetence with regard to the accounting.'

'I could demand that an independent audit be done.'

'You'd need an order from a magistrate for that.'

'I am a magistrate.' At least, he would be in a few weeks' time.

Avery began to bluster. 'Her sister and mother were spendthrifts.'

'I have copies of the wills, and every account you ever presented to Miss Price or her late mother. She has also kept an account of her own expenditure – a set of books which is a meticulous record that follows on from those she kept on her mother's behalf.'

'Harriet kept records for her mother?'

'Her accounting is excellent, the receipts go back for several years.' And so the man wouldn't think he was bluffing, which he was, he added, 'It includes an amount paid to you by Mrs Price two months before her death, which doesn't appear to have been repaid.'

'An investment that went wrong, I imagine.'

'Or which didn't take place at all. My partner will follow every bill of sale through to the source for comparison, and will personally interview every person concerned. He has already approached several people, only to discover misrepresentation such as a nought added where there shouldn't have been one, or a charge for services that were never ordered, or which never took place.'

'A slip of the pen, I imagine. We all make mistakes from time to time.'

'There were several slips of the pen – too many to be mere coincidences. It's thievery, Mr Avery, pure and simple. You've fraudulently dealt with a client who trusted you – one who you thought you could squeeze the last brick and nail from.'

'Miss Price is a spinster I offered marriage to in exchange. She should have been grateful someone was interested in her. I felt sorry for her.'

For the first time in his life James felt like punching someone. But the man was older than himself, and he looked unfit. Besides ... Harriet wouldn't have approved.

He sucked in a breath, slowly exhaling it. 'Despite the fact that I have a personal interest invested in this matter I'll let that remark pass, since I know the client concerned is a decent, caring, and useful member of the community in which she resides. However, should the matter go to court, Miss Price will be represented by my partner, Charles Curtis, who is fast gaining a reputation amongst his peers. Believe me, he will leave no stone unturned, and all will be aired.'

'It would ruin me.' Arthur paled as James' former words sank in. 'What personal interest are you talking about?'

'Miss Price and I are to be married. So there you are, Mr Avery. Now you know exactly where I stand, and where you stand. If you'd prefer to do the gentlemanly thing and quietly settle out of court – an action that would protect Miss Price from the unwelcome publicity that would ensue, and save your own reputation from complete and utter ruin into the bargain – you may submit your offer to my clerk. If the offer is realistic, then our client will be advised to drop the matter.'

Arthur Avery's face had turned the colour of clay, and his hands trembled so much that James almost felt sorry for him.

'I'll do what you ask.'

James stood, smiling a little, for his business had progressed faster than he'd imagined it would. On the strength of it he intended to visit his lady on the way home and sweet-talk her into a kiss or two as a reward.

'I promise you it's the wiser of the two options. Good day, Mr Avery.'

Fifteen

1855
The first of Thomas and Celia's readings was at
the home of a poetry society. About fifty people
attended the meeting where members read their
own work, either too timidly to have any performance value, or in voices shaking with ner-
vousness, or with too much drama, waving their
arms about and bellowing.

Celia recognized her own early appearances to
the public in them and stifled her laughter.

One young mother called Addie was so shy
and choked up that Celia felt sorry for her.
Joining her, she stood beside her and began to
read with her, a lovely poem dedicated to her
child that she'd called Cradle Song.

> *Hush, hush, my baby fair.*
> *It's mamma playing with your hair*
> *And smoothing those curls so golden bright*
> *In evening's soft and mellow light.*

As Addie's voice strengthened Celia retreated
to her chair and left her to it. She read the
remaining five verses with such emotion in her
voice that even Thomas had tears in his eyes.

Afterwards there were refreshments.

When Addie approached her for a signature in her copy of the book, and expressed her gratitude at being rescued, Celia smile and whispered, 'I enjoyed your poem. I thought it the best of the poems read out. What's your baby's name?'

'He's called Edward, after his grandfather. He's so sweet.'

'I'm sure he is. Would you like me to introduce you to Reverend Hambert. I know he enjoyed your poem.'

'I don't think I'd know what to say, since I'm totally in awe of him. Your story was wonderful, Miss Laws. It was so sad that the little girl died of starvation, though a fitting end for an unwanted child who has no relatives to care for them.'

Thomas, who stood within earshot, cleared his throat, and Celia bit back an urge to shoot the woman with a hot and hasty retort, saying instead, with a sugary sweetness that was alien to her thoughts, 'Thank goodness your own dear child will never be in the position to need the charity of strangers.'

'Yes indeed,' she said, and Celia felt the young woman begin to quiver as they neared Thomas. 'What shall I say to a learned man like him?' she whispered.

'Oh, the reverend won't be lost for words, I assure you, Addie. He's very sweet, and will be happy to personally sign your book for you, too.'

Thomas, who Celia knew always kept his ear cocked for what he described as her misplaced crumbs of wisdom, raised an eyebrow at her and smiled when she introduced Addie, saying, 'Ah my dear lady, such a lovely poem, so moving and full of motherly love.'

He soon had Addie talking, if a little shyly, and he autographed her book and kissed her hand.

Something drew Celia's glance across the room and there was Charles, half a head taller than most of the men in the room. He was conversing with another man near the door, his face tilted slightly down towards him, grave and in a listening attitude. The wintry grey of Charles' suit was warmed by a silk, burgundy waistcoat over a pleated white shirt and bow tie. His hair was shorter than the last time she'd seen him and curled crisply.

The air around her seemed to vibrate with danger. Her heart plunged, then each beat swooped it up into her throat, where it spread in both directions to stroke in noisy panic at the depths of her ears. She tasted salt on her tongue as her wayward heart settled back into a more normal rhythm.

'Charles Curtis, how can the sight of you affect me this way,' she said under her breath, and he chose that moment to look her way. His smile was a white gleam in the sensual curve of his mouth. Without being obvious, he placed a finger to his lips and sent a tiny kiss quivering across the room towards her. Her body came alive, but she resisted the urge to touch her mouth.

The contact between them held for several seconds. Celia felt it in a shockingly physical way, the peaks of her breasts pushing against her bodice and the secret woman part of her swelling between her thighs and achingly moist, so she wanted to place her hand against its sudden and seductive invitation. She'd never felt like this before, so aware of herself ... of him ... so knowing of where this arousal in her would lead if it were pandered to.

She didn't know who moved first, him or her, but he was standing before her, gazing down at her and saying softly, 'I haven't been able to get near you in the crush until now.'

'They're here to admire the reverend really. He's immensely popular, and I'm lucky to be part of his circle of friends, even though I often feel out of place.'

'I'm here to admire you, Celia, ' he said softly.

A fragrance lingered about him, a faint warm touch of sandalwood, and underneath – underneath was a note of something sharp and lemony. Charles was attractive; he must have experienced relations with certain types of women. Was he aware of her feelings? Did he know how she reacted to him?

Suddenly it hit her. She was now thinking about women like her mother, who did what they did to stay alive! Regret roiled in her when she remembered that Charles Curtis was like any other man, and had been willing to buy her services for a week when she'd been hardly more than a child. Who'd been the whore in that case?

He took her hands in his, this devil of persuasion, bore them both to his lips and left the imprint of his mouth on each one, like a brand. His cufflinks were small gold shields attached to posts and, while he looked into her eyes, her fingerstips strayed to them, to the pulse pounding life through his wrist under his shirt cuff and tickling her fingertips. While he was distracted, it would take just a moment to slip them out and into her pocket, and she already knew which pocket he kept his card case in. The temptation of it was almost overwhelming, and she knew she missed the excitement and danger of her former occupation.

She remembered him telling her she'd had sensitive hands, and he'd enjoyed the feel of them when she'd lifted his card case before. She recalled the beat, beat, of his heart under the silk of his waistcoat, the way it quickened against her fingertips at that moment when he'd realized what she was up to.

She became aware that he was now standing too close, not only for her own comfort but for the sake of propriety – as if they were the only two people existing in the room. She took a step backwards, removing her hands from his before anyone noticed them, trying not to grin at the thought of robbing him.

The amusement in his eyes spoke of the awareness she'd feared – but it was not of her past life as a dip in the London slums, or as the daughter of a seamstress and occasional whore – but of her present life as a young woman he desired. Was this a light-hearted flirtation on his part, or a serious attempt to court her? She must not encourage him in either course of behaviour. If he got too close to her, James Kent was bound to warn him of her past, and Charles would begin to despise her.

'You look warm, Celia; shall I fetch you a glass of lemonade?'

Lemonade? A full tub wouldn't quench the fire he'd lit in her! She sighed. This sort of problem she didn't need. 'Thank you, Charles.'

She sipped it as fast as she dare.

'I hate these literary circles where the intellectual try to outdo each other with their cleverness and those not so intellectual pretend to be,' he remarked, and she nearly choked on her last mouthful.

'Then why did you come?'

'I told you ... it's because I wanted to admire you.'

She noted the gleam in his eye and laughed. 'I don't want to be admired by you, Charles.'

'Nonsense, you're a woman; of course you do.'

'You look very fine. Perhaps it's the other way around and you've come to be admired.'

'Do you think so?'

'It wouldn't surprise me. You think far too much of yourself.'

Thomas joined them. 'Ah ... Charles, I thought it was you. Celia, dear, it's about time we departed so we can be home before dark. You're enjoying being in London again, I trust, Charles.'

'I'd forgotten how many social occasions one is obliged to attend, and I do miss the countryside. You don't seem to notice the glory of the seasons in the capital quite so well. There, I believe I have turned into a country bumpkin.'

'The air is certainly more agreeable there ... on the whole.'

'Perhaps you'll allow me to call on you now you're home, Reverend. Would Thursday be convenient?'

Before Thomas could nod, Celia said, 'Let me reassure you, Charles, you are under no obligation to call on us, at all.'

When Thomas gazed at her in surprise, Charles gave an easy laugh. 'Celia is convinced I'm here to be admired rather than admire her. My dear Celia, in your case the visit will not be an obligation, but an extreme pleasure.'

'Come for dinner, Charles,' Thomas said, gazing with interest from one to another.

'Thank you, I will. I'll regale you with who said what about you after you've departed from here.'

And he did. Celia had dressed for the occasion of his visit in a modest blue skirt and bodice, a lace collar its only adornment.

'You should avoid that large woman in the purple frock ... she sings most excruciatingly out of tune, and we had to sit through half an hour of her warbling. She wouldn't be quiet, until someone stuffed a hand muff in her mouth.'

'You have a wicked tongue, Charles. What do you say to them about the reverend and myself when we're not present?'

The chuckle he gave was almost a purr. 'I tell them the reverend is a saint and Miss Laws is an angel. A couple of husbands were browbeaten by their jealous wives for praising you too much, Celia.'

She laughed. 'I don't believe you.'

242

'The draughts from all those swaying crinolines caused smoke to bellow into the room, and when Mrs Eggleston stood, she needed five yards of space to accommodate her skirt in every direction. She was mistaken for a table, and six gentlemen drew up their chairs around her and began to play cards on her skirt.'

Dissolving into giggles, Celia spluttered, 'Nonsense.'

'Not at all.' Charles' eyes gleamed. 'As for you, Reverend, you were quite the celebrity. Several of the widows fainted clean away after you left, and they enjoyed the experience so much that they plan to go to the next reading to repeat the experience.'

Thomas laughed. 'Then you must come to the next meeting and point them out to me so I can escape while they're still unconscious.'

'Oh, I intend to be there. I wouldn't miss Celia's performance for the world. As a spectacle you'll have competition though; they are hanging the Frenchman Emile Barthelemy on that same day.'

'Wasn't he suspected of being a spy for the French?'

'He shot a policeman in France and was jailed for life. After the uprising Barthelemy was released. He came to England a couple of years ago, fought a duel with a naval officer and was sentenced to two months for manslaughter. The death sentence was handed down after he shot and killed his former employer and the man's neighbour, who tried to prevent his escape. I have no sympathy for Barthelemy. He had several chances to reform.'

Thomas sighed. 'It will be a popular hanging that's well attended. I'll pray for his soul.'

'I doubt if he has one,' Charles replied.

Celia shuddered. The lad who'd killed her mother would have been given a death sentence, or so she'd been told by the constable, a decent man who'd retrieved and returned her mother's wage to her. On his advice she hadn't gone to the trial in case her mother's name was slandered, and by people who could only see what was obvious. All the same, the killer had only been young, and her mother wouldn't have wanted him punished in that way.

'Is that what happened to that lad, Reverend?'

Thomas' glance came to her, his expression puzzled. 'What lad was that?'

'The one who killed my—' No! Charles didn't know the nature of her mother's death! 'The one who killed that *woman* in London.'

Because she'd denied her mother in this instance, Celia felt like a Judas. Grief for her was a sudden, depressing sea of misery into which she plunged head first. It wrapped tight tentacles around her and held her fast in its sticky folds.

The cup clattered on her saucer as her hands began to tremble. She stared at him, stricken by her slip of the tongue and unable to overcome the almost overpowering need to weep. Then she realized that she'd have to go on denying her mother were she ever to wear the guise of respectability.

Thomas took the cup and saucer from her and placed it on the table, awareness in his eyes. 'My dear, this is not a subject that we should have discussed in front of you.' He began to gently pat her hand, to what purpose she couldn't imagine. 'See how upset you are.'

As if the hanging of a vile man who'd deliberately killed several people would upset her.

She'd attended a hanging once. It had been conducted early Monday morning and the roads surrounding Newgate prison had seethed with people who'd pushed and shoved for a view of the event. Celia had been too short to see anything from her position, but she'd heard a verse of a hymn sung by a single voice in one of the spectator windows in the building behind her. The hymn had been taken up by the crowd, raising the fine hairs on her neck and arms, then a bell had chimed and a great triumphant roar had filled the air.

Celia had been almost trampled underfoot as the spectators had dispersed, some hurrying to their place of work, others to their homes or the nearby markets, where she'd intended to do a little work of her own. Even at the tender age of twelve, she'd reached the conclusion that a public hanging was a form of entertainment. It was the last indignity for the criminal, who'd been hunted down like a fox, questioned until he'd confessed, then punished by the public spectacle of hanging at the end of a rope and jerking about until there was no life left in the body.

Charles looked utterly repentant. 'It was entirely my fault and I can't apologize enough. I forgot that my own study of the criminal under-

245

class is not to the taste of everyone, especially someone ignorant of their ways.'

Ignorant of their ways ... Hah! It was Charles Curtis who was ignorant of their ways. Wasn't she one of the people he studied, the unfortunate *underclass!*

'I'll go and find Mrs Packer and see if she has any smelling salts,' Thomas murmured.

She did feel rather drained at this moment, but struggled against it. 'I'll be all right in a moment or two.'

But Thomas had gone. Charles took his place. He slid his arm around her and supported her head in the crook of his shoulder while he gently stroked her hair.

Celia enjoyed the closeness for all of ten seconds while her trembling eased, then said, 'I feel stronger, so you may release me now.'

'Such a miraculous cure. Perhaps I should have taken up doctoring instead of the law,' he whispered into her hair. 'Does my proximity disturb you?'

'Yes ... no you don't ... why should you think that?'

'No reason at all. Look at me, Celia dear, allow me to see if the colour has returned to your face.'

She looked into his melting eyes and was lost because she knew exactly what he was going to do next, and said on her next outward breath, but not very convincingly, 'No, Charles...'

'Yes, my sweet Celia.' His mouth touched a tender kiss against her mouth, as soft as a butterfly. When she closed her eyes he placed a kiss against each lid, then her mouth again, firmer this time, leaving his claim there because she hadn't repulsed him that first time.

She wanted to cry even more because that kiss told her she'd fallen in love, but it was a love that could never be. No matter how much she tried, she wasn't good enough for someone like him, and he'd spurn her once he learned of her past – break her heart.

When they heard a footfall, Charles laid her gently back against the cushions. A smile played around his mouth as he said with complete disregard of Thomas Hambert's sensibilities, 'My diagnosis is that your corselette is too tight. There ... that's brought colour to your face.'

His words certainly had. She did feel better, and when the smelling salts were passed under her nose her eyes widened and her head cleared with a sudden jolt. She felt skittish afterwards, as though the salts had blown the cobwebs from her brain in all directions with one mighty puff. It left her mind so sharply honed that she wanted to leap from the sofa, stamp her feet, and box his ears all at the same time, for taking such liberties with her.

She had a sudden urge to laugh at the thought, and only just stifled it.

Charles smiled, as if he knew her thoughts exactly. 'Perhaps you'd both be my guests at the theatre while you're in London,' he said. 'There's a new play on at the Adelphi by Boucicoult which I think might pander to Celia's taste of the dramatic. It's titled *Janet Pride*.'

'I'd heard it has a rather long prologue.'

'Oh ... a real play ... that would be wonderful.

I've never been to one, at least, not a professional one on a proper stage. Please may we go and see it, Reverend?' she said, and her eyes began to shine.

Thomas gazed from one to the other and sighed. He was not immune to what was going on under his nose. Charles Curtis was a personable and charming young man, Celia, incandescent in his presence. She would be vulnerable as well as susceptible, having spent her childhood absorbing a standard of moral behaviour lower than now expected of her.

It was a complication he'd rather not have. He reminded himself that although Celia was not his responsibility, he'd assumed the role of mentor to her. She was in London at his behest, and it was his duty to look after her, though he had to admit that she probably knew the dangers of London better than he did.

But she was a young woman, and her eyes were brimming over with such excitement at the thought of going to the theatre that he didn't have the heart to refuse. What had she done to raise this protective fatherly feeling inside him? Nothing he'd observed to be untoward, except her smile was too bright when she looked at Charles, her cheeks too pink, and her manner too self-conscious.

He was not her father, but, Thomas wondered, should he have a word with her? But with what words did fathers caution young ladies about gentlemen like Charles? Indeed, he knew hardly anything about his guest and might do him an injustice.

His glance flicked to Charles and he smiled. Perhaps it would be better if he had a word with the young man, instead.

Sixteen

After Celia had retired for the night, Thomas said to Charles, 'I do believe you're trying to turn the child's head.'

Charles didn't bother to deny it. 'Celia is hardly a child, but a beautiful young woman with a lively mind, whose company I enjoy. It's she who is turning mine.'

'Celia is only beginning to venture into society, and it's very different to the one she grew up in. She's susceptible to flattery.'

'From what I see of her family background, it's sound.'

Thomas had forgotten that Charles knew nothing of Celia's background except what he saw and assumed. He remembered it now, and told himself he'd have to be careful. 'Which is why I'd rather not see her encouraged to attach her affections to a man whose intentions are spurious, to say the least.'

'An assumption in itself, Reverend. May I enquire; what motivates your own interest in Celia?'

'My interest in her is purely academic. She has skills I've been encouraging.'

'For whose benefit, hers or yours?'

'I beg your pardon,' he spluttered.

'Come, come, Reverend, I've been to one of two of your gatherings. While Celia seems unaffected by the fuss – indeed she's unassuming where her own creative talent is concerned – you bask in her reflected glory, and as her mentor take credit.'

Thomas was horrified by such a notion. 'You think so? I'm immensely proud of her, you know. Oh, dear ... I'm mortified to think that I should appear prideful on my own account, and for my own small contribution. If you'd known her when—' Aware of his slip of the tongue, he shrugged. 'I will not excuse my behaviour, but rather I'll try and change it. Celia has such a thirst for knowledge, and her welfare is dear to my heart.'

'I apologize, Reverend; I spoke out of turn, and as a reaction to your accusation that my own interest in her is spurious. As a matter of curiosity, why do you feel you must nurture her mind?'

'Some things come about without reason, Charles, as though God meant them to be, but with Celia it's different.'

'Like love?'

'In one of its many forms. If you're asking if I hold a great affection for Celia Laws, the answer is, yes, I do. My own daughter bore the same name, and would be about the same age had she lived. That's why I asked you not to try and turn Celia's head. She's already had enough problems in her life. How well do you love her, Charles?'

The man spoke without thinking that Thomas' phrasing was odd. 'How ... with my body and my heart. She is rapidly becoming an addiction, like opium is to the soul, or like one more glass of wine intoxicates the brain.'

Thomas hummed softly in his throat. 'Love is not to be found in the gratification of one's appetite, however strong the turmoil of that feeling, or the instant, but temporary relief brought by satiation of the flesh.' Thomas smiled when his guest appeared a little uncomfortable. 'Would you like a glass of port?'

Charles rose. 'It's about time I left, so I think not, Reverend. My ears are already glowing. You're skilled in verbal sparring and would make a fine legal advocate if you didn't allow your heart to rule your head.'

Thomas followed him into the hall and, when Charles shrugged into his coat, said, 'And Celia Laws ... what of her?'

'Neither of us can profess to be experts in the art of love ... you taking a spiritual approach while I'm at the opposite end, by needing to express it in a more ungodly manner.'

'Ah yes ... The blood runs hotly when one is young.'

'In deference to yours, I was not going to mention age, Reverend. Be reassured though, your words have not fallen on deaf ears.'

'Then you'll no longer pursue Celia?'

'I didn't say that, Reverend – I didn't say that, at all. I imagine I'll simply change my tactics. Like that glass of good wine, it's become obvious that Celia needs to be allowed to breathe for a short time before being savoured. Good-night, sir.'

Placing his hat on his head Charles gave him a grin, picked up a silver-topped cane and went out into the night – leaving Thomas with a broad smile on his face.

Celia donned her favourite blue dress with the lace collar for the theatre and Mrs Packer dressed her hair, using the tongs to create side ringlets.

Charles had taken a box at the Adelphi Theatre and had invited his family to join them. Celia received a shock when she was introduced to his mother and stepfather.

Like all the men, Joshua Harris was elegant in his evening suit. Charles' mother, Imogene, was beautifully and finely gowned in pale lilac. Her eyes flared in a moment of uncertain recognition when they were introduced. 'Miss Laws ... I feel as though I've already met you. Have we been introduced before?'

Celia blessed the dim light, and not only because it hid the fact that her gown was a little shabby. She didn't want to lie; she'd told so many to conceal her past, and they now seemed to be expanding with every breath, she thought, as she twisted her answer in a way designed to avoid being entirely untruthful. 'I think you're the first people I've met with the surname of Harris. It's a Scottish name isn't it?'

Joshua smiled and said in a perfectly modu-lated English, 'I think my family may have origi-nated in Scotland, but it was a long time ago.'

'I'm so pleased to meet you, Mrs Harris.

Charles has told us he has a baby sister. He seems to be very fond of her.'

'My son has always liked children. I understand you've made yourself responsible for your late mother's ward.'

'Lottie is six, and I love her dearly. I rarely think of her in terms any less than my sister.'

'You're young to have responsibility for a child of that age.'

Celia vaguely remembered that this woman had been susceptible to flattery on the previous occasion they'd met. 'You must have been extremely young when Charles was born.'

Her mouth curved in a smile – a smile so like Charles' that it nearly robbed Celia of breath. 'I was barely seventeen. I'm truly blessed with my children. Charles is so clever and well mannered. He never gave me a moment of unease when he was growing up, and I'm so proud of him. As for Adelaide, she's a joy.'

'She certainly is.' Charles lifted an eyebrow and gave a long-suffering sigh. 'There are problems attached to being the only son of a devoted mother. The motherly praise is quite unwarranted if you did but know it, Celia. I'm far from perfect.'

Celia offered him a faint grin. 'As you say ... and I imagine that both you and your mother know you better than I do. Which version to accept could prove to be the problem.'

He chuckled. 'I stand willing to be convinced to the contrary.'

'You mean you were hinting to be complimented? What a conceited creature you are,

Charles Curtis ... there, that is my opinion. By the way, thank you for the Christmas gifts. Lottie adores her doll.'

'And you?'

'I love my little bird, though I prefer to see them flying free than penned in a cage.'

'Which is exactly why I bought you a metal bird. However, if you think you can make it fly...?'

His mother laughed.

Thomas gave one of his behave-yourself reminder coughs and stated to nobody in particular, 'I have a theory that parental praise from an early age imbues a lad with self-confidence. Alas, I've never had the chance to put the idea into practice.' He held the back of a chair. 'Will you sit here next to Celia, Mrs Harris? You'll have an excellent view of the stage.'

Joshua took the seat next to his wife. Charles and Thomas seated themselves behind.

Celia immersed herself in the programme, familiarizing herself with the characters.

When the curtain began to rise, Charles leaned forward and breathed against her ear, 'I hope you'll enjoy the play.'

'I will ... I know I will. Thank you so much for inviting us, Charles; you're so kind, and I'm looking forward to it so much.'

Her words filled Charles with such tender pleasure that he could hardly breathe. Odd that something so commonplace as going to the theatre could raise such interest in her, and right from the beginning.

As soon as the scenery depicting Paris was

revealed she gave a quiet little gasp of delight, and during the long prologue she leaned forward, as though determined to catch every word, and oblivious to those around her.

She cried over the fate of Richard Pride, and whispered under her breath, 'Oh, no, that's not fair,' when his daughter, Janet Pride, was convicted of the crime.

Charles watched the emotions come and go on her face, heard her sigh with relief when Richard Pride confessed to the crime, and heard her trying to stifle a sob when he died.

He handed over his handkerchief for her to mop her eyes with.

When the play was over, she asked him, 'Does the Bailey courtroom really look like that inside?'

'It's a fairly accurate depiction. I'd say the scene painter had been inside, or at least had a sketch to work from.'

They paused at the top of the staircase, the other three going ahead.

'And do barristers and judges wear those wigs?'

'Yes, they do.'

'Do you wear one?'

'During a court trial, yes, just a short one. It's a tradition.'

She nodded. 'I really enjoyed the play. The scenery was very good. It made me feel as though I was there. I should like to go to Paris one day, and also to the wilds of Australia. I know someone whose father was sent there for stealing a pair of boots from a dead man. I thought that was unfair, because the dead man didn't need them, and his young son was forced on to the streets and left all alone to fend for himself.'

'Stealing is a crime that shouldn't go unpunished,' he said.

She knew that to be untrue, for he'd made an exception in her case. But that had been a long time ago and his thinking would have since been influenced by others. 'What if a friend stole something from you, then confessed and gave it back somehow ... would you have them arrested and charged?'

He gazed at her, his glance intent on her face then coming up to her eyes, where they held her trapped in their darkness. He appeared interested in the conversation, his head slanting a little to one side as he gave a faint smile and made a little murmur deep in his throat before saying, 'I don't imagine my friends would ever steal from me. They're trustworthy.'

Guilt swallowed most of her breath, and although she tried to shift her eyes away, she couldn't. She would hate to be prosecuted by Charles Curtis, she thought. 'What if they were hungry and had no choice?'

'Then they'd only have to ask me, and I'd share with them what I had, including money, which they could repay when their circumstances had improved.' He tucked her arm through his. 'Does that answer your question?'

'Yes,' she murmured. No, she thought, for he'd never regard her as trustworthy now, even if she repaid that large amount of cash he'd given her.

But she'd feel better about herself when she did, she mused, especially since its presence still tempted her sorely at the times she remembered it.

'What happened to the friend of yours who was left alone to fend for himself?'

She didn't want to tell him anything of her background. 'Johnny was taken in by a couple who'd lost their own son.'

'A little like your sister Lottie.'

'Johnnny was older, about twelve. The couple had an inn so he was able to offer them his services in return for his home. I was pleased to find him so settled, when I visited recently.'

'So you see, there are people who do care about the welfare of abandoned children. That couple at the inn, your mother ... you ... Reverend Hambert. And there are church committees and boards that support and run workhouses. Where did you say the inn was?'

'Oh, in the New Forest,' she said carelessly, and returned to the conversation. 'Despite that, people still die on the streets from starvation and cold, and they have to steal to stay alive. And women are forced into selling—' She bit down on her lip. 'Sorry,' she said, her voice faltering a little. 'I shouldn't have ... I'm sorry.'

'You don't have to apologize, Celia. The simple fact is that there are too many disadvantaged on the streets now, and that's partly because the rail network gives easy access to London, and the unemployed swarm here looking for work. If law and order isn't maintained there will be more crime. At the same time, the innocent are going to suffer along with the guilty. That's why I thought this play would interest you.'

'Instead, it made me cry and fired my anger,' she said ruefully.

'You're sensitive to the plight of the needy. I found it interesting. Have you had much to do with them? Your stories, the settings in particular, seem to have an edge of truth to them.'

She folded up his handkerchief and handed it back to him, attempting to distract his train of thought away from herself. 'I'm afraid it's a little damp.'

'You didn't answer my question.'

'Goodness, didn't I?' She groped words out of the air. 'I imagine the reverend's views have rubbed off on me a little.'

'That must account for it, since Reverend Hambert is well known for his views on reform. James Kent takes after him somewhat, for he often intervenes in cases where children are handed down the death sentence.'

If Celia had intended to confide in him over her mother's death, now would have been the time, but they'd reached the bottom of the stairs and were about to join the others, who were waiting for the carriage to arrive. He smiled at her. 'I'm aware this subject distressed you the last time we were together. I'll try not to raise it again.'

'No ... I'm quite all right. Thank you for an enjoyable evening, Charles.'

'I enjoyed it, and I sincerely hope there will be more like it.'

She hoped so too, but didn't see any point in

encouraging him, since she was as poor as a church mouse, and had nothing to wear. She looked around at the crowd pressing around them, the men with fat wallets and gold watch chains, and the women richly dressed for the most part. As they jostled against her they were almost begging to be relieved of their riches. It would take but a few moments to help herself.

'What are you smiling at?' he asked.

'Must I have a motive? Don't you ever smile for no reason?'

'Never. I keep my smile for special occasions, but the one you displayed was a cross between a grimace and a leer, like a wolf, which having run its prey to ground then discovered it lacked the appetite to eat it.'

She giggled, because his analogy, had he but known it, was so apt. 'I've never seen a wolf smile, but then, I've never seen a wolf – not a real one, though I've seen a picture of one in a book in Reverend Hambert's library. They're beautiful, even though dangerous. It's a pity they're extinct in England.'

He smiled. 'I've never met a woman who reads books about wolves before?'

'The reverend says I should read everything I can if I want to expand on my education. You have a nice smile, Charles. However, the only animal I can compare it to is a cat – a cat quite pleased with himself.'

'Smug?'

'As you please.'

'I do not please. I'll never smile again.'

And he didn't, not until the carriage reached

Bedford Square and he helped her down while Thomas opened the front door. When Charles kissed her hand and smiled at her everything inside her melted.

'Goodnight, Celia. I enjoyed your company tonight.'

'Thank you, Charles.' She remembered Mr and Mrs Harris, and hoped she hadn't been too careless in her conversation with their son. She smiled past his shoulder into the interior of the carriage. 'Goodnight, Mr and Mrs Harris. Thank you for a perfect evening.'

Charles leaned back into the cushioned interior where Celia, sandwiched between himself and the reverend, had recently rested her head. He could almost smell her perfume, and said to his mother and stepfather as the carriage proceeded, 'What do you think of Celia Laws?'

His mother spoke first. 'My first impression is that she was out of her element. I'm surprised a girl of her age has never been to the theatre, and I thought her attire inappropriate; in fact it was a little shabby. Oh dear, Charles, I'm ashamed to say that I lived in fear that she might have booed and hissed out loud.'

Charles laughed as he hastened to defend Celia. 'Her aunt, Miss Price, is not well off.'

'The girl's manners are a little gauche, I feel, and sometimes she seems out of her depth. What of her background ... has she a father?'

'I know nothing about her except she lives with her aunt and has a young girl in her care. Her mother is now dead, but both the Reverend and James Kent were acquainted with her when she was a child. Thomas Hambert took it upon himself to mentor her.'

Joshua offered, 'Reverend Hambert is an interesting man, and I was pleased to meet him at last. He has the reputation of being a bit of a reformer, and his methods of teaching are unorthodox. He also has a half-share interest in a publishing venture, which supports his views. Sometimes his essays are rather radical, and they put him at odds with his bishop. He was a little different to what I'd expected to find. Your young woman seems comfortable in his presence, and has a mind of her own, a rather lively one judging from your exchanges.'

Imogene sighed. 'And she's emotional; she cried over the play.'

'I believe she once wanted to act, but the reverend thinks her talents lie in the written word. That's her work in the book I gave you. He's found a kindred spirit I feel, for she certainly depicts life in the London slums sensitively, and well. It's as if she's lived amongst the poor.'

'She's certainly a beauty. What did her parents die of?'

Charles shrugged. 'I've never asked her. Celia has never mentioned her father in my presence.'

His mother frowned in concentration. 'Laws ... Where have I heard that name before? I believe there's an opera singer called Daniel Laws. I've heard he's very good. How did she come to be acquainted with Reverend Hambert and James Kent?'

'I believe she met them when she lived in London.' His frown crinkled. 'You said she seemed familiar to you when you first met. I formed the very same impression when we were introduced.'

Those close to Celia guarded her background very well ... too well he was beginning to think, because the evasion and the odd slip of the tongue he'd noticed, though carefully covered up, had now piqued Charles' curiosity.

His mother leaned forward and placed a hand on his arm. 'I can see that Celia Laws intrigues you, Charles, and I can understand why, since she's lovely as well as being intelligent, and she has an air of innocence about her that's very refreshing.

If you are thinking of asking me if I approve of her, the answer is yes. Your judgement has always been sound, and, Lord knows, I came from a modest background myself. Just exercise some caution, my dear. You know very little about her. Perhaps you should ask James Kent when you return to Poole.'

That could prove to be a problem, since James was also afflicted by love. Not that Charles was in love with Celia – he was just interested in her.

He prompted himself. Because?

Detouring around the question, his next thought was: Show me a man who wouldn't be interested in Celia Laws?

That answer brought a frown to his face. Other men could stay out of the equation or answer to him. All the same, she'd attracted attention at the theatre during the interval. The lawyer in him stepped forward. Don't answer a question with a question, Mr Curtis, especially one designed to evade. You know you hate someone doing it to you.

He gave in to his inner man with a sigh. All right, I admit it. I've fallen in love with Celia Laws. There. Thinking it wouldn't commit him to do anything rash, though he noted that a poetic little dove had loosened itself from the confines of his heart and had gone off winging and wheeling into the sky like a glowing silver star. He became aware that his manly urges were reminding him they'd been neglected.

He ignored them and grinned in Joshua's direction. 'For what it's worth, because James has been walking around with his head in the clouds since he met Harriet Price – yes, I will ask for his opinion when I get back. In the meantime, I've been thinking about buying a house.'

'Have you found a place you like, then?'

'There are a couple of houses in Poole I've been considering.'

'And there will always be a room for you with us when you come to London.'

Charles settled back into his corner thinking of Celia Laws. A woman's input would be useful, since, if his limited experience was anything to go by, they always managed to notice the impracticalities of a house, like the kitchen might be too far away from the dining room, or the ceilings were damp-stained, or there were silverfish in the carpets and mice in the walls. The latter was usually accompanied by the exposure of ankles as skirts were lifted slightly.

He must ask Celia to accompany him and offer an opinion, in case she also expected mice to scurry from the wainscot to take refuge under her skirt.

He grinned. He'd wager she had pretty ankles.

Seventeen

Celia slid her feet into the footwear Mrs Packer had bought on her behalf, and gazed down at her feet. She couldn't remember having a new pair of boots, and these had dainty heels and buttons. 'They're so pretty, Mrs Packer.'

'As well as being serviceable, Miss. I was instructed to buy boots, and a gown you could wear in the evening as well as the day. This one has two bodices, the pale-blue one for evening with some lace at the sleeves and neck, and the other, as you can see, is quite plain, except for the watery pattern on the taffeta. Modest, the reverend said it was to be, but that doesn't mean it has to be plain, does it?'

'It's so pretty, and I'll never be able to repay him.'

'Bless you, but you won't have to do that. The reverend believes in the power of giving a gift. He said he paid scant attention to your appearance, and it wasn't until you wore the same gown to the theatre that you did for the performances, and somebody commented on it, that he

264

realized how at a disadvantage you were. He wanted to surprise you, so I used your other outfit for size.'

'I'm not as disadvantaged as when I first showed up at your door in my rags.'

'Aye, and I'm right ashamed at the uncharitable things I said about you, especially after what happened to your poor mother ... well, you know ... and you being left with your baby sister to care for, the poor, dear little thing.' Tears came to the woman's eyes. 'I didn't know what to make of it when Mr Kent managed to get his sentence turned around – that lad, who did her in, I mean. Still, Mr Kent doesn't believe in children being given the death penalty. Being hung is barbaric, he says. I don't suppose being sent all that way to work off his sentence in that inhospitable country is much better. I've heard that there are poisonous snakes, giant lizards and spiders everywhere. I don't know why anyone would want to live in Australia, when it's full of scum from the prisons.'

Celia's eyes rounded. 'You mean James Kent saved that murderer's life, when all this time I thought he'd been hung ... and I felt sorry for him.'

'How could you feel sorry for him, after he killed your mother?'

'I know my mother wouldn't have wanted him to die on her account. He was too young.'

'He was a black-hearted villain, that's what he was. If he carried a knife, he intended to use it. Types like him never reform.'

Mrs Packer was probably right. Celia had an

instant image of a young man in a red kerchief, his face etched by crime, and already hardened to life on the streets. He would have shown no mercy to his victims. It crossed her mind that he might die as he'd lived, violently, because now he was in the company of older, more vicious criminals. Then again, it was possible that his narrow escape from the gallows had made an impression on him, and he'd decide that living was a preferable option.

But she wished James or the reverend had told her. But perhaps they hadn't wanted to upset her.

If it hadn't been for her mother's guidance, and Thomas Hambert's interest in offering her a way out, Celia knew she'd probably be one of Bessie's girls by now. She shuddered at such an awful fate, and hoped Charles didn't find out about her past. Although she was not good enough for him by far, she enjoyed his company and didn't think she'd be able to bear seeing his regard turn to disdain.

Celia hugged the woman and gazed at her careworn face. 'You needn't be sorry. I knew there was a compassionate person under your gruffness ... it shone through. I'll miss you when I've gone.'

'It might not be for long. The reverend has offered me a job in Dorset if he decides to move, and I'm considering it.'

Celia hugged her. 'I'm so glad.'

'I haven't agreed to it yet.' Mrs Packer managed a faint smile and suddenly became brisk. 'There's this embroidered jacket for warmth. It's a darker blue, and very pretty. And here's the bonnet. I've sewn a little bunch of violets each side, to pick up the colour of your eyes. The reverend won't mind that. He always gets a twinkle in his eyes when he's in the company of a pretty woman.'

A little later she presented herself to him in the library. 'Thank you for the clothing, Reverend. I've never had anything new before, and I feel so grand.'

He looked up from his book and smiled almost absently. 'I should have thought of it earlier. You look quite delightful. Have you finished the episode you were writing?'

'The third one? Almost. I'm afraid I blotted it.'

'That doesn't matter, since Mr Parkinson will edit it before it's printed, so it will end up messy anyway. He wants to meet you, so if you can have it ready by the end of the week I'll take you to see him. I daresay he'll be pleased to get the episodes in advance, and you can see how the printing press works.'

'Thank you. That should be interesting,' though she didn't always like to know how things worked because it spoiled the sense of wonder. 'When are we returning to Dorset?'

His eyes twinkled when he smiled. 'Had enough of London, have you?'

'A little, though I'm seeing a different London to the one I knew before, and I'm realizing how places and people add colour. You and Charles seem to have peeled back the layers for me. Poor people seem to have a multicoloured vitality that blends into shades of grey. The wealthy practice frugality, yet can be charitable in unexpected ways. People have been so kind, but I miss Lottie and my aunt. I'm so pleased Aunt Harriet is to marry James, though.'

He closed his book. 'So am I; they seem ideally suited. Have you thought of where you'll go when they are married?'

She gazed at him, uncomprehending.

The man explained, 'I understood from James that he intends to move into Chaffinch House when he and Harriet marry, since it's situated halfway between Poole and Dorchester, which is handy for his profession. He intends to buy the house from Harriet ... and Harriet intends to give half of the proceeds to you. She said you're to have what your mother was entitled to, through her legacy – and James agrees that is how they should go about things.'

'But I thought ... Mr Avery said there was no money left.'

'Mr Avery was mistaken. He and James have negotiated a settlement.'

'Did Aunt Harriet ask you to tell me she wanted me to move out?'

He gazed over his glasses at her. 'Harriet doesn't want you to move out, my dear, and neither does James. It came up in general discussion. As you know, James has taken over your aunt's affairs. She said it was up to you, and I should sound you out if the opportunity arose.'

'I think you created the opportunity, Reverend. Harriet would not be so devious. She would have sat me down and discussed the situation.'

He gave a faint smile. 'Of course she would have, exactly as I am doing. But newly-weds appreciate their privacy, and Harriet loves you and she wouldn't want to hurt your feelings. It's likely there will be children from the union, and they will need more servants, who will need to be housed. James will hold social evenings because his position will demand it of him.'

'Enough!' She laughed, even though colour rushed to her cheeks. 'I admit, I've not given it much thought, because the engagement is so new, and it happened so quickly and unexpectedly that even Harriet was taken aback.'

'I've discussed the situation with my sister, Abigail, and she suggested that you and Charlotte might like to move in with us ... that's if you don't marry yourself, in the meantime.'

'I won't marry ... I cannot! You know that. What if he discovered my past and began to despise me? I couldn't bear it.'

'What if *who* discovered your past, Celia?'

She swooped in a breath and felt blood creep into her cheeks. 'Oh, nobody in particular ... a prospective husband, I suppose.'

Quite gently, he said, 'There's that. But if a man loved you enough to offer you marriage, surely you would tell him the truth about your upbringing.'

'That I begged, picked pockets, and recited poetry badly on street corners?'

'That you spent some of your life in straightened circumstances and were forced to live on your wits. If the man truly loved you it wouldn't make any difference to him, surely.'

Head slanting to one side she thought about it for just a moment, then said, 'What if it did make a difference?'

'It's a possibility.'

She appreciated the fact that Thomas Hambert didn't give her false hope, but recognized the reality of life. 'If I didn't take you and your sister up on your generous offer, when my mother's legacy is settled on me, and if it's enough, I could buy somewhere for Lottie and myself – a small house with a yard where we could keep chickens and grow vegetables. Perhaps I could support us through my writing. That way we wouldn't be a burden to anyone.'

He smiled at that. 'On the other hand you could become my secretary. You could help me in the morning, and have the afternoon to yourself for your own writing. With Lottie at school, you would have plenty of peace and quiet, because there's a room with a small sitting room attached that you could have for your own use.'

'If I bought a house not far from where you live, I could still be your secretary. When you've begged for food to fill your stomach, you don't feel inclined to live on another's charity if you can manage not to.'

'Eating pride doesn't satisfy an empty stomach.'

She persisted with her reasoning. 'When you're used to the freedom of the streets, you're bound to find chaperonage irksome. I cannot fit comfortably into a mould of somebody else's making.'

'You've fallen into the trap of romanticizing your former life, and we've strayed from the point.'

'Being?'

'Charles Curtis, I believe. He's incurably romantic, and you intrigue him.'

Her next breath was a long and heartfelt sigh. 'I'm nowhere near good enough for him.'

'Celia dear ... don't talk nonsense. Poverty is a state of being, not of inferiority. You've changed from a grubby, awkward child with a thirst to learn, into a graceful and intelligent young woman. You've learned much from your aunt, including patience, and as each day passes you will gain in sense and wisdom. Be careful that the need for independence doesn't make you headstrong.' Rising, he gently kissed her cheek. 'Your mother would be proud of you, my dear. As for Charles Curtis, beware, for he will seduce you if you allow it.'

Celia knew he would, and the very thought of being seduced by him was sublime. Her initial distaste at the thought of the method of mating between men and women had gradually become curiosity as she'd come to realize it was meant to be that way, and nothing to be ashamed of. Sometimes, and unaided, her body indicated an eagerness to experience it in a way that made her blush, and she wondered if it was normal to be so needy of something she'd never experienced – like an addiction waiting to happen for her.

But the innocence of women was an asset highly prized by men. They were less careful of their own though. Goodness ... Charles had offered her money when she was hardly more than a child, and himself so callow there was barely a stray whisker on his chin. What was more, she'd found his kiss so sweet that she'd dreamed of it for years. If he seriously turned his charm towards seduction she doubted if it would be easy to stand up against such a sweet assault.

The reverend had been right. She did need an older and wiser head to chaperone her, and it was sweet of the reverend and his sister to be concerned about her.

'Thank you for your offer of a home, Reverend. Lottie and I will be happy to live with you and Mrs Kent if the need arises. I do like your sister, and her gossip. She told me that you were often naughty, and caused your father no end of despair.'

'No wonder he wanted me to be a soldier.' He laughed, then said, 'Why do you always put up an argument, Celia?'

'Because you expect me to.'

'Expect you to?'

'Oh, don't look so innocent. You usually tie me in a knot and I have to think in several directions to find my way out of all the tangles in it, and come to the right conclusion – which is usually your opinion. That's the way you taught me to think for myself, though I didn't know it at the time. I thought of you often when we were apart. I missed our conversations where you encouraged me to speak my mind. I think I shocked Aunt Harriet a few times.'

He nodded. 'The life you and your mother led, and the reason behind it, is not something that can be easily understood and absorbed without making judgement.'

'Yet you would expect me to tell Ch ... someone who loved me of my past, and risk losing that love.'

'There is no love without trust, my dear. What's the alternative?'

'Not to love in the first place, for to love and lose would be to suffer the pain of having it dashed in your face and regarded as worthless.'

'My dear, you're too young to be so pessimistic. Not even you can guard your heart from the ache of unrequited love.'

'I can try.'

'You should allow a man to show what he's worth rather than judge him in advance. I think your mother's experience may have coloured your thinking.'

Celia had not considered that, but she would, and now her mother had been mentioned she said, 'I would like to visit the site of her grave while we're in London, if you don't mind. It might reassure her to know that Lottie and I are well and happy.'

'I imagine she already knows that, my dear, but I'm sure we can find time to fit in a visit.'

'And, Reverend ... I want to look for Daniel Laws.'

This time he did look slightly shocked. 'Are you sure this is wise?'

'I'm only sure it's something I must do. If he's my father I need to know it. Or if he's dead I need to know that too ... in which case I can safely bury him in my mind.'

'And if he is your father and denies knowing your mother?'

She shrugged. 'Then he won't be worth knowing. My mother said his eyes were the same colour as mine.'

Thomas gave a sigh, then grumbled, 'I know a theatrical agent. He'll be able to locate him and arrange a meeting, I imagine. And Celia, put any romantic notion you may have about long-lost daughters from your head. I almost wish Charles had chosen a different play to take you to. *Janet Pride* was bound to give you ideas.'

Eighteen

'Mr Laws can give you five minutes before he has to warm up his voice,' the theatre manager said.

They found him in his dressing room. Daniel Laws was in his mid forties. He had greyish hair and eyes the colour of amber. First disappointment. He was slightly rotund and of medium height. Second disappointment. He was altogether more ordinary-looking than Jackaby Laws was in her mind. She had a picture of a larger-than-life gentleman who was tall and handsome, and had a booming laugh.

Daniel Laws was dressed in an evening suit, and applying greasepaint to his eyes with his fingertip, making his eyes look bigger. Those eyes widened as they fell on Celia and he said, 'What can I do for you, Miss ... and you, sir? The theatre manager said you were a relative.'

274

His voice was soft and cultured, so it flowed more smoothly and warmly than that of the average Englishman.

'We're looking for Jackaby Laws,' Celia said.

'Are you? Are you, now?' His eyes speculated on her. 'May I ask why?'

She didn't wait for the reverend; after all, they only had five minutes. She blurted out, 'Jackaby Laws is my father, and I thought—'

A smile spread across his face and he held up a hand, palm foremost. 'You assumed that, because my second name is Laws, I'm your father?'

'Are you?'

'There are hundreds of people with the same name, and I assure you I'm not your father.' Picking up a glass of water he gargled, then sang up and down the scale in a soft voice that was perfectly pitched, and rather beautiful.

'We're sorry to have wasted your time, Mr Laws,' the reverend said, and they turned away.

'Wait ... I didn't say I'd never heard of Jackaby Laws.' He took another sip of the water and repeated the exercise, going slightly higher and louder.

There was a knock at the door. 'Two minutes, Mr Laws,' someone said.

The man gazed into her eyes for a moment, contemplating what he saw, then said, 'I suppose you could be his daughter, at that, but it's a long time since I set eyes on Jackaby. Look, I can see this is important to you, young lady ... I haven't got time to explain now. Come into the wings and watch my act, the pair of you. We can talk afterwards.'

Daniel Laws was good. His voice soared to the ceilings and the clink of the cutlery against china plates of the diners became subdued, then stopped altogether.

He sang three songs, one of them a popular aria. Celia was entranced and the applause was deafening. Then she spotted Charles seated at one of the tables with a small group of men and women, and she shrank back in case he saw her. He looked her way a couple of times, placing his hand across his brows so he could peer into the darkness of the wings better.

Daniel Laws' body came between them.

'I don't know how you can sing so beautifully with all that cigar smoke drifting about,' Celia said, when Daniel came off stage.

'Sometimes it's difficult, but you get used to it. I have half an hour before I'm on stage again. Let's go to my dressing room and talk.'

There was only one chair, and the singer pulled a small wooden bench inside for them to seat themselves on. He offered the reverend a brandy, which was declined. 'Now, young woman,' he said. 'How well did you know your father?'

'I didn't know him at all. He went away before I was born, to America. He was a famous impresario in the theatre, and had been raising money for a show.'

Daniel Laws gave a faint smile and slowly shook his head.

'He told my mother, whose name was Alice Price before their marriage, that he'd be back. She waited for him.'

276

'Yes ... I thought that might have been the case. You see, my dear, Jackaby Laws died when the ship he was on sank in a storm with the loss of all on board ... It must have been about nineteen years ago now.'

She gave a distressed little cry, even though such news was half expected.

'Perhaps there's something else I should tell you,' and he gazed at the reverend. 'With your permission, sir, since it might prove to be upsetting to the young lady.'

'I want to know the truth, whatever that truth may be, Mr Laws.'

He took her hands in his. 'I do believe Jackaby fathered you, since there are similarities, especially your eyes, which are an unusually striking colour, and the darkness of your hair. Jackaby Laws was my cousin but we were not close. He wasn't an impresario; he was a confidence trickster who posed as a Southern gentleman, and he also had a wife he left behind in Boston. She was very young ... not much older than you. Jackaby was a thief and a liar who preyed on women without compunction. He was deeply in debt when he died, and his widow was left destitute.'

'So was my mother,' she said bitterly, and despite wanting to know the truth, found it unpalatable. She'd rather he'd been a dead hero than a criminal. 'We ended up living in the slums begging for food, even though she came from a good home. He ruined her, then brought her down. My mother was killed for the few shillings she'd earned sewing trouser seams.'

He looked shocked. 'I'm so sorry, my dear. If

you don't mind me saying so, you're better off without Jackaby Laws in your life.'

Celia felt like crying. It was not what she'd wanted to hear. Then hope flared in her eyes. 'Did they have any children?'

There was sympathy in the gaze he bestowed on her. 'You have no siblings, I'm afraid. His widow married again and she has two sons from her second husband. The only kin you have left on your father's side is me, and that link is so remote it's almost non-existent.' He cocked his head to one side. 'I'm sorry I couldn't have been more helpful, but at least you know where you stand now, and won't waste time looking for somebody who no longer exists. Jackaby is not worth breaking your heart over, but I'm sorry you and your mother suffered at his hands.'

Celia smiled, even though her heart ached and she felt like crying. 'I'm glad you're my cousin, even though it might be such a tenuous link. And I'm pleased you're so talented. I once wanted to make my way on the stage, but thanks to Reverend Hambert here, I became an author instead.'

He smiled at that. 'You became an author ... at your age?'

He sounded so disbelieving that the Reverend reached into his pocket, where he always kept a cloth-bound version of their book. 'This contains several of Celia's stories. You will learn something of her life by reading it.'

A new respect filled his eyes and he whistled. 'A published writer ... well done, my dear. May I keep this?'

'We'll sign it for you.'

When they'd done that it was time to go. 'You've been very kind. Thank you so much, Mr Laws. I'm sorry I took up your time with this matter.' She kissed his cheek.

'I was pleased to have been of some help. If you ever come to Boston, look me up.'

'I will ... I promise,' she said, as he shook hands with the reverend. 'Good luck with your tour.' She had tears in her eyes as they left the theatre in the same way as they'd arrived, through the stage door in the back alley, which was lit only by a sputtering gas lamp.

Like most alleyways in London it afforded room for the underclass to squat or sleep. There was a group of several men and women passing round a stone jar containing gin, their shadows leaping and dancing in a demented dance against the alley walls. Children wandered amongst them, some staggering a little, for tuppence worth of gin in empty stomachs dulled the hunger pangs and brought forgetfulness.

A couple of light-skirts leaned against the wall, and there was the scrape and rattle of rubbish as a breeze circled the alley and swept the dust out of the dark corners.

'Do you need a woman? I've got starving children at home,' one of them said to the reverend.

'You know very well that I don't, Rosie.' Fumbling in his pocket he brought a coin out and spun it through the air. 'Buy your children some soup.'

'Bless you, Reverend,' one of them said.

The other one stared hard at Celia. 'Hello, dearie, don't I know you? Didn't your mother work for Bessie?'

She was grateful for the darkness when her face flamed. 'I don't know what you're talking about.' She took the reverend's arm. 'We should have gone out of the front way. Let's hurry.'

Two small lads detached themselves from the group and casually followed after them. One of them held out cupped hands to Celia, and the other one jostled the reverend.

They were in sight of the main thoroughfare. Celia smiled as she stepped in the path of the second lad, dislodging from his cuff the coin he'd stolen from the reverend's pocket and catching it. Hissing with menace she handed the reverend back the shilling they'd taken from his coin pocket, then turned back to them. 'Get going, else I'll shout for a constable.'

One backed off, the other stood his ground. 'We're hungry.'

'Here then, buy yourself and your companion a meal.' Thomas handed the boy the shilling. They ran back to the light-skirts; the one who'd remembered Celia's mother took the coin from the older lad, then whispered something in his ear. A quick glance came their way.

'If word gets round you'll be besieged by beggars every time you come here,' she told him.

'Stop fussing, Celia,' and he gave a chuckle. 'I've walked amongst these people without suffering harm for years. Would you deny me the pleasure of offering the price of a meal to the hungry?'

She remembered him buying her a bowl of soup once, and felt ashamed – but still, she felt safer when they turned the corner into the crowd of pleasure-seekers queuing for the second sitting of the supper hall.

'I was afraid for you.' She shrugged. 'Or perhaps I was being selfish and didn't want to share you with anyone.'

'You're angry, and are reacting to that. I'm sorry your search for your father was fruitless. Are you very disappointed?'

'I wanted a hero, preferably a live one.' She offered him a quick smile. 'I used to rehearse what I'd say to Jackaby Laws if we ever met. At the moment I feel like a cat must when its prey disappears down a mouse-hole and escapes for good, just as it's about to pounce.'

'A good analogy.'

'I think I'm disappointed on behalf of my mother, rather than me. After all, I never knew him. At least I know what he was like, and his fate. My mother didn't. She always hoped he'd come back into her life. She would have been heartbroken had she known for certain she'd been duped, that he was married and that I ... I'm *illegitimate*.'

'Your mother married him in good faith, my dear. There's proof of their marriage in the parish records of the church they were married in. Only you, Daniel Laws, and myself know the truth of the matter, and that doesn't reflect on you in any way. Were I you I'd leave it at that, otherwise it might upset others who loved your mother.'

He meant Aunt Harriet. She nodded, willing to

bow to his superior wisdom in this. It wasn't until later, as the reverend hailed the cab, that she realized it was yet another unsavoury part of her past – and another reason why Charles Curtis would turn away from her.

It wasn't until they reached their destination and the cab turned to retrace its steps that Celia thought she saw the boy from the alley clinging to the back of the cab like a fly on a wall. Then they were gone from sight round the corner and she heard the horses pick up speed.

Charles could have sworn that he'd caught a glimpse of Thomas Hambert in the wings at the theatre, and he wondered if Celia was with him. As soon as he could he excused himself from the company of his companions and hurried backstage. His way was blocked by the figure of the stage manager. 'I'm afraid the public are not allowed backstage, sir.'

'I was looking for someone.'

'I daresay. One of the lady performers, was it?'

'It was the Reverend Thomas Hambert. I thought I saw him in the wings.'

'If I were you I'd try the church down the road.'

'He would have had a woman with him – a Miss Laws.'

'A pert little piece of goods with blue eyes and dark hair?'

Charles smiled at the description, and nodded.

'They were here ... They wanted to speak to Daniel Laws. They spent half an hour together, now they're gone ... It must be fifteen minutes, since.'

'What did they want with Daniel Laws?'

'I didn't ask them, sir, since it were none of my business. Because of the similarity in name, I assumed they were relatives. Now, would you mind leaving, sir? I have a theatre to run.'

'Could I speak to Daniel Laws then?'

'Not at the moment, sir, he's resting before the next show. If you'd like to buy a ticket for the next show you can see him afterwards perhaps.'

'I've just come from the first sitting, and I have companions waiting.' Charles slid his hand into his inside pocket. 'Just one minute with Mr Laws, perhaps.'

The manager smiled at the gesture. 'I don't take money for favours, so you're wasting my time as well as your own. That way out, sir, if you please. You'll be able to catch Mr Laws at the stage door when he leaves after the show. He'll be last on because he's top billing. Watch out for the beggars.'

Charles shrugged. They were attending the same musical function tomorrow evening. He'd simply ask Thomas Hambert, or Celia herself come to that, what they were doing backstage at the theatre. He was surprised that Celia hadn't mentioned having a relative who was a singer.

The next morning Thomas and Celia visited Potter's Field, where her mother was buried in her rough wooden coffin. Celia tried not to think of her lying beneath the earth in her ragged clothing, one of the many poor of the parish who were buried in great numbers, but without pomp.

Gone and forgotten quickly, their memories were lost in the ongoing need of their families to survive.

'I don't even know where she is now,' Celia said sadly, the tears gathering in her eyes. 'The grass has grown over her.'

'The earth has reclaimed her body, and her soul is in heaven.'

'Now you sound like a real reverend, sort of pompous.'

'It can't be helped since I am a real reverend; and my faith sustains me.'

'Tell me this, then, Reverend Thomas Hambert. What does a soul look like?'

He gazed sideways at her, grinned and murmured, 'You have to be initiated to be trusted with that secret.'

She dashed away her tears and grinned at him in return. 'What you mean is that you really don't know?'

'I didn't say that. Tell me about your mother's funeral while I gather my thoughts on this, Celia.'

'It was a sad day; the grass was soaked through from the mist rising from the earth. The ravens were cawing, and the bare twigs on the trees scribbled on the sky as if it were a slate.'

He gave a faint murmur of appreciation at her description.

'There was a gravedigger here with his son. He was gnarled-looking, and had calloused hands from working hard. Because there was no preacher here to say the words over the dead, he asked me if I'd like him to say a special prayer for my mother. He asked his dead wife to look after her in heaven, and his son told me that his father had always wanted to be a preacher. Then they wished us well and went off home. Lottie didn't realize what was going on. She needed...' Celia huffed out a laugh. 'Lottie said she needed ... to relieve herself.'

Thomas chuckled. 'About the soul, Celia ... it's one of God's great mysteries.'

'So you really don't know what a soul looks like ... admit it?'

'I do not think a soul has a shape and entity. It just is – and it's too complex a concept to really grasp, except we know it when it touches us. What was the name of the man who said the prayer over your mother?'

'Bert.' Her face screwed up in concentration. 'He called his dead wife Mary Holloway, so he must have been Bert Holloway. His support was comforting. It was nice to think that his wife might be waiting to look after my mother.'

'He offered you comfort, and in doing so his own soul was comforted. Mankind has pondered on the soul since he realized there was a God. Years ago a man called John Dryden wrote:

'Our souls sit close and silently within, and their own webs from their own entrails spin; and when eyes meet far off, our sense is such that spider-like, we feel the tenderest touch.'

She closed her eyes and thought about it, and the wind was a soft caress against her face and she remembered her mother alive, her beautiful

285

face illuminated by the candlelight as she bent to her sewing. She thought she felt her mother's fingers smooth the hair back from her face, remembered her smile and knew she was standing there beside her. For the briefest of moments Celia felt the touch of her lips against her cheeks and her name carried as a whisper on the wind. *'Celia ... my sweet Celia.'*

She opened her eyes and gazed at him through the tears flooding them. 'John Dryden was writing about love.'

'The line is from a play, a comedy called *Marriage-A-la-Mode*, which doesn't really relate to what we were talking about. But that line is so beautifully written and evocative, and as good an explanation of the existence of the soul that I've ever come across.'

'Can a soul feel the *tenderest* touch of those gone from us?'

'My dearest child, you're asking me if contact can be made with the dead. Tell me ... did you feel a connection here with your mother?'

She nodded. 'For just a moment I heard her whisper my name, then it slipped away like a wisp of smoke in the wind. It left me feeling ... oh, I don't know ... happy and sad at the same time, and reassured.'

'Then you have your answer. The soul is something so ethereal it can never really be understood. It's faith ... a mystery—'

'A secret known only to those initiated,' and she giggled. 'Sometimes I think you pretend to be one person when you're really another. You have answers for everything.'

'I just wish were there more people like you around, who can supply questions for those answers.' He gazed at her, half-smiling. 'There will be other times when you'll feel your soul at work, Celia. It's nothing tangible, just emotion, but experienced at a level so deep that we're incapable of understanding the source of it. We just have to accept that it's there.' He held out his arm. 'Now we must go. We have a musical evening to attend tonight, and tomorrow is our final engagement. But before we go I just want to say that knowing you has brought me great joy.'

'I treasure your friendship, and I always will.'

He gave a bit of a sigh. 'I think my work here in London is done. I'm looking forward to moving, where I'll be nearer to my family.'

He looked tired and Celia felt guilty for taking up his time and making him walk so far. 'You must rest before we get ready to go out tonight. I'm so looking forward to it.'

'Are you familiar with the works of Bach?'

'My Aunt Harriet has played a couple of pieces on the piano, and I liked them.'

'Then you're in for a wonderful evening, for an orchestra, soloists and a choral society will be performing his work. Charles Curtis mentioned that he might attend the performance.'

'Really,' she said as casually as she could, and her heart leaped, so she missed the faint smile he gave.

Nineteen

On the way home from Potter's Field Celia devised a plan to return the money to Charles. She'd never felt easy keeping it in her possession, knowing it was his, and what it represented to him.

When they returned to Bedford Square she wrapped the satchel in brown paper, tied it with string and wrote on it in her best hand, *Charles Curtis esquire*. Hesitating for a moment, she added in smaller letters, because he'd probably forgotten the beggar girl he'd given the money to, and she wanted him to think kindly of that girl she'd been, *from Lizzie Carter*.

She waited until the Reverend was asleep in his chair in front of the fire before fetching her parcel and concealing it under her shawl. 'I'm going out for a short while, Mrs Packer.'

'If you don't mind me saying so, the reverend wouldn't like you going out by yourself.'

'I'm going to buy him a book he was admiring and I want it to be a secret. I'll be back in time to take him his tea tray.' Indeed, she did have her eyes on a collection of the work of the poet, Edgar Allan Poe, as a gift for the reverend. She'd overheard him saying to someone that he'd heard that Poe's work had an uncomfortable dark edge to it that scared people, and he must read the American one day, and discover it for himself. Celia had checked his bookshelves and discovered he was indeed lacking a volume of Poe.

Reassured, Mrs Packer smiled. 'I won't tell him if he wakes up, but he usually naps for an hour or so after luncheon.'

Celia took Charles' card from her pocket and looked at the words scribbled on the back before replacing it in her purse. 'Oxford and Cambridge club ... Pall Mall,' she muttered.

She considered walking, but knew it would take her too long. With the latest royalties from the sale of the book she took a cab to the address. It was a men's club, and several of them were lingering in the porch. Celia kept her head down as she handed the parcel over to the doorman, for she didn't want to be noticed.

'You'll make sure he gets it, won't you?' she said, for it was a lot of money to hand over.

'Don't worry, Miss. We're expecting Mr Curtis. He's dining with some of his friends, so I'm sure he won't be long. If you'd like to wait for a few minutes you could hand it to him yourself ... We can't allow you inside the club, of course. Gentlemen only, you see. It would be against the rules.'

The breath left her body, and with some alarm in her eyes she gazed up at the man. 'I don't want to come into the club, and no, I can't hand it to him, and he mustn't see me,' she said, and she turned and ran back down to the waiting cab.

As they turned into Bedford Square Celia felt

jubilant. She'd paid it back. She no longer owed Charles Curtis anything, and a great weight had fallen from her shoulders.

'Lizzie Carter?' Charles tasted the name on his tongue as he turned the parcel over in his hands, trying to trigger his memory from the hand-writing, which seemed familiar, though he couldn't place it at the moment. 'What did the girl look like?'

'I only saw her for a moment, sir. She was a slim young woman with striking eyes, sir. Her dress was ordinary, not at all smart, and a little shabby. She kept her face shielded by her bonnet and only looked up once. That's when I caught a glimpse of her eyes. Very appealing, they were; the colour of cornflowers.'

'Ah yes.' Charles grinned as he remembered them, and the sooty sweep of her eyelashes against her cheek ... and the muddy face and tangled dark hair, of course. 'Don't wax too lyrical about her, Barton. The woman who left this parcel was a first-class pickpocket.'

Barton's mouth pursed, as though he'd swallowed a sour plum. 'And she looked like such a sweet young woman.'

Charles grinned, remembering his youthful lust for the girl who'd stolen his card case and returned it to claim a reward. He'd admired her spirit, and had discovered that, although she was a thief, she also had a moral code, and was not about to sell her body to him for any amount of money. Not even a bribe of one hundred pounds had tempted her to stray from the straight and narrow, it seemed.

'She *was* sweet, and innocent, but you'd better check your pockets anyway.'

Was she innocent still? Charles wondered, as he unwrapped the parcel. He encountered a small satchel that was very familiar to him, for his initials were tooled into the surface in gold. He hadn't expected her to return it, and he'd recalled that he'd asked her to get in touch when she was ready.

He smiled, hesitated, then smiled again as he gazed inside it to see if she'd written him a note. There wasn't one; the contents of the satchel were the same as when handed to her. The sharp folds and creases spoke of the notes being kept under something weighty – a book perhaps?

'Well, well ... you're an enigma, Lizzie Carter,' he murmured about the ragged young woman whose services he'd once tried to buy, and who'd placed such value on retaining her purity over a promise made to a dead mother. That was something he'd found touching at the time – still did. 'You must have decided I wasn't worth waiting for.'

Or perhaps she'd lost the satchel and someone honest had found it and returned it. But over three years had gone by since then. Although Charles had never really expected Lizzie to honour the bargain they'd made, he'd never expected to get the money back, either.

He'd entertained his friends and acquaintances with the story of the expensive beggar maid he'd tried to buy over the years – now he'd have a fitting ending to the tale.

He couldn't help wondering what had happened to the girl after all this time, though, and felt a twinge of conscience at making her the object of his jokes as he passed through into the dining room to be greeted by the laughter and chiding of his friends for his lateness. After all, it hadn't been Lizzie Carter's fault that she'd been born poor.

Celia had ordered the book she'd wanted from a bookshop not far from the house, and had been told they'd keep it under the counter for her. She left the cab there, and hurried home, relieved to find the reverend still sleeping off his lunch.

Head leaning against the right wing of his armchair, his sparse grey hair was disarranged, as though it had relaxed along with his body, and he gave an occasional quiet snuffle. His shoes stood side by side on the floor, while his feet rested on a shabby footstool. Affection for him raced through her when she saw a small hole in the heel of his black hose. The lump damming the tears in her throat was threatening to burst.

Taking in a deep breath to dispel the feeling, she wrote a note to go with her gift and tucked it under the red ribbon she'd tied round it. It read: To my beloved and finest friend, Reverend Thomas Hambert. No doubt you'll ask me why I've bought you a gift, so here is the answer – it's because you are you. Celia Jane Laws.

Being careful not to disturb him she picked up the fire tongs and carefully placed coal on the ashes so he wouldn't be cold when he woke. Positioning her gift in a prominent position on the table in front of him, Celia went to the writing desk, where she took out paper and ink and began to write part three of her magazine serial.

When the clock chimed three Thomas woke with a grunt. 'Goodness, is that the time already? I must have drifted off to sleep.'

'I'll go and prepare the tea tray.'

'Thank you, dear. Ask Mrs Packer if there's any of that delicious fruit cake left, if you would.'

'I'm sure there is, since she hid half of it in the larder, so you wouldn't eat it all at once.'

'I do like fruit cake,' he said with a laugh. His glance fell on the book with the gaudy ribbon bow. With a puzzled expression on his face he reached into his pocket for his reading glasses and said in a wondering manner, 'Hello ... What's this parcel doing on the table?'

'Waiting to be opened by you,' and Celia kissed his forehead and left him to it.

The music recital was held in the hall of a large home of an earl, on the west side of Belgrave Square. He was a patron of the arts as well as the Poor Reform Society, and he'd sponsored the concert ... or so the reverend had told her.

The orchestra was seated on a raised dais along with the solo artists. The choral singers were ranged up the staircase.

Celia had felt quite the lady in her blue skirt and evening bodice, until she set her eyes on the fashionable women with their satin, lace and feathers, flashing diamonds and affectations.

The chairs were numbered, and arranged in a fan shape. Their seats were near the back, a few seats away from a plinth – one of many that supported sculptures of composers, now long gone. There was an empty chair beside them. For Charles, she guessed.

The reverend named some of the sculptures for her, Ludwig Van Beethoven, who glowered at the assembly of people. Then there was George Frideric Handel, Wolfgang Amadeus Mozart, and Johann Sebastian Bach, whose music she was going to listen to before too long. He had rather an austere face, and his hairstyle – a wig, she imagined – was dressed in precise rolls that reminded her of sausages.

The air was becoming warm with all the people crowding in, and the hall that she'd first considered huge, now seemed a great deal smaller as everyone scrambled to find their seats. Thankful for the small fan she carried in her reticule, she slipped the cord over her wrist and put it to good use as she tried to make sense of the printed programme. What on earth were oratorios and cantatas? She must ask the reverend to explain the terms to her tomorrow. More and more she was realizing how wide a gulf existed between different social environments, and the opportunities available to them.

Celia was glad she wasn't sitting amongst the ladies in their finery, where she would have contrasted badly, despite wearing her best gown – the one the reverend had bought for her, with a pretty lace collar. She wore short gloves too, and an embroidered shawl that Mrs Packer had lent her, because Celia had been worried that the neck of the gown was lower than was decent. Now she was here, she needn't have worried, since most of the other ladies' gowns were much lower.

The audience was a pickpocket's dream, she thought irreverently, and she glanced over the crowd wondering if anyone was working it. But no, this audience was too expensive and too rarefied for the average dip, who wouldn't be able to afford the entry fee, or get past the doorman even if they could. There might be a few beggars in the street when the concert was over and the guests were all waiting for carriages to arrive.

There was a buzz in the room that affected her like a glass of wine. She smiled happily at the reverend, distinguished-looking in his evening suit, and wondered if Charles was in the audience.

The crowd was soon settled, the conductor came on to the dais, bowing to much applause before turning to face the orchestra. There was a breathless hush, then he lifted his baton and the music began – glorious music that instantly transported her from being a mere mortal into a world of sound so enthralling, that she wondered if she'd ever breathe again.

Standing a little to one side, for he'd been a little late and didn't want to disturb the row to reach his seat, Charles stood, partially concealed by the plinth, where Beethoven frowned upon him for his tardiness.

He could almost smell Celia, the occasional drift of roses teasing at his nostrils. He wryly congratulated himself on being able to single her perfume out in a hall filled with ladies, when, in fact, the massed fragrance was more like a flower garden in high summer.

He had a good view of her lovely profile, and a good view of some of the men stealing looks at her, some more assessing than they should be. He blessed the fact that he'd been born a hunter instead of the prey. As most people were acquainted with and respected the reverend, he knew she would not be approached within these walls.

Unlike the play, where Celia's face had reflected the drama, and she'd leaned forward to offer little comments under her breath, she was completely absorbed by the music. She sat upright, but relaxed, smiling a little, or giving a small nod when she was transported into the arrangement of notes. Sometimes her eyes closed, or a runaway tear escaped from under her lids to be captured on the square of lace-edged lawn she carried, and he wondered what was going on inside her head. She clapped enthusiastically when the interval was announced.

Charles joined them at the refreshment table, handing her a glass of lemonade. 'I'm sorry I was late ... in fact I've been running late all day. I'm pleased to see you kept my seat vacant, Reverend.'

Celia had a slightly wary expression on her face. 'Did anything exciting happen today to make you late?'

'I dined at my club with some friends, then we went to the Bailey to watch a fraud trial. Time slipped by. Are you enjoying the music, Celia?'

Her face lit up. 'It's wonderful; I've never heard a real orchestra and choir before, except in Hyde Park. The notes have such clarity, as if...' Her eyes began to shine. 'As if icicles were dropping from a branch into a pond, making perfect ripples. It's precise, yet relaxing ... so exquisite that I feel like crying. This is the best night of my life and I want it to go on for ever.'

Charles exchanged a smile with Thomas. 'Bach will be dancing in his grave at that endorsement, I imagine.'

She gave in to a moment of flirtation when the reverend turned aside to greet someone, spreading her fan and gazing over it at him from wide eyes a mesmerizing shade of blue that were circled by a sweep of sooty lashes. Cornflowers, the porter had said. *Cornflowers!* No, it couldn't be his Lizzie. He was being ridiculous. Yet the handwriting had seemed familiar. He couldn't help but ask, 'What did you get up to today, Celia?'

She started, as though she'd just realized that her gesture might be misconstrued as personal interest in him, then folded her fan and averted her gaze. 'Very little. We visited my mother's grave this morning.'

'How long has your mother been gone?'

'Getting on for four years. I do miss her.'

'It wasn't a good age for a young woman to lose her mother, I imagine.'

'No it wasn't, but then, when is any age a good

297

one? I understand you lost your father when you were younger, so I expect the same applies to you.'

He gently touched her hand. 'You never get over losing someone you love, but the pain does grow less over time.'

'After our visit to Potter's Field, Celia was kind enough to keep an old man company for the rest of the day,' Thomas interjected. 'And she gave me a gift, a volume of Edgar Allen Poe's work.'

'I wouldn't have thought that the darkness of the human spirit would be of interest to you, Reverend. Some people regard Poe as being not quite sane.'

'An interesting man for that reason alone, I'd say, and his work might offer some insight into that unhappy condition. He seems a very accomplished poet nevertheless.'

'Perhaps he has an unhappy soul,' Celia said giving a huff of laughter, which caused Thomas to chuckle, as if each had complete understanding of the other.

Thomas allowed Charles the privilege of sitting next to her in this public setting. Charles was very aware of her by his side, but involved with the music as she was, to his chagrin she didn't seem to notice him at all.

She pandered to her own senses, feasting on the music like someone who'd been totally starved of such a delight in the past. Idly, he wondered if she'd indulge in lovemaking with such an all-absorbing passion. One day he hoped to find out.

Her eyes were full of dreams when the music ended. They fetched their cloaks and went out into the street – walking into a thin fog that had crept out of the River Thames to try and rob the streets of their identity.

Charles managed to find a cab. 'I'll accompany you all the way home, since it's a long way and this will probably thicken.'

The reverend protested. 'Charles, your home is the closer, is it not? We could leave you there and travel on.'

'I was going to sleep at my club tonight, but I wouldn't be able to sleep if I didn't escort you both safely to your destination. No doubt you'll offer me a bed for the night should it be needed.'

The fog did thicken, and the cabbie said apologetically, 'Sorry, sir, but I'll have to leave you here. I was on my way home when I picked you up. If I'm lucky I'll just have time to get there in time to bed my horse down before it worsens. Luckily, the horse knows its own way home.'

And worse the fog got, pressing against the house like a clammy mustard-coloured shroud, a bare ten minutes after the sound of horse and cab disappeared.

Her little reticule still swinging from her wrist by its loops, Celia turned back the cover in the second guest bedroom, her fingers unconsciously smoothing the pillow where Charles' head would rest. She lit the fire, placing the spark guard back around it before going to her own room to remove her bonnet and cloak.

The two men were in the library sipping at a

brandy when she went down. 'Would you like some supper? I expect Mrs Packer has left something cold in the larder for us.'

The kitchen was in the basement, and was a large room hung with shining copper pots. The house was built to accommodate a large family and a staff to match. The reverend barely occupied the first two floors.

The cellar she'd once lived in with her mother and Lottie would have fitted in this domestic kingdom twice over.

Through the door was a second room with a copper tub, under which a fire could be lit to boil the water. There was a mangle with big wooden rollers that squeezed water from the garments once they were clean. Overhead were some racks, with pulleys to lower them down, so garments could be hung to dry. The ironing was done on a padded table, and there was a place down here to bathe in private ... something Celia loved. When she was married and had her own house she intended to take a bath every day and wash away the memories of the dirt of her childhood. And she'd have pots with bright flowers on every table, if she could afford them.

There was a plate containing slices of pork pie, cheese, pickles and bread on a covered marble slab in the larder. The tea tray was laid, the black iron kettle warm and set to one side of the stove so it wouldn't boil dry. Celia lifted the kettle on to the hob, then added a third cup and saucer to the tray. She was not hungry herself. Her head was full of the music, which had given her a sense of contentment as well as wonder that a man could create such delight from just a few notes of music.

Just as the kettle began to sing she thought she heard a noise outside the window. She drew aside the lace curtain that hid the interior of the room from outsiders and pressed her face against the glass. All she could see was the bottom couple of steps and a railing.

Her heart began to thump. Then she heard a plaintive whine, followed by a yelp. She smiled when she saw a puppy on the step. The poor creature must have lost its way. Well, Frederick's basket was vacant, and she was sure he wouldn't mind her lending it to a poor lost pup for the night.

Unlocking the door she pulled it open and stepped outside, stooping to pick it up. Arms closed around her and a hand covered her mouth.

'Got you,' someone grunted.

Celia lashed out with feet and her hands; her reticule was ripped from her wrist and thrown aside, scattering bits and pieces. Her hair came loose.

Something dropped on Celia's head and a peculiar numbing pain shot through her. Her knees gave and she slumped against a man's body. She wanted to scream, but all she could manage was a sigh before all consciousness fled.

A little while later, Thomas gazed at his watch and frowned. 'Celia is being a long time.'

'Perhaps she's forgotten us and has decided to write an account of the concert instead.'

'No, she'd be too excited after the concert to

settle to that.' He rose to his feet. 'I'm going to check on her.'

'I'll join you. If nothing else I can carry the supper tray up.'

They felt the clammy cold that was pervading the house before they reached the kitchen, where the door stood wide open inviting the fog inside. The trays stood ready, the kettle was boiling, and had been for some time, for the lid was giving off a furious rattle.

Thomas moved it to one side and called out Celia's name as he went to investigate the laundry room.

Charles had gone outside. He was filled with unease. Something had happened to her ... he sensed it. The night pressed in on him. There was a yap, and he saw a pup on the step. In the act of picking it up he noticed her reticule on the step, the string broken and the contents scattered over the steps. He scooped it up along with the pup and inspected his immediate surrounds, walking up and down the fog-shrouded street.

He found no sign of Celia, only a metal button ripped from a man's coat at the top of the steps, which could have been anyone's. There were also signs of a handcart having been there, the line of a wheel and a heel mark in some horse dung.

They'd not heard a horse and cart, or any signs of a struggle, but they'd been in the back room, and the fog muffled most noises. It would be useless trying to find her in the fog, since Charles couldn't see more than a yard in front of his face. Even the street lamp was a sickly, yellow glow suspended above, and it sent out no useful light.

'I think she may have been abducted,' he told the worried-looking Thomas, 'and by somebody who knows his way around, even in a fog such as this one. My guess is, this pup was used to lure her out. I found her purse on the step, and the ribbon is broken.'

'Why would anyone abduct Celia?'

'For ransom, I should imagine.'

'I must search the entire house. She may have fallen somewhere.'

They searched it together, and there was no sign of her. They searched it again, with the same result, then went back down to the kitchen again.'

Thomas took the pup from Charles, gave it a dish of milk to lap and settled it in Frederick's basket afterwards. There, it curled up and went to sleep. 'It's a pity the animal can't speak,' he said. 'We must inform a constable of what has happened, Charles.'

The unconscious gesture of caring for the puppy touched Charles. The reverend was a gentle and sincere man who acted from the dictates of his heart.

He spread the contents of Celia's bag on the table to see if they held any clue – a pencil and diary, a handkerchief and a couple of coins. He picked a card up and gazed at it. It was his ... an old one, black on white. He used gold-embossed now, to impress his clients. It also looked more professional. He flipped the card over. The name of his club was scrawled on the back in his own handwriting.

There was an instant recall ... of the beggar girl called Lizzie who he'd lusted over; she with beguiling blue eyes ... of a satchel containing one hundred pounds or so, that he'd won at the card table.

'Contact me when you're ready,' he'd said after he'd kissed her, all arrogance, and not even bothering to act the gentleman, because he'd not long been initiated into the delights of love-making and had been suffering all the tortures of a randy tom from the moment he first set eyes on her. He hadn't known much about attracting women apart from paying for the services of a professional, something that satisfied his body and left his heart untouched.

He'd initially asked Bessie to approach the girl for him with an offer no self-respecting beggar, or brothel owner, could refuse.

But Lizzie Carter *had* refused.

Lizzie Carter! He remembered it now. It *had* been Celia's writing on the wrapping paper!

As he thought of Bessie his blood ran cold. The pimp wouldn't have forgotten the money he'd dangled under her nose, nor forgiven the girl who'd deprived her of it.

'No constables please, Reverend. Not yet. I think I know where Celia might be and it would only put her in more danger. There's nothing we can do until morning, except wander around in the fog. Now ... I'm of the mind that we need to have a chat. I want to know everything there is to know about Celia Laws and her background ... including the reason why you were both at the

304

theatre visiting a man called Daniel Laws.'

Thomas looked troubled. 'I cannot break her confidence.'

'You might have to if you don't want her fate on your conscience. If it will help, I'll tell you where and when I first set eyes on her. It was about four years ago. I was with a group of my acquaintances and we were making bets on the outcome of a rat and terrier contest. Celia ... though I didn't know her name then, was reciting poetry. She was none too happy with the terrier promoter for moving in on her patch, but there was nothing she could do about it. I tossed her sixpence and she smiled at me and walked off. I was enchanted by her, and hung around the place at every opportunity, hoping I'd see her again.'

'She was just a child then, you a fully grown man.'

'I couldn't tell how old she was because she wore some shapeless rags. I thought she was older. It wasn't until later that I realized how young she was ... that was after she'd stolen my card case. But she didn't lack in ingenuity; she returned it and claimed a reward for finding it.'

Thomas started, then chuckled. 'I've had that experience myself.'

A tender smile spread across Charles' face, though he wasn't about to tell Thomas about the one hundred pounds he'd given Celia. 'She told me her name was Lizzie Carter, and that her mother had just died and she had a baby sister to raise. She said she was going to the country to live.'

'That's exactly what she did.'

'I finished my education, did the tour and then moved to Dorset to join your nephew's practice. You know the rest. Lizzie Carter often came into my mind, but I didn't realize that she and Celia Laws was one and the same person, until tonight. She's changed ... grown into a beautiful woman. Now ... perhaps you'd tell me about Daniel Laws. Who is he?'

'Celia thought he might be her father.' Thomas sighed. 'He isn't her father, just a distant relative. He did know her father in the past though. Jackaby Laws died before she was born.'

He made the tea, and the two men sat at the kitchen table and ate the supper Mrs Packer had provided. Though both were frantic with worry and neither of the men were really hungry they knew there would be no sleep for them that night.

'I'm taking it as read that Mrs Laws was left destitute by her husband.'

'Mrs Laws was a decent women who came from a good home, Charles. Having met her I can vouch for that. She fell on hard times, and did her best to cope with her situation.'

'I've seen that home for myself, and met Celia's Aunt Harriet.'

'So you have.' Thomas folded his arms on his chest. 'That's all I'm prepared to tell you. It's up to Celia if she wishes to confide in you in the future ... but don't count on it. I'd advise you not to push her.'

When Celia woke it felt as though her head had been pulped. Blackness pressed in on her. Cold

306

invaded her bones and she began to shiver, so her teeth chattered together like a bag of loose bones. She was in a cellar, she thought. The damp air contained all sorts of foul vapours, most of which she'd smelled before, and had tried to forget.

She was on a pile of rough sacks. Lifting one arm her fingertips touched against the ceiling. She swung them outwards and touched a wall either side. Squeaks and rustles scattered before her as, getting to her knees, she crawled around her prison, exploring the slimy wall as she measured the space. There was hardly any headroom and she couldn't stand.

And her beautiful gown would be ruined, she thought, the female in her coming to the fore, because when all was said and done it was the least of her worries.

Panic nearly overtook her when she discovered there was no door, so no way to get out – and that thought made her feel as though she was suffocating.

'Be sensible. There must be a way out, otherwise they wouldn't have got you in here,' she whispered, the sound of her own voice calming her a little.

And there was a draught, from above. Feeling along the ceiling, she traced the directions of the floorboards, and two cuts across, where a trapdoor had been fashioned.

Lying on her back in the dirt she placed her feet against the trapdoor and applied pressure. It didn't give an inch. There was something heavy over it.

If they'd intended to kill her she'd be dead by now, so whoever had abducted her would be revealed sooner or later. In the meantime she intended to conserve her strength in case she got the chance to escape. One thing was certain. If they demanded a ransom the reverend would pay it, and he'd call out the constables and have them all arrested.

Sinking back on to the sacks she curled up, and, ignoring her aching head and the other long-legged inhabitants of her prison, she thought of something more pleasant, the music she'd heard earlier...

Twenty

It was still foggy the next morning, but it had thinned enough to be able to see a few yards in either direction.

Word was circulating underground, for a private event was to take place just after dark, and was to be settled quickly before the authorities got to hear of it.

The amusement was only for a select few ... those gentlemen who could afford to pay the large price demanded for a certain pleasure. They would examine the goods and place their bids independently. The whole business would be over and done with in half an hour.

The merchandise they bought would be

spirited away and, if taken on board one of the ships that pushed and shoved at each other in the crowded river berths, would probably never be seen again, until years later, when they might turn up in some foreign bawdy house, coarsened and diseased.

Charles sent a note to Thomas Hambert informing him of his suspicions. He begged him to leave the matter in his hands and remain patient. Then he gathered his colleagues together, men he'd spent his learning years with – men he could trust.

'It could be dangerous. Bessie will have her wolf pack hidden around every corner, and they'll be armed to the teeth. If they smell a rat we'll be done for, so if any of you want to back out, do it now.'

Bart Granger, crack pistol shot, fencing champion and physician, examined his nails. 'Are we allowed to know who this girl is, Chas?'

'I would rather she survived this without the embarrassment of knowing others were aware of her identity, or what's taken place.'

'I see. Am I to understand that your heart is engaged here, not just your balls.'

'It is.'

'Commiserations.'

'You won't say that when you see her.'

The two men picked up their cloaks, and Bart said gently, 'All the more reason to rescue the maiden then. There are eight of us. They'll go in two by two, and take out the wolves while you're placing your bid. We've emptied our strong-boxes. What will you do if it's not enough?'

'Abduct her, or die in the attempt,' Charles said grimly. 'You may present your notes to my step-father if I do. I've made Joshua Harris aware of the situation.'

A wolfish grin crossed Bart's face. 'Nothing will happen to you, not while I'm guarding your back. You know, I'm quite looking forward to this.'

'Who's driving the carriage?'

Edmund Sedgley, breeder of thoroughbred horses, thwacked a sand-filled leather ned against his palm. He was enveloped in an old cloak and wore a ragged fabric cap for his role of cab driver. 'Me, of course. We'll be exactly where I said I'd be ... at the back entrance. There will be several soldiers standing about, courtesy of my cousin's regiment, with side arms ready to use, or to cause a little mayhem with, while the escape takes place. You know, Chas, this is typical of you if your tale about that girl you told us is true. What's the problem, can't you get yourself a woman in the usual manner?'

Charles shrugged. 'This is no ordinary woman.'

'Poor Chas, he's in love, and needs us to help him get the girl,' one of the others said and they all laughed. 'All right, let us go about our business, gentlemen.'

They patted him on the back, then Charles and Bart left together and climbed into the waiting carriage.

'Where you going, Guv?' Edmund asked gruffly, getting into his role.

'Seven Dials, my man,' Bart said. 'His highness has business to conduct there.' He turned to his friend. 'May I know her name, Chas? If you are incapacitated—'

'You must get her out, Bart. Her name is Celia Laws. Take her to my mother and stepfather, they'll know what to do, and inform the Reverend Thomas Hambert.'

'Edmund is right, you know, this does have a sameness about it. It's not the same girl as before by any chance, is it?'

Charles gave him a wry smile. 'She handed my money back, and I fell in love with her all over again.'

Bart whistled. 'You're faithful ... I'll give you that. I hope this girl is worthy of you. You'll never live this down, you do know that.'

'I will if you don't tell anyone.'

'In that case you have my absolute confidence. Have you got a weapon on you?'

'My fists.'

'You weren't the college boxing champion for nothing, I suppose,' and as the cab began to slow down Bart took two masks from inside his cloak, handing one to Charles. He held out his hand. 'Are you ready, Your Highness?'

Charles managed a faint grin as he took it. It seemed childish, dressing up, but necessary if they were to remain anonymous. He admitted to a vague sense of excitement at the thought of the coming stoush. 'Ready.'

If her seething fury got any worse than it was at this moment, she would explode!

Earlier, Bessie and a couple of her employees

311

had dragged her out of her dirty tomb, and into a room with nothing but a red-velvet chair, a bed, and a few drifting curtains as furnishings. There, she'd been told to remove her clothing.

When she'd put up a struggle the clothes had been ripped from her back. Water was poured over her to get rid of the dust. Then Bessie Jones instructed two of her hard-faced whores to hold Celia down. The whoremonger had stuck her dirty hands up Celia's skirt. The examination had been intimate and horrible, causing Celia to squirm with embarrassment.

'She's still intact,' Bessie said with satisfaction.

They'd dressed her again, in a virginal white gown of opaque fabric. One of Bessie's girls had brushed her hair out so it fell in shining ripples down her back.

'Lie on the bed with your arms behind your head and one knee up,' Bessie said.

'Go to hell, you witch.'

'Don't make it hard for yourself.' Bessie slapped her face, but lightly, so as not to mark it, then pushed her on to the bed and manacled her wrists with a short chain to a metal ring at the top of the bedhead. 'Now, girl, either you cooperate, or I'll chain your ankles as well and invite a couple of my men to take a whip to you. My clients will like that.'

There was a small window in the wall, curtained on the other side with the same opaque material. Now and again, someone's face would appear, usually a man.

'Help me,' she shouted out when this happened, then realized from the leers and the excitement in their expressions that they were bidders, and enjoying her predicament. From then on she closed her eyes and was able to calm herself. It was some sort of act Bessie had put on for their benefit, and she didn't intend to knowingly be part of it.

Celia was dying of thirst, and now she was unable to scratch, she itched all over. The furniture was probably full of fleas.

'Undo the manacles and I'll behave,' she pleaded when she saw Bessie at the window, for she felt at a decided disadvantage with them on. 'And give me something to drink. I'm parched.'

The curtain closed without an answer.

'What's going on?' she said when the woman came in, carrying a jug of water. 'Are you charging those pigs a fee to look at me?'

'I'm auctioning you off to the highest bidder.'

The colour faded from Celia's face as her fear came back. 'You can't.'

Bessie chuckled. 'Try and stop me.' She tipped the jug of water over Celia's breasts and it ran down over her stomach and thighs, and soaked into the mattress. Goosebumps raced over her as the material clung. 'There, that shows your assets off a little better for the clients.' Tipping the jug the rest of the way she held it against Celia's lips. Celia greedily lapped up the mouthful she managed to get before Bessie removed the jug. It was hardly enough for a good swallow. 'At least take the manacles off,' she pleaded.

'They stay for the moment. They add a nice touch, I think. I've got my two best gentlemen about to bid. One of them is an aristocrat from Venice. They both want to come in and get a closer look at you. Here's your drink.' The rest of the water hit her in the face with such a rush that Celia gasped as she nearly choked on it.

When she recovered she set eyes on three men. All wore black dinner suits, and two wore identical masks. The third man had a paunch and wore a bushy moustache. He looked to be about fifty. The expression on his face was wolfish. He came to gaze down at her, then leaned forward and reached out towards her breasts, his mouth almost slavering.

One of the masked men said with soft menace, 'Keep your hands off zee merchandise if you value your life, my friend. The final bids aren't in yet.'

The second masked man placed a restraining hand on his arm. 'Allow me to gut him for you, Highness.'

His Highness threw a disdainful 'Hah!' into the air, as if he was some amateur thespian hero in a melodrama, with more dash than acting talent.

Her eyes narrowed in on him. She'd give him melodrama – she'd give them all melodrama when she got these damned manacles off. Celia shuddered at the thought of any of them touching her. She kicked out at the man with the paunch when he leered at her. He grunted when her heel connected with his knee. She would have aimed it higher, but she couldn't reach.

He laughed the attack off. 'I'll soon have you tamed, girl. I'll take a riding crop to you and ride you from here to John O' Groats.' Turning to

Bessie he whispered something in her ear. His offer for her, she supposed.

Eyes gleaming, Bessie beckoned to the other two men. The taller man strutted forward. His hair curled from under the brim of his hat, and his eyes glittered darkly through the slits as he gazed down at her.

'Lay one finger on me you Venetian turkey cock and I'll kick you so hard you won't be able to fluff your tail feathers for a week,' she hissed. She remembered her feet were bare and it would hurt her more than him. 'After that I'll gouge your beady chicken eyes out – Highness or not.'

The noise he made was halfway between a growl and a laugh. He reached out anyway, and his finger traced a path down her cheek and over the contours of her mouth – his touch so gentle that it raised little shivers at the nape of her neck. It might be preferable to have a man who touched her gently, if she couldn't find a way to escape.

Then again, it might not. He was like all the others, except he smelled better.

A sardonic twitch pulled his lips sideways and his gaze ran over the clinging garment she wore. 'Iz zat so, girl? I shall haff to be careful then.' Lazily, he said to Bessie, 'The girl izza sweet little trollop. I'll take her.'

'You haven't put in a bid yet,' Bessie said, her fists going to her hips.

'Name zee price you want and let's be done wizz it, woman.'

The other man gave a bit of a snort that turned into a cough.

Bessie became all business. 'She'll cost you one thousand pounds, Highness.'

'Zat is perfecto.' The man didn't so much as blink, but waved a languid hand towards the other masked man, who was probably his servant. The stone in the ring on his little finger picked up a beam of light from the candle, and dazzled her eyes. 'Pay zee old crone. Take zee manacles off her, Mizzis Bessie.'

'Money first.'

'The foreigner has more money than sense,' the paunchy man sneered. 'You wouldn't catch me paying that amount of money for a common whore.'

'No decent whore would want you,' Celia spat at him, and the masked servant guffawed with laughter.

The man walked away, banging the door behind him.

The servant removed a roll of paper money from the top of the satchel he had hidden under his cloak. He handed the satchel containing the rest to Bessie, who began to count it. Celia recognized that satchel with its gold lettering, and her heart began to thump. She'd seen it often enough.

Charles was either very brave, or very stupid to have walked in here and put in a bid for her. Then she remembered the state she was in. She was practically naked! What would he think of her now?

It didn't matter, because Bessie had finished her inspection of the satchel and was leaning over her. Celia could see the bulging satchel stuffed down her bodice. She was not going to allow the woman to get away with this—

When the manacles dropped from her wrists she lunged upwards, giving a scream as she let her anger free, and grasping Bessie by the hair, she wrestled her to the floor. Sitting astride the woman's stomach she began to pummel her.

Bessie heaved about, throwing threats and foul curses into the air. Her skirt edged up and there was a knife strapped to her thigh. It came from its sheath with hardly a whisper when Celia's fingers closed around it.

'This is on behalf of my mother,' Celia said, twisting Bessie's nose between her finger and thumb, so she gave a nasal scream.

'Your mother had too many airs and graces. She thought she was better than the rest of us but I soon showed her who was boss.' Bessie managed to get a couple of slaps in, which incensed Celia even more.

'She was better than you, you heap of...' Something warned her not to be too vulgar. *'Rubbish!'* To hell with it, this was not the time or place to act the lady. Celia dug the blade into Bessie's bodice and deftly slashed it from bosom to waist.

'She's killed me,' Bessie screamed.

'Not yet, I haven't.' Celia pricked the knife against the whore's neck. Suddenly she remembered a line from a play in her time with the Wentworth Players, and said with great menace, 'Stop squawking, you heap of flea bites, else I'll carve a smile where one wasn't intended to be.'

Bessie fell quiet.

Charles' glance fell on the knife, and he cursed

soundly before he said, 'She's not worth swinging for.'

Celia felt hysterical laughter building up inside her, because he'd forgotten his accent. 'She thought nothing of selling me to you. For that, I'm going to kill her. Then I'm going to kill you for buying me from her. How dare you ... *Your Royal Highness?*'

Bessie began to wriggle. 'Don't kill me! Don't kill me!'

Charles' voice mirrored his irritation. 'For pity's sake, shut up, woman. She's not killing anyone. Drop that knife. *Now!*' He roared.

Celia dropped the knife, and Charles kicked it aside.

The man with him began to laugh.

Bessie took the opportunity to start struggling again. Celia didn't quite know what to do, since she'd achieved her objective. The matter was taken out of her hands when Charles pulled Bessie out from under and winded her with a punch. Then his cloak dropped over Celia and she was wrapped in a tight bundle.

Still struggling, despite her arms being immobilized, she was scooped up and thrown over his shoulder. Bumped along a corridor and up some steps, after a few seconds she felt cold damp air against her face. He placed her down, and the cobbles were rough and clammy under her feet.

There came a gunshot then, from not far off, followed by the sound of a police whistle.

Celia was pushed into a carriage head first and a pair of feet pinned her to the floor by her shoulders. 'Keep your head down,' he warned, then said, 'Bart, are you still with us?'

'Of course. That was my shot ... a signal to the others. What are we waiting for Edmund? I'm hanging off the back of the carriage like a fly on a donkey's tail. Let's go before the old hag marshals her forces.'

'She'll have the constables to contend with as well, now,' Edmund said, roaring with laughter. 'Look at them all spilling into the street. There's quite a melee going on, and the soldiers are in the midst of it.' He raised his voice and cracked his whip over the horse's head, shouting authoritatively, 'I have His Royal Highness in my cab and I'm coming through – so out the way, unless you want to end up under my wheels.'

The horse gave a surprised, whinnying dance, then they were off at a trot, rocking over the cobbles. Within seconds the fog had swallowed them up and the conveyance was forced to slow down as the driver tried to get his bearings, and began to pick his way more carefully. As soon as they got out of the slums and into the wider streets, the fog thinned.

Celia's shoulders were beginning to hurt from the pressure of the feet keeping her pinned to the floor. Feeling slightly savage over the way he was treating her, she turned her head and bit Charles' ankle.

She was pulled up on to the seat. 'Ouch! What did you do that for?'

Celia found herself pulled up into the seat. 'You were treading on me, and it was painful.'

'I'm sorry. I wanted you out of the way of any flying bullets.'

She shrank into the corner, gazing at him. The excitement of the rescue had turned to sludge in her stomach, and she felt sick. She didn't know what to say to him – didn't know what he must be thinking. Charles still had his mask in place. Did he think she hadn't recognized him?

She tried a little humour, though her emotional state was as far from amused as it could get. 'You can take zee stupid mask off now, Charles.'

He gave a low chuckle and removed it. 'I'd forgotten I was still wearing it.'

The hysteria she'd been bottling up exploded from her in a welter of tears and laughter. 'I hate you, Charles ... I hate all men. I want my aunt.' She gave a short scream of frustrated rage. 'I'll never speak to you again ... never!'

'Enough, Celia,' he said sharply. 'You're safe now, and you're being hysterical. Take in some deep breaths and gather your wits together.'

It was enough to bring her to her senses. 'I feel sick,' she said, her voice shaking.

He shouted for Edmund to stop the carriage, and opened the door for her. She could only dry retch. She hadn't eaten or drunk anything for a while, so that explained why. She gave a small scream when a figure appeared from behind the carriage.

'It's all right. It's my friend, Bart. I'll introduce you properly some other time.'

Bart gave her a smile then turned to Charles. 'I'm going back to the club while I can still find my way. I'll see you later.'

'Ask them to put some champagne on ice.'

As soon as the man disappeared the carriage

began to move again. Charles gathered her against him and she could feel the steady beat of his heart against her ear. 'Are you all right ... were you *ill-treated?*'

'I was kept in a hole under the floor. I had nothing to eat or drink and I was stripped of my clothing and made to wear that ... *garment.* Bessie put water on it so it would cling to my body. I felt so ashamed.'

'From what I saw you have nothing to feel ashamed of.'

'You don't understand, Charles. It was the faces of the men as they looked at me through that window ... as though I was nothing but a piece of meat for sale. Only another woman could understand the loathsome feeling that comes with it. They made my skin crawl ... saw me as something I didn't want to be.'

'Of course you didn't.'

'But I would have been if I hadn't fled from the slums to leave my past behind.' But for all this time, the past had been waiting to remind her of what she was and where she had come from. She started to shake as the horror of her ordeal began to sink in. 'I don't want to talk about what happened. I just want to go home, go to bed, go to sleep and forget about it.'

'You can't sleep for ever.'

'I can try.' She realized she was being churlish. 'I haven't thanked you for rescuing me. Thank you, Charles. Thank your friends on my behalf, as well. I'm truly grateful and I hope nobody got hurt.'

There was a quiver of a smile in his voice. 'My

friends can take care of themselves. Believe me, they would have enjoyed that little brawl.'

'I'm glad somebody did. The reverend must be sick with worry about me.'

A smile touched his lips. 'I imagine he'll be relieved to see you. You've made a good friend there.'

His breath stirred warmly against her scalp. 'Charles ... let me go,' she pleaded, for she didn't want to feel close to him.

'Let you go? But I've just paid one thousand pounds to get you back.'

She knew the remark was an attempt at humour. It was a great deal of money – a great deal, and if love was measured by money she was worth a lot to him. But it wasn't. Love had no price. It was an exchange of emotion and trust. At the moment she no longer trusted anyone, including Charles, for he'd looked her over in exactly the same way as the other men had, with the need to conquer and possess in his eyes.

'I was never yours to begin with,' she said dispiritedly.

'You've been mine since the first moment I set eyes on you, and you know it, *Lizzie Carter*.' He tipped up her chin, placed a brief kiss on her mouth and allowed her to remove herself from his embrace.

They turned into Bedford Square, stopping outside the reverend's house. Tiredness crept over her when the door opened and the reverend stood there in the misty yellow light. He looked like her guardian angel.

'I'm not yours, Charles. I can never be yours.'

She shoved the satchel into his hands and sniffed back her tears. 'Here's your money. I always knew my skills would be used for good one day.' She gently kissed his cheek, knowing she was heartsick. 'You've been a good friend and that's all you can ever be. Go back to your club and celebrate with your friends ... Goodnight.'

He looked at the satchel, clearly astounded. 'How did you get hold of this?'

'Did you really think I attacked Bessie Jones with no purpose in mind but to kill her?' Tears beginning to trickle down her cheeks, she descended from the carriage when the reverend opened the door for her.

Thomas had a relieved smile on his face. 'You're safe, Celia.'

'Yes ... I'm safe.'

'Thank God, my prayers were answered.'

Somehow, Celia rustled up a smile to match her mentor's. 'Thank the Prince of Venice, instead.'

He looked puzzled. 'The Prince of Venice?'

'No doubt Charles will enlighten you.'

'Charles, I cannot thank you enough,' he said effusively. 'Will you come in?'

'I've arranged to meet my friends, sir,' the man who loved her more than an astounding one thousand pounds said.

His friends would laugh over her predicament and the evening's events would become an adventure to laugh over, then they'd drink themselves into insensibility to celebrate, no doubt.

'Rest assured, this affair will not become public knowledge.'

This affair! As though they were lovers, furtive, so any feelings that might develop between them must be kept secret from the eyes of decent folk and would shrivel up inside her – and because she was not fit to become wife and mother, only a bed partner.

'Thank you,' Thomas Hambert said, and the pair of them shook hands.

He was a hypocrite ... they both were. She had never felt so low. Never wanted to howl so loudly, so that her self-pitying tears and mindless rage would wash her rescuer from her mind. Charles was so sure of himself – of what he wanted, and of his ability to get it.

Well ... so was she! She hadn't come this far to slip back into the mire. So she called on some false courage, snorted, and walked past them, away up the stairs and into the room she called hers.

The two men gazed at each other when the door shut after her with a rather definite thud.

'She's upset,' Charles said ineffectually, and swiftly outlined what Celia had been through. 'With your permission, I'll ask my mother to call on her in the morning. I think she needs a woman's counsel.'

Thomas could feel only relief at the thought.

Charles thought, as the carriage left Bedford Square, that Celia's smile had been as brittle as the first crazed layer of ice on the window in winter, and as brilliant as the most delicate shard of crystal when it caught the light. One tiny crack would shatter her, and then she'd be lost to him forever.

A lonely ache throbbed inside him at the thought. Celia was emotional and sensitive. She found pleasure in music and books, responded to his overtures with a shy eagerness. Tonight he'd seen another side of her, a poor, hunted creature with enough courage in reserve to take on a predator. She'd been magnificent in both her courage and her temper.

Where had he taken the wrong turn tonight? When had the game turned away from him? What had she said in the carriage...? That the expressions on the faces of the men had made her skin crawl?

Had he made her skin crawl? He'd been acting a part, she must be aware of that. But no ... he'd seen what the other men had seen, Celia in her nakedness, her small waist and long elegant legs, the tilted breasts jutting against the fragile shift. He'd wanted to tear the filmy chemise from her body, and kiss the triangle of dusky darkness guarding the prize he'd been willing to pay one thousand pounds, or more for. Hell, he'd have handed over his entire fortune for Celia Laws. She was perfection.

He'd not listened to what she'd said. He'd been too insensitive to her feelings, seeing the object of his desire through the heated eyes and throbbing loins of his lust.

She'd thrust the money at him, and by doing so had regained her pride. He'd never be able to buy her, as he'd never been able to buy Lizzie Carter – that had been made perfectly clear to him. He would have to take her on her own terms. As yet, those terms had not been made clear to him.

Some women didn't like intimacy, he'd heard, and he frowned. What if someone had violated her while Bessie had her held prisoner?

What if someone has? the voice in his head mocked. What will you do then?

He put the question from his head. He needed advice. His mother had always been there for him in the past, but he was no longer a boy; he was a grown man. Still, he needn't be specific with his questions. His mother would instinctively know what he meant. She always did.

He shouted to Edmund to be dropped off at Hanover Square. 'I'll try and get to the club a little later, Edmund, but in case I don't, the drinks are on me tonight.'

Drawn by the sound of music, he found his mother and stepfather in the drawing room, where a fire burned cheerily in the grate. As he waited for her to complete her piece, he answered the enquiry in Joshua's eyes with a slight nod.

'Charles, we weren't expecting you,' his mother said when she'd finished, and he crossed to where she stood.

He smiled as he kissed her, elegant in her gown of dark rose, and always serene. 'I was on my way to my club and thought I'd drop in.'

'Is the fog clearing?'

'A little. How is my baby sister?'

'Beautiful, just like her mother,' Joshua said proudly.

Tenderly, Imogene touched Charles' cheek.

'Your face is bruised, my dear.'

'It's nothing, and it's not the first bruise I've ever had.'

'You have dirt on your suit, your jacket has a tear, your shoes are scuffed and your hair is messy. You've been in a scuffle?'

He shrugged. 'It was nothing.'

'I'm relieved to hear that.'

How calm his mother was. She had never been one to fuss unnecessarily about him when he was growing up, but allowed him to progress through childhood with his scrapes and bruises worn as a symbol of his maleness, he thought.

'Are you staying the night? Your room is kept ready.'

'I thought I might stay at my club. We have a little celebrating to do. Have you anything arranged for the morning, Mother.'

She gazed up at him, head tilted to one side like an inquisitive bird, suspicion forming in her eyes. 'What's on your mind, Charles?'

'There's a young woman I'd like you to call on. She's had a hard time of late, and I think she needs a woman's counsel.'

'I take it the young woman is Miss Laws?'

He nodded. 'How did you know?'

She laughed. 'You're my son. My instincts are alerted when you have something on your mind and I've seen the way you look at that young woman.' Her smile faded as she indicated a chair. 'Do stop looming over me, Charles, it gives me a crick in the neck. Have you got this young woman into trouble?'

Joshua got to his feet and casually stretched. 'I

think I'll go and find something to do.'

'You most certainly will not, Joshua Harris. You'll stay here. You've been restless all evening, gazing out of the window and fidgeting, so I knew something was up. Now Charles has turned up looking as though he's been run over by a horse and cart, and you've exchanged enough significant looks to alert the whole of London to the fact that there's a conspiracy between you. I intend to get to the bottom of it. After which, he may go off and celebrate with his friends, and you can damned well go with him, if you feel you must.'

The two men grinned sheepishly at each other.

'Fetch Charles a brandy, and pour one for yourself, Joshua. In fact, you can pour me a small one, too. Make up your mind to it. Neither of you are going anywhere until I know exactly what has been going on.'

Twenty-One

The morning dawned brightly.

Celia was late down to breakfast. Mrs Packer had gone off to the market. Puffy-eyed from weeping half the night, Celia faced Thomas over the breakfast table as she chased a piece of bacon round her plate with her fork. 'I must apologize for my churlish behaviour last night.'

He touched her hand. 'It's all right, Celia my

dear. Charles has told me what happened, so I quite understand. I don't blame you for being upset.'

'Do you want me to leave your home?'

'Leave? Why should I want you to do that?'

'I was rude, and you've always been so very kind and charitable to me. However, after what has happened...'

'What happened was not of your doing, and you are back amongst those who love you, and unharmed. Celia, my dear ... It will take a little time for you to recover from your ordeal, but you eventually will.'

'When are we going home?'

'Tomorrow. We'll be catching the eleven o'clock train. I have to visit my printing shop this morning. I wanted you to meet my partner in the venture, but it would be better if you spent a quiet day, and rested. I believe Charles has asked his mother to call on you.'

Damn Charles for his presumption, she thought. How many more people were to be told of her escapade? The elegant Imogene would probably look down her nose at her now.

There was a yap from below and something furry rubbed around her ankles. She gazed at the black puppy with the white spot, then smiled and scooped it up into her lap. It licked her hand and yawned before snuggling against her with a whine. It was odd how something so small, warm, and silky had such a calming effect.

'What happened to me is all your fault,' she told it, then smiled at Thomas. 'You're such a dear. I'm glad you took the puppy in, though

Frederick will be annoyed when he discovers he's been usurped.'

'Frederick is mature enough to cope. In fact, I thought Lottie might like to take care of him. She seems to like animals. I've called him Spot.'

'Very original,' she said drily. 'Lottie will be delighted with him. She has a lovely nature and the little things in life please her.'

'I imagine it's because she didn't have much to begin with. You're exactly the same, my dear ... only you delight in the emotional, such as the pleasures of music and the written word. It's as though by being denied proper access to them, you now have a thirst for them.'

'You read me too well, I think ... and you're easily swayed by a sad story, Reverend.'

He got to his feet. 'I do know the difference between genuine need and self-interest, my dear.'

'You make me feel ashamed.'

'For what ... your vulnerability? I think we both needed each other when we met. I imagine the almighty had a hand in bringing us together, don't you?'

'Are you saying he helped me to steal your watch?'

He chuckled. 'An interesting concept, but hardly.'

'You know, very few of the poor would consider the almighty a benefactor, unless they can take more out of the offertory plate as it's being passed around than they put in.'

'Out of personal interest—'

She grinned at him. 'No ... I certainly did not

steal from an offertory plate, which is not to say that I wouldn't have, if I'd been in need and thought of it at the time. Stop being such a provocative creature, and don't forget to wear your topcoat. You *will* be careful while you're out, won't you? I feel uneasy after what happened, especially since Bessie knows where we live.'

'I'll take a cab and ask the driver to wait, if that will reassure you. Just make sure you keep the doors locked while I'm out. Mrs Packer won't be long and she has her instructions.'

'Why don't you invite your partner to dinner tonight? I could meet him then.'

'That might be a very good idea.' He brightened her mood with a smile, and was gone.

Celia didn't want Charles to think her ungrateful, so she wrote him a letter, and placed it on top of his cloak.

Imogene Harris arrived at eleven, and Mrs Packer let her in before going to the kitchen to arrange some refreshment. She settled herself on the sofa in a skirt the colour of toasted almonds, scattered with delicately embroidered sprigs of lavender. The same shade was picked up by her bodice.

Celia found herself the object of a thorough inspection, then Imogene gave a short huff of laughter. 'You do not look as ill-used as Charles suggested you might be.'

Feeling at a disadvantage in her skirt, which was no longer fresh, Celia managed a smile. 'Your son worried needlessly.'

'Needlessly? Charles tells me that he and his companions marched into that woman's establishment and rescued you. Were you aware of the danger you were in?'

'Yes, but I would rather die than have him endangered.'

'Tell me what happened, then.'

'Your son was magnificent. He pretended to be a Prince of Venice, and wore a mask.' The horror of it suddenly came back to her, and along with it a touch of hysteria. She found it difficult to breathe, until the woman waved a small vial of smelling salts under her nose. The smell exploded in her head and her eyes widened. 'Charles was so very brave ... and I'll be forever grateful.'

'I take it that you're aware of my son's feelings towards you?'

This woman would not want her for a daughter-in-law, and Celia attempted to put her mind at rest. 'I cannot help but know, when he has declared them. But you needn't worry. I've resolved never to marry. I'm not good enough for him, especially now.' She began to hurt inside at the thought of never seeing Charles again. 'He cannot want me now, anyway. I'm too much beneath him.'

'Yes ... I suppose you are. Are you going to indulge in self-pity?'

Dashing away the tears that threatened to engulf her, she said heatedly, 'I am trying not to, but you needn't worry about Charles making an unsuitable marriage. I've decided never to marry, but to act as companion to Reverend Thomas Hambert and his sister, Abigail. I intend to live quietly in the country and bring up my sister.'

'How very noble of you. On their largesse, no doubt.'

She bowed her head. 'It is as you say, for I'll have very little money of my own. But I will do my best to justify their trust in me by being useful to them in every way that I can. The alternative is to return to the slums.'

'So ... You intend to discard the man who risked his life and reputation to pluck you from life in a whorehouse.'

'*Mrs Harris!*' She blenched at the woman's frankness, and was equally frank. 'You are too outspoken. And just because he rescued me, it does not mean I am, or ever have been a whore. Surely you cannot want me for a daughter-in-law.'

'Not in particular. There is a certain amount of grubbiness attached to your background, and I don't think Charles knows it all. I don't want him to marry in haste, then see him ruined by his folly. But neither do I want to see his regard for you cast aside, as though it was worth nothing.'

Neither did Celia, but she said nothing.

After a while, and with some exasperation, Imogene asked, 'Why did you return that money to my son? You could have kept it, and nobody would have been the wiser.'

Celia retreated into herself. 'You're being inquisitive, and I don't feel the need to answer any more of your questions, Mrs Harris.'

'Answer me one thing. Do you love my son?'

Did she love Charles Curtis? Yes, with everything in her that lived and breathed. Not a minute passed when she didn't think of him. In front of her was his mother, the woman who'd given birth to him, and had loved and nursed him through childhood, as only a mother could. It was understandable that she wouldn't want him to marry a woman from the slums.

She drew in a deep breath. 'You must understand, Mrs Harris, that Charles pursued me. It was not the other way around. Twice now, he has attempted to buy me, and in doing so has made it very clear that the price he paid gives him possession of me. Not once has he thought that this attention is less than flattering to me. Were I a woman from a more respectable background, he would not have presumed on such a bargain being anything more than an insult.'

'Do you love my son?' she asked again.

Celia didn't want to disappoint the woman. 'In all honesty...' and a lie had never been harder to utter. 'I cannot bring myself to tell you that I do.'

There was silence for a few moments, in which time Imogene rose to her feet. Scornfully, she said, as she picked up her son's cloak, 'You are not worth the money Charles was willing to pay for your favour, and I will tell him so.'

A sob tore from Celia's throat. 'Do you think I don't know that? I've already told him so. It's in that letter on top of his cloak. Perhaps you would be good enough to take it with you.'

The young woman's heartbreaking sobs followed Imogene into the hall, and guilt beset her. She'd been there to counsel her, not accuse.

Celia Laws had already been through enough.

There was more than met the eyes about what was going on. A girl with Celia's background should have jumped at the chance to marry someone like Charles, whether she loved him or not.

Whose side am I on? Imogene thought. Charles, who had always been a good judge of character, had asked her to help him, not crush the young woman, who seemed very low in spirit at the moment.

Placing the cloak on the hallstand she went back into the drawing room. 'You do love Charles ... I know it.'

'With my heart and soul ... That's why I must let him go.'

'Oh, my dear.' Imogene took the girl in her arms and held her tight. 'You will do no such thing. You're too distressed to even think coherently, let alone make a decision that will make you both miserable. Come, we will throw the letter on the fire, and you will tell me all about it. What happened to you in that dreadful place?'

Did she really want to know what happened to Celia? If the girl had been forced into ... well, if she'd been *used*, then she'd be duty bound to inform Charles.

A shuddering sob went through the girl as she imperceptibly drew away, in both body and mind. It was though she'd pulled an invisible door between them and stood behind it for the few seconds it took to compose herself. 'I have no intention of discussing this any further with you, Mrs Harris. My decision is made. Please do not try to push me any further.'

'Is it now?' Imogene whispered as her carriage bore her away. Celia Laws knew very little about her son if she thought she could discard him so easily. To start with, she wouldn't be able to avoid him socially, since they'd be connected through James Kent. Charles would not let Celia slip through his fingers.

Imogene smiled, having no doubt that if Charles wanted Celia, he'd get her. She discovered that she didn't mind the thought of having Celia Laws for a daughter-in-law – she didn't mind it at all. The girl was interesting, and there was nothing insipid about her.

On the other side of town, Charles was waking from his slumber. He had no choice. Someone was pounding on his head with a mallet.

He opened one eye and quickly closed it again. The sun was up.

'Charles ... Are you going to open this door or shall I fetch the porter with an axe.'

It was Bart's voice ... and the pounding came from Bart applying his fist to the door panel. 'Let me in; the constables are after you for impersonating Venetian royalty.'

Charles opened one eye again, mumbled something uncomplimentary, then croaked, 'There's no such charge, is there?'

'How would I know; you're the lawyer.'

The lawyer grimaced, for he felt more like what remained of last Sunday's dinner than a legal gentleman of note ... or even one without note. 'I'm coming.'

Bart carried in a tray of coffee, and poured them both a cup. A cursory glance came his way and Bart handed him the cup and saucer. 'You look like death while its decomposing a body. Drink up.'

Charles shuddered at the image Bart had conjured up. He was still fully dressed, his evening suit crumpled, while in contrast Bart looked as though he'd just stepped out of a tailor's establishment. 'Why is it you sound so cheerful?'

'Because I know I don't feel as ghastly as you do. I stopped drinking when it became obvious you intended to drink us all into the ground. Someone had to look after you.'

'Well, you don't have to look so bloody smug about it. Where's everyone else?'

'Gone ... There was a bit of a riot over at Bessie's, I hear. She's been arrested.'

Alarm jiggled painfully through him. 'What for?'

'Everything you can think of. The authorities have had enough of her, and she'll be going to prison for a long time. We were lucky we got your poppet out in time before the raid took place, else she'd have been arrested along with Bessie's girls. They've closed the house down.'

Thank God, Charles thought, though he knew it would soon reopen under another proprietor. At least Celia would no longer be in danger from Bessie and her crew. He nearly scalded his throat as he swallowed down his coffee and gave a surprised yelp. 'Celia told me she didn't want me.'

'So that accounts for the attempt to drink yourself under the table.' Bart shrugged. 'Women change their minds all the time. Ignore her for a week, and she'll come running.'

'Do you think so?'

'It stands to reason. I admire your taste though, and who can ignore a damsel in distress, who also happens to be an all-in-wrestler. I thought she was going to use that knife on Bessie; the way she sliced her bodice open would have put any surgeon to shame. Bessie's breasts sprang out of the top like monkeys out of a barrel, and they blacked both her eyes. It was fascinating.'

Charles managed a short-lived grin, mainly because the movement of his mouth sent a pain soaring into his head. 'Shut up, Bart, it's too painful to laugh.'

'And your lady-love has a nice turn of phrase when she's pushed to it. Bessie will never get over being called a heap of flea bites.'

Charles chuckled. 'I thought that to be a nice touch, myself. It's a line from a play, but I can't remember where I heard it.'

'Finished that coffee? Right then, I'll take you home to your mama, delightful creature that she is. You were blessed when mothers were allo-cated. Can you stand?'

'Just about.' The world spun around him and he groaned piteously. 'I'll never drink again ... well, not to excess anyway. Have you seen my other shoe anywhere?'

'If you open your other eye you'll discover you have two legs, with a shoe on each foot,' Bart said helpfully.

'I thought they were already both open.' He

gazed blearily at his friend. 'What's the time?'

'Noon.'

'Already? Good God!' he groaned, hoping he didn't look as pathetic as he sounded and felt.

'Do you have an appointment then?'

'No ... I was hoping it was bedtime, that's all.'

Dear Charles,

My sincere thanks for the assistance rendered by you and your friends in securing my release from my abductor. I'm appreciative of the danger you were placed in, and sincerely apologize. It was rude of me to compare you to vari-ous fowls. At the time, I was pushed past the point of endurance and my temper was overheated. I should have controlled it, and I can only hope that you'll forgive me for what would be to anyone else, unforgivable.

On the matter of our relationship, and your declaration. I will always regard you with great affection, Charles, but any relationship beyond friendship will not be encouraged. No doubt you have rethought your impulsive words and now regret them, so it will be as if you never spoke.

Sincerely,

Celia Laws.

'Good God!' he said for the third time that day, amused that Celia had mentioned the turkey she'd compared him to. He gazed at his mother. 'Celia can't really believe that I'm given to empty utterances.'

'No, Charles, she doesn't think that. After talking to her this morning, I have reached a conclusion that the young woman's confidence is badly eroded. She's had a great shock, and anyway, is very unsure of herself, I suspect. She's coping with things in the best way she can. She was kept under the floorboards in the dark for several hours, and in a space hardly bigger than a grave. Can you imagine how that must have felt?'

Charles shuddered. He could imagine it only too well.

'It would be a mistake to mention your feelings again until she has recovered, and is thinking straight. Give her a little time, and I believe she will come round. I formed the impression that she has something more on her mind than she's willing to discuss. She does care for you, though.'

'Did she say so?'

'Yes ... she did, in many more ways than one. I do believe you've overwhelmed her. Allow her to recover ... to get used to you. Women enjoy romantic gestures. Show yourself to advantage, buy her a posy of flowers.'

Charles' mind sifted through the information and stored it tidily away with the similar advice. He would make a list. 'You'll have me under her window singing a serenade in the moonlight, next. Hmmm ... yes, not too bad an idea. Celia likes music.'

Laughter trickled from his mother. 'With your voice, music would be a misnomer, and might be a bit too much to expect. Be of support to her, nothing more. Be patient, Charles. When Celia begins to trust you, and she will, I'm sure she'll confide in you.'

'I never thought I'd need a lesson on courtship from my own mother.'

'Your father was a romantic man, you know. Like you, he had a bit of the wolf in him.'

Such a comparison pleased him. 'Did you love each other?'

A smile flirted around her mouth. 'We did. It took me a long time to recover from his death. Sometimes you're very much like him. I'm so very proud of you, you know, and so would he be.'

'And Joshua?'

'It's a different kind of love, less hot-blooded, but more affectionate. He's a good man.'

She reached out to touch his face. It was reassuring that his mother could still express love for her child, who was now a man, and how he could draw on it for comfort. He took her hand and kissed it, saying gruffly, 'I'm glad you're my mother.'

'So am I. You look rather pitiful, you poor boy. Now, go and get yourself a wash and shave and tidy yourself up while I ask the cook to warm some chicken broth for you. I have guests coming this afternoon. You can stay and help me entertain them if you wish.'

His heartfelt groan clearly expressed what that wish was worth at the moment.

'Don't worry, dear. Stay long enough to be polite, and I'll ask Joshua to find some urgent business to discuss with you.'

Twenty-Two

September

Poole smelled of fish and the harbour was in its usual bustle of swaying masts and swooping seagulls as the fishing boats were being relieved of their catches.

The journey from Hanbury Cross had been a delight. The air was redolent of nuts and apples, and the trees, crowned in their autumn glory, were a sight to behold. Those leaves that had already lost their hold on the branches drifted in the air or were crunched under foot. There was a soft mistiness to the day that was altogether pretty.

The market stalls had a riper aroma, of horse and cattle dung. Men and women shouted their wares and dogs and children ran between the bustle and thrust of people's legs.

'Are you looking forward to your visit to Italy with James,' Celia asked her aunt.

Harriet's smile emerged like the sun from behind a cloud. 'I've been told it's the most romantic place on earth for a honeymoon.' Pink tinted her cheeks. 'I'm so happy.'

Celia envied her that happiness. The wedding was to take place at the end of the week in the village church. There she would see Charles again, but she didn't know how she'd be able to look him in the face. Now he had observed her in her true colours, he obviously despised her.

'You won't mind being alone at Chaffinch House for a month, will you?'

'I won't be alone. Lottie and Millie will be there for company.'

'Shall I ask Charles to look in on you from time to time?'

'Certainly not.'

'He's asked after you several times, Celia.'

'Only because he thinks he's supposed to. He would have sent me a note if he'd been that interested.'

'It sounds as though you still care for him.'

'It cannot be, Aunt. You know why, and so does the reverend. You are the only people I can trust with my secret.'

'Why don't you confide in Charles, and allow him to make up his own mind?'

'Because I know what the result will be. Remember how shocked you were when I told you that my father had duped my mother into marriage, and of her need to earn enough money for food to keep us all alive.'

'From what you tell me she was forced into it, and that must never become public knowledge. Not because I'm ashamed, but because I don't want other people to think badly of her. The real Alice was the one who loved you enough to send you to me in your time of trouble, and who found it in her heart to give Charlotte a home.'

Harriet tied the donkey to the hitching post next to a handsome gelding. The two bared their teeth at each other and whuffled a greeting. Harriet slipped a coin to an enterprising lad to give Major a drink and keep an eye on him.

'We shall go to the courthouse first. James will meet us there and take us to lunch.'

They slipped into the public gallery, where a gypsy was being tried for stealing apples from an orchard.

Charles was defending the gypsy. Dressed all in black he looked slightly intimidating, and wore a pale wig, curled at the sides and with a little pigtail tied at the back. Charles was in the process of saying: 'So you were working for the fruit grower, Mr Reeves, and you asked the man if you could take some windfalls home for your family.'

'Yes, sir. And when it came time to pay my wage, he deducted the price of the apples. It were little enough as it was, seeing as most of the apples were rotten from the core out, on account of the wasps had been at them. When I told Farmer Dent that I wanted my money in full, less my wife and child starve that week, he got into a temper and hit me with his riding crop. He said he wasn't going to pay me at all, and would have me arrested and charged with stealing the apples. And here I am.'

'Mr Dent, is this true?' the magistrate asked.

'No ... He's a bloody gypsy and they're all liars. I didn't say nothing like that.'

A man sitting next to Harriet jumped to his feet to state angrily, 'You did so, Dent. I heard you with my own lugholes. You told him his wife and child could starve to death for all you cared. I don't go much on gypsies, but he put in a good week picking apples, and with no shirking. I reckon he gave you more than his eight shillings' worth.'

Charles had turned towards the man's voice, and his glance fell on her. His smile came to rob her of breath, and everything Celia had ever felt for him came rushing back to her like a spring tide.

The magistrate yawned. 'I think I've heard enough of this case, Mr Curtis. I find the defendant not guilty, and the next time you're in front of me, have your witness properly instructed in court protocol. Do you have anything to add on your client's behalf?' There was a short pause then louder. '*Mr Curtis!*'

'Yes, my lord.'

'You're not usually quite so dim-witted, Mr Curtis. Do you have anything to add? *Compensation* for your client, perhaps.'

Celia giggled.

Charles' smile became a wry grin and he turned his attention back to the magistrate. 'I request that my client be awarded his wages, plus an extra pound for the trouble he's been put to.'

'A pound!' Dent shouted. 'Not bloody likely.'

The magistrate would not be dictated to. 'Let us make it eight shillings wages and twenty-two shillings compensation. That's a total of thirty-shillings to the gypsy, I believe.'

'That's daylight robbery,' shouted Mr Dent.

'Mr Dent will also pay to Mr Curtis the sum of his account for representing the accused. Have you got anything else to say before I fine you for contempt of court, Mr Dent?'

Dent pressed his lips tightly together.

'See to it, clerk.' His gavel descended with a bang. 'Court is adjourned.'

'I was hoping you'd accept my invitation,' Charles said, when they got outside.

'Invitation?' Celia admired a posy of purple verbena and yellow asters he'd given her. They were very pretty.

'To help me make up my mind about a house I'm thinking of buying. Didn't Harriet tell you?'

'No.' She slid him a shy glance, for he'd taken a small notebook from his pocket and was in the process of ticking off an item on a list.

'That's the second time you've done that.'

'Done what?'

'Ticked that list.'

'Ah ... I suppose you're curious as to what's written on it.'

'Not at all.' He hailed a cab, and he helped her inside. She gazed out the window. 'James and my aunt seem to have disappeared.'

He gave an address to the driver. 'Never mind. You'll be safe with me.' He tucked the notebook and pencil back in his pocket and his smile captivated her.

This was going to happen again, she thought. Just when she thought she was over him, she'd fall in love all over again. They set off up a long hill. 'Why didn't you invite them?'

'I think they wanted to be on their own. I imagine they'll catch us up when they're ready.' He took her hand in his when they turned into the

346

short carriageway of a comfortably large house, lined with elm trees and lilac bushes. It looked a little neglected, but had a spectacular view over the harbour.

'This is the house you're thinking of buying?'

'I've been living in rooms for the past two years or more. Do you like it?'

The house was of regency design. The garden was overgrown and it had an air of waiting about it. 'It has a great deal of charm.'

'That's what I thought. The furnishings are optional, since the present owner lives abroad, and has no intention of returning – which is ideal for me, since I only own a gentleman's dressing chest and a desk.'

Inside, the furniture was shrouded. They wandered from room to room. Charles opened the French windows to the terrace, where the view over the harbour was exposed to their gaze.

'It would be a wonderful home.'

Out came the book again, a tick was added. The book was put away with a flourish that she pretended not to notice.

Halfway up the stairs was a small landing where they turned at an angle. Above, a window of multicoloured glass let in the light. He pulled her down on to a stair. 'You look pretty in blue.'

'Charles—'

'I know. I know. You don't want to encourage me in case I'm disappointed. Do you think I'm so shallow that I can fall out of love so easily?'

'No, I—'

'I know everything about you, Celia.'

'You don't know about my father.'

'What of him?'

'He duped my mother into marrying him, when he was already married to someone else. I'm illegitimate,' she blurted out.

'I don't give a fig about your father ... or your mother, except she must have been an exceptional woman to have raised you so nicely under the circumstances.'

He pulled her against him. 'I've come prepared for every eventuality. If you feel the need to cry I have handkerchiefs. If you want to curse, I promise not to be shocked. If you want to make love, I will find us a soft bed.'

Her hands flew to her cheeks. 'Charles Curtis, you are making me blush.'

He gazed at her cheeks and grinned. 'So you are.' He took out the book and gazed at his list, then at his watch, then fell to one knee. 'Dearest Celia, my love. Will you marry me?'

'What is on that list?' She plucked it from his hand and read it. Her eyes met his. 'You have it all planned. Don't contact her for a while, then she'll miss you ... give her flowers ... show yourself at work to your best advantage so you impress her with your skills. Apples?' she spluttered.

'Sorry, it was supposed to be a fraud trial, but the court list was switched at the last minute.'

'I was impressed. You look sweet in your wig and gown.'

He winced. 'I was supposed to look professional and in command of myself. Dearest Celia. Is it to be yes or no?'

Her eyes scanned down the rest of the list.

'Show her the house you want to buy for her, and see if she likes it.'

'She does.'

'Charles. This is a big house.'

'Big enough for a man and his wife, plus a little girl called Lottie and a dog called Spot ... and one or two other small creatures in time, perhaps.'

'It will need servants to help look after it. Can you afford it? There must be something smaller around. There's a pretty cottage for sale in the village.'

He grinned. 'I earn five thousand pounds a year.'

She blinked. 'Well ... if you think that will cover your expenses ... but you might have to economize a bit. It's a lovely home though. It just needs to be loved.'

'I need to be loved.'

'I love you. I've always loved you, from the very moment we met ... which was why I couldn't spend that money. I didn't want you to think I was a gold digger, and it gave me an excuse to see you again, because I always knew I'd give it back.'

'Number Five: Propose marriage. Number Six: Kiss her. Seven...'

'Charles Curtis ... I could shake you. Of all the conniving, cold-blooded creatures.'

'Not at all. I just followed the advice offered by Thomas Hambert, my mother, and my friend Bart. Yes or no!'

'I give in,' she said faintly, and threw the notebook over the banister into the hall below. 'Can we get on to the kissing part now.'

He took her face in his hands and his mouth came down to hers. His fingertips slid into her ears and his thumbs caressed the edges of her smile. He kissed her slowly, tenderly, and she nearly fell apart with the ache of wanting him. Her arms slid round him.

'I love you so much,' he whispered against her scalp.

'And I you.'

He held her at arm's length. 'Did you read the last item on the list?'

'About the ring in your waistcoat pocket? I read that first.' She held out her left hand, where a sapphire surrounded by diamonds sent out a loving glow.

He began to laugh. 'That's going to be the last thing you steal from me, Lady Lightfingers.'

'Except for your heart.'

'You stole that years ago,' he said, and kissed her again.